D1294877

Aunt Arie

A FOXFIRE PORTRAIT

A
Foxfire Press
Book

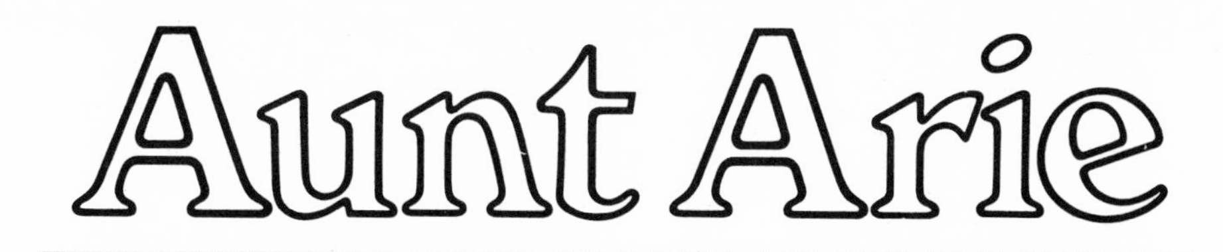

A FOXFIRE PORTRAIT

Edited by

LINDA GARLAND PAGE

and

ELIOT WIGGINTON

E. P. Dutton, Inc. | New York

Published in the United States by
E. P. Dutton, Inc., 2 Park Avenue, New York, N.Y. 10016

Library of Congress Cataloging in Publication Data

Carpenter, Arie, 1885–1978.
Aunt Arie, a Foxfire portrait.

"A Foxfire Press book."
1. Carpenter, Arie, 1885–1978. 2. Macon County (N.C.)—Social life and customs. 3. Macon County (N.C.)—Biography. I. Page, Linda. II. Wigginton, Eliot. III. Title.
F262.M2C37 1983 975.6'98204'0924 [B] 83-1474

ISBN: 0-525-93292-5 cl
0-525-93291-7 pa

Published simultaneously in Canada by
Clarke, Irwin & Company Limited, Toronto and Vancouver

Designed by Nancy Etheredge
Production manager: Stuart Horowitz

10 9 8 7 6 5 4 3 2 1

First Edition

This book is dedicated
to those who accepted Aunt Arie's love,
and are passing it on.

Contents

CONTENTS

Credits

Numerous students interviewed and photographed Aunt Arie, worked in her garden, helped her cook, organized parties for her, and kept her company. Those whose names follow are some of them. There were undoubtedly others, and to those whose names we have inadvertently omitted, our sincerest apologies; there were simply too many of you to keep track of. Jan Brown, Laurie Brunson, Andrea Burrell, Vivian Burrell, David Bush, Kaye Carver, Phyllis Carver, Vicki Chastain, Mike Cook, Karen Cox, Stan Darnell, Roy Dickerson, David Dillard, Stan Echols, Susan Farr, Ernest Flanagan, Mary Garth, Paul Gillespie, Anita Hamilton, Kathy Long, Don MacNeil, Ray McBride, Gina McHugh, Carol Maney, Gary Ramey, Annette Reems, Claude Rickman, Steve Smith, Randy Starnes, Cheryl Stocky, Greg Strickland, Annette Sutherland, Barbara Taylor, Mary Thomas, Gary Warfield, Rose Wells, Frenda Wilburn, Craig Williams,

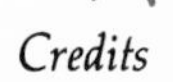

David Wilson, Tommy Wilson, Allan Woodward, Greg York, Carlton Young, and David Young.

Additional tape recordings were furnished by John Hart of CBS, Steve Hill of Odyssey Productions, Emil Willimetz of Audio Visual Productions, and Bess Keller. Additional photographs were furnished by Richard Swanson, *Life* magazine; Jay Leviton; and John Pennington, Atlanta *Journal and Constitution.*

Foxfire staff members who accompanied students on interviews include Suzy Angier, Margie Bennett, Pat Rogers and Eliot Wigginton.

Funding for the first year's operation of the Foxfire Press was provided by the Georgia Council for the Arts. This book was developed during that year.

Introduction

Of all the people my high school students, my staff members, and I have documented and shared with the outside world since 1966, none has been more warmly embraced than Arie Carpenter. Though she has been dead for years, wherever I go with my students on speaking engagements—be it Alaska, Oklahoma, California, Maine, or wherever—someone will surely come up to one of us and inquire about her health. She is the only person we ever wrote about whose personality was so strong and whose face was so compelling that she literally walked off the pages of *The Foxfire Book* and into the lives of the millions who read it. I've looked at that modest chapter about her in wonderment scores of times since that book's publication, trying to unravel the mystery of the reception she received, and it still eludes me. Of the fact that an afternoon with her was magic there is no question. That so many others who never met her responded to her—apparently as strongly as we did—through a mere ten pages of cold type and five two-dimensional black-and-white photographs is a mystery I'll continue to probe for the rest of my writing and teaching career.

Arie Cabe was born on a farm on December 29, 1885, in Macon County, North Carolina, to Christine Tilithia Henson and Davie Leander Cabe. She had four brothers—Mount, Lindsey, Randy, and Hillard. In her ninety-two years, she never left Macon County except on short visits, and if these ever took her farther than thirty-five miles from home, she never told us about it.

She married for the first and only time when she was thirty-eight. The man she married, Ulysses, was also from Macon County, the son of Avie and Bud Carpenter. He had been married once before, to Ada Garland. Ulysses and Ada had moved to the state of Washington, where they had a daughter named Dovie. When Ada died of tuberculosis in Washington, Ulysses and Dovie moved back to Macon County, and shortly thereafter Ulysses and Arie married. Dovie grew up, married, moved away and virtually disappeared, returning for a brief visit about a year before Arie died. She did not return for the funeral.

Arie and Ulysses tried to have children, but she was beyond childbearing age. Their one baby was premature and stillborn—probably when Arie was forty. Supposedly it was a boy. It is rumored to be buried somewhere on the ridge behind their house, but there is no sign of a grave, and Arie never talked about the experience.

Ulysses died on November 19, 1966, and left Arie living alone on their eighty-acre farm in the log house they had built together.

We first met her in the fall of 1970. By that time, *Foxfire* magazine—the first issue of which had been a collection of high school poetry, short stories, essays, and one small section of local folklore and tales—had established its shaky identity over the preceding three school years as a magazine almost exclusively devoted to the recording of area personalities and culture and tradition. It was not particularly well known outside a twenty-mile radius—in fact, there were still many people in our own rural county who had never heard of it—but those who did know about our work were beginning to send us ideas for future stories, and we were working as hard as we could to pursue those, knowing that only by giving our readers what they wanted could we survive economically.

At that time, I was teaching eleventh- and twelfth-grade English. I walked into class one day and Andrea Burrell, one of my students, introduced me to Patsy Cabe, a friend of hers who attended the Macon County Public School and was visiting Andrea for the day and going to her classes with her. At the end of the period, Patsy came up with Andrea and said something like: "You know, since you're interested in old people and what they used to do around here, you might be interested in my great-aunt. She still lives in a log house and does a lot of that old stuff." I asked Patsy if she'd be willing to introduce some of my students to her great-aunt; she agreed, and several days later she took Andrea, Mike Cook, and Paul Gillespie up the winding dirt road to meet "Aunt Arie." The next day in class, Mike came up to me and said, "You're not going to believe this."

That was all the confirmation I needed to want to go and meet her myself. Paul offered to go with me that Thanksgiving weekend and show me the way, since his parents were out of town and he had no plans; and so we got the reel-to-reel tape recorder that we had bought, used, from Bob Edwards at the local Kodak shop, and the camera my uncle had brought home from Germany after World War II and passed on to me, and shortly afterwards found ourselves knocking at the front door of a weather-worn log house, the tilting porch of which looked out over miles of the mountain ranges that had drawn me back to this part of the country immediately after college. No one answered, so Paul and I walked around to the one-story kitchen that was tacked onto the end of the two-story house. We could hear noises inside, so we eased open the door. Aunt Arie leaped in fright when she suddenly realized we were there; then she relaxed and began to laugh—a mixture of relief and music. In a washtub on the table before her was a fresh hog's head from which she had been struggling to remove the eyeballs in preparation for cooking the meat off the bones and fixing canned souse meat for the coming winter.

A rush of impressions hit me. First, for some inexplicable reason, I was enormously embarrassed. It was almost as though I had inadvertently intruded on a stranger who was in the grip of a very private moment. The image of the raw, severed hog's head—coming as it did on the heels of my just completing *Lord of the Flies* with my students—in the clutches of a tiny, white-haired lady in a long shapeless dark dress protected in front by a flour-sack-patterned cloth apron (a lady with the most disarmingly bright eyes and beautiful smile I had ever seen on any human in my life), grasping a butcher knife and standing at a handmade table covered with a five-and-dime-store oilcloth in a dark, smoke-stained kitchen with a fireplace and a wood-burning stove and a sagging wooden floor—this image was unforgettable. It was harmony and discord, resonance and dissonance, peace and chaos. At that moment, on Thanksgiving of 1970, it was almost unbelievable.

We all relaxed. I know I apologized. I don't know whether she recognized Paul or not. She asked for help. Paul balked. He was sixteen years old. I had been a pre-med student at Cornell for two years before changing my major to English and teaching. I had dissected all sorts of animals in pursuit of that early goal, so I figured the present task couldn't be that different. I offered. Paul got permission to set up the tape recorder and plug it into her recently-acquired "electric." I went to work. Paul, eyes averted, held a Shure microphone in our general direction. The first chapter of this book is a transcription of the tape we made that day, a small portion of which, edited and rearranged for clarity, became that ten-page Aunt Arie chapter in *The Foxfire Book.* It is somewhat fragmented and disconnected here. You'll see why we chose to edit it for its original publication. But we thought it ought to be presented here virtually intact—for the record, as it were.

During that first visit, as I became permanently drawn to this frail/strong woman, I can remember being inwardly furious at the fact that this gift she so apparently prized—this stubborn head—was only that and nothing more. No ham. No shoulder. No tenderloin. No ribs. I immediately flashed back to boyhood memories of Athens, Georgia, where possums and Oconee River catfish and other disreputable pieces of trash were given away or sold to supposedly grateful blacks in "Niggertown" by white boys fresh from the hunt who laughed all the way home at the thought of the primitive beings who not only accepted such merchandise, but actually ate it.

As we talked on, I can also remember being equally furious at the antique dealer she told us about who so frequently visited her and so obviously, after every visit, must also have laughed all the way home at the loot he had talked this stupid mountain woman out of. This was the man who had given her five dollars for her mother's handmade spinning wheel.

But a hog's head *was* meat, five dollars *was* five dollars, and Arie seemed grateful. I could only sulk silently at what I imagined were less than truly charitable motivations on the part of those who would have her believe they were "good neighbors." But perhaps they were. The only thing I knew for sure was the sense of being acutely aware of the gulf between our two worlds as I held one of those eyeballs in my hand and wondered aloud what I should do with it.

This little woman confounded me that way constantly. After the black washpot she kept on her kitchen porch disappeared and she told me about it, my first reaction was to get angry. Aunt Arie simply laughed at the scene only she would have imagined, when the thief would stand before St. Peter having jeopardized the quality of his eternal life for want of a washpot. "He's goin' t'look mighty funny comin' up before St. Peter with that old pot on his hands," she laughed. "Now how's he goin' t'explain that?"

And of course, that was it. She was safe in the everlasting arms. A gift was a gift. No question of its value or quality. Only gratitude at the giving. A cheater or a thief could only traffic in those material possessions, which were of little consequence anyway. What mattered, truly, was the record with which one approached the ultimate tribunal. Her concern was not for the stolen possession, but for the thief.

Well, I had been to church myself, and I had heard those pious sentiments before. But this woman meant what most of the Christians I knew only said.

That's not to say she was a saint. In fact, one of the things most compelling about her was that she was also so very human. When she felt she had been truly wronged for no justifiable reason—generally on a matter having to do with an interpersonal relationship which she valued—she could also be vindictive. As she told me once:

"I wish you'uns could've see'd Ulyss's daddy. I always called him Uncle Bud. Well, he was th'devilishist man I ever see'd in my life. All kinda trouble in th'world. And he didn't much like t'hear me laugh. And I've been awful t'laugh in my life. That's th'truth. I have. I've been awful t'laugh. He'd say, 'Listen at that ol' Cabe laugh.' And I'll tell you I didn't care n'more'n spit in th'fire. But still that resentment's there. Right there. And when he was layin' on his deathbed—now, I'll tell you children this so you'll see how all things end for th'good. That's what I'm a'tryin' t'bring over t'you'uns, but I hope with my heart that you'uns don't have t'go through with what I went through with—on his deathbed, Uncle Bud said, 'Arie, you'll have t'forgive me, th'way I treated you.' Boys, I never said nothin'. I stood there, I couldn't say a word, and never did. Stood there and never said a word. He didn't *have* t'treat me that way, cause I was as good t'him as a baby. Washed his clothes, made his clothes, and waited on him just as good as, well, more'n I waited on my own daddy."

We visited Aunt Arie for years. We fell into something of a routine, if visits to her mountain could be called routine. Lift one visit out of the middle of the stream of encounters and document it, and it would look pretty much like this:

Yesterday after school, I loaded four students into my Bronco and turned left onto Route 441. Eight miles north, we stopped at a small, neon-lit food mart to load several cardboard boxes with groceries. The clerk, who recognized the buying pattern at once, grinned as she added up the figures and said: "Heading for Aunt Arie's? Stop in again next week and we should have some fresh sausage that I think she'll like. Here, take this too [throwing in a sack of Brach's jawbreakers]. You know she likes hard candy."

Another few miles and a left off 441 and a right past the graveyard where Ulysses was buried, and we were on a gravel road; then a narrow, tree-lined, rutted lane that crossed a creek and wound up the edge of a long narrow valley past the Dills' log barn, and their pasture and cow and squawking guineas, to her house. Before we got there, we could see the smoke curling out of the stone chimney from the fire in her living room.

The driveway stopped right in her yard near the uncontrolled mass of hydrangea bushes and a log pile. We pulled up, grabbed the groceries, the tape recorder, and the camera, and walked across the yard to the front, noting that the pile of wood on the porch needed some attention. We could hear the sound of the radio coming from the living room—a radio preacher shouting to the mid-afternoon flock. We banged on the front door—single-thickness vertical gray boards and a white porcelain knob—heard her "Come in," and walked into the living room. Along the porch wall on our immediate right was a lounge and, at its head, a table and the radio. On the wall at the right end of the room was the fireplace and hearth, the mantelpiece with its hand-crocheted fringe hanging down and the clock in a wooden case on top, and a set of double-hung windows, one on either side of the mantel. Straight ahead, opposite the front door, was the dark hallway that went to the dining room and kitchen, and a large double bed to the left of the doorway. The bed was piled with paper sacks, clothing, and newspapers. On the left wall was a handmade bureau and the door into Aunt Arie's bedroom. In the center of the carpetless floor, facing the fireplace, were four or five handmade chairs with white oak split bottoms, each covered with a square, flat cushion.

Aunt Arie was sitting near the radio and in front of the window in the chair she always sat in—the chair whose bottom round was nearly worn through in the two places where she always hooked the heels of her shoes when she was sitting in it. She looked at me quizzically, realized who I was, threw both of her arms in the air, and let out a whoop of relief and joy. We set the groceries on the lounge, I hugged her—still seated—and she gave me a wet affectionate smack on each cheek and pounded on my back; then she turned to grasp the hands of each of the students in turn—still seated—and exclaim over every one of them. What followed was a torrent of exclamations as she looked into each student's face: "Where have you been so long? I give out a'th'notion you was ever comin' again!" "What's th'matter with your eye? It's as black as a man's hat!" "What's your name, honey? Have you been here before? Take this piece of paper and put your name on it for me, and I'll try to remember it. Here. Ever'one of you'uns put you'uns names down and I'll save this. That way I'll know who come to visit me!" "You'uns know what popcorn looks like? Go get some out'a that box and we'll shell it out and after while we'll parch us some popcorn! You'uns love popcorn? Yeah-h-h. I do! You'uns does too! I know." "Now, get you some chairs. Here. Come right up here where I can see ever'one of you'uns."

The students, none of whom had ever been to Aunt Arie's before, were awed, drawn inexorably into the little circle of activity that surrounded this five-foot-six-inch dynamo who laughed and pecked on each of them and tapped their shoulders and grasped their knees and tried to remember their names and loved them, instantly and without reservation—strangers all.

As usual, it was the damnedest thing I'd ever seen.

Before long, she asked, "Will you'uns eat dinner with me?" Four heads nodded and smiled, turned to look at me to make sure I wasn't going to refuse, and, reading my face, began to laugh. Aunt Arie was delighted. "Well, let's go t'th'kitchen! I've got beans cooked already. My stomach's undone. I've eat a little too much grease th'last few days. I know what done that. But we'll get out some cabbage and Irish taters and sausage and make some bread, and that'll be just as good as wheat t'th'mill. I can eat that. Boys, I'm gettin' sorta hungry. Reckon that'll be enough?"

The kids helped her up and followed her through the narrow hallway into the kitchen. Mystified at first by the wooden meal bin and wood cookstove and lack of a sink, they were soon drawing water from the well outside, peeling potatoes, opening a glass canning jar filled with balls of sausage and dumping the contents into a black iron skillet, and taking turns helping her mix up a stiff bread dough of several spoonfuls of lard, some powdered milk and soda, and a dipper of water. At one point, everything stopped as Aunt Arie dumped some kindling into the wood stove's firebox, splashed a cup of kerosene on top, struck a match and dropped it in, and flinched as a muffled "whump" sent flames into the air. As the flames settled down to a satisfying roar, the students glanced quickly at each other, grinned, and turned back to the work at hand, which soon resulted in the oven and all four stove eyes being jammed with food.

Standing around the stove stirring, adding wood occasionally, and orchestrating the movement of pots and pans from one eye to another, Aunt Arie continued to chatter on: "Take this water we washed th'taters in and throw it out the door. You'uns remember, though, don't throw water out before breakfast on New Year's Day. If you do, you'll have bad luck with chickens." "We've got t'empty th'stove's ash box later. Don't let me forget that. Mommy wouldn't never let me take th'ashes out between Christmas and New Year's. I don't remember why, but you'uns remember that." "See th'smoke from th'chimney goin' past th'winder there? If it comes out and goes right t'th'ground, that means they'll be fallin' weather in three days." "I'm goin' t'shake hands with a stranger, I reckon. My hand's just a'itchin'!"

While she added several cups of fresh water to the pot of this morning's coffee and grounds sitting behind the food on the stove, Aunt Arie asked one of the students to remove the tablecloth that covered the stacks of dishes and bowls and the tin can full of silverware on the dining room table and bring her some bowls and a plate. She opened the oven, grasped the squat pan of browned bread with a cloth, rapped it smartly against the stove several times to loosen the loaf, and dumped it upside down on a waiting plate. Along with the other bowls of food, it went out to the table as they were filled; and when all the food had been removed from the stove, we seated Aunt Arie, found chairs for ourselves, and waited silently for a volunteer when she asked softly, "Will one of you'uns say grace?" Finally one of the students responded, and when he was finished Aunt Arie looked up with a huge grin, spread her arms in a gesture that took us all in, and said: "Now you all know what you come for! Just help you'uns'selves!" Platters were passed and emptied: corn on the cob, beans, fried potatoes, fried cabbage, sausage. As the bread came around, following Aunt Arie's lead, each person simply broke a chunk off the flat loaf and added it to the pile of food on his plate. Some got glasses of water to drink. Others, more adventurous, sampled the thick black mixture from the coffeepot. Aunt Arie poured her coffee a sup at a time into a saucer and sipped it from that. We ate, and kept on talking. This evening she was concerned about the fact that some folks had moved into a rented house down below her over a month ago—a house we had passed on the way in—but had not yet put up a mailbox, that rural stamp of permanence and respectability. She wondered if we had seen anyone there as we'd driven in, and if so, what they were doing.

For some reason, as we rested from our meal and sat around the table and continued to talk, she was also preoccupied with friends she had known who had lived a hard life and recently died. One was an uncomplaining friend she particularly admired, of whom she said, "Viola had as hard a time as 'ary black nigger in th'world, and she kept it to Viola." Of another, the daughter of a local sheriff, she exclaimed: "She prayed a many a prayer for her daddy's protection. She'd get down beside th'bed and pray until she froze t'death, and she didn't live no time, neither." Of yet another, she concluded quietly and movingly: "Poor ol' feller died out. He was a good ol' John, though. Take a man that's done that much work and helped that many people, and it leaves a vacant spot that's hard t'fill."

A dinner at Aunt Arie's was always a special event for the Foxfire students.
FROM LEFT TO RIGHT: Mike Cook, George Freeman, Greg Strickland, Laurie Brunson, and Craig Williams serve themselves from a meal they helped to cook.

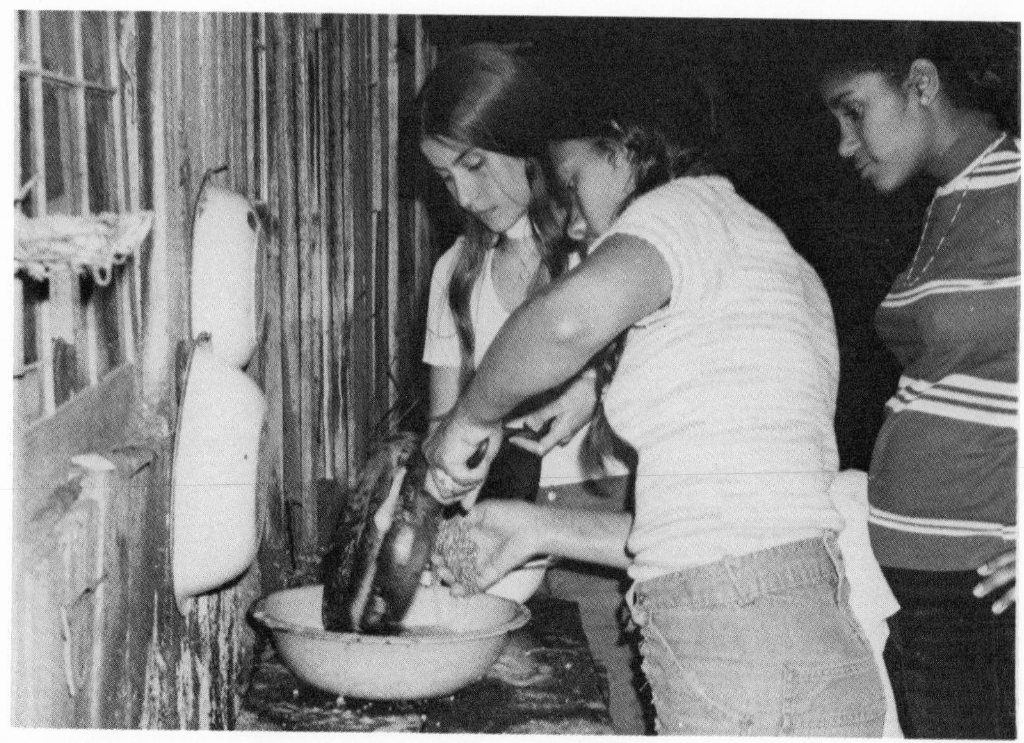

At the instigation of Diane Churchill, a Georgian teaching on New York City's Lower East Side, we initiated an exchange program through which rural Rabun County students were able to spend a week in an urban environment and a group of Puerto Rican students shared a week with us in Rabun County. A day with Aunt Arie was of course a priority for the visitors. Here Elsie, Miriam, and Carmen plumb the mysteries of washing dishes without running water.

The kids were subdued as the dining room became darker. Eventually one reached up and switched on the single bare bulb over the table and went into the kitchen to add more wood to the stove to keep the dishwashing water hot. Aunt Arie began to laugh again, and we all went into the kitchen, set two pans on the shelf outside the door, filled one pan with hot soapy water and one with clear rinse water, and washed and dried the dishes as best we could in the growing darkness.

Then we closed the outside kitchen door, pushed the end of a small log into the cat-hole cut into its lower corner to keep the cat outdoors, replaced the tablecloth over the freshly washed dishes and bowls, and went into the living room, where we added a log to the fire and pulled up chairs before it to "parch" popcorn in the tin "capper" wired to the end of a broomstick. The popcorn fired away inside the tin box, and Aunt Arie continued to talk almost nonstop as she passed the capper on to another student to shake for a while and tapped another student on the arm as she made a point, and then suddenly began to laugh at herself for talking so much. "Do you'uns love t'talk? I do. I've always been sorta blowy. Mommy always said that, with me, whatever come up, come out! Wouldn't pay me a bit more attention as if I was th'wind a'blowin'. I'm pretty good t'bridle my tongue now, though. More than I used t'be. It's pretty long yet, but I bridle it pretty well now. Yeah-h-h. You don't believe that, do you! [Laughing.] Well, I do love it when we're all sittin' around thisaway. It's th'joy of my life. It is. When you'uns is all here, it's just a joy."

The end of a winter visit was invariably the popping of home-grown popcorn in a tin box, wired to the end of a broomstick over the living room fire.

"I don't reckon th'Devil'll get me fer laughin',
but if he does, he'll *shore* get me 'cause I've always done
more'n'my share a'th'laughin' in the world."

INTRODUCTION

Outside, it was dark and chilly. I found myself imagining what someone from the world down the mountain would have thought had he been drawn by the fireplace glow through the window of this log house, looked in, and seen the incongruous sight of those kids in Adidas and Nike running shoes and jeans and Izod shirts hunched around a fireplace with an old lady eating popcorn.

Aunt Arie's stories became shorter, her laughter somewhat more agitated, as she sensed that I was working my way up to saying that I thought it was time we left. I had kids to deliver home, papers to grade, another day of work ahead. As always, I tried to make the break as gently as possible by involving the students in one last round of activities that we hoped would make life a little easier for this lady. We turned on the porch light and replenished the supply of firewood next to the front door. One of the students brought in a large back log and wrestled it into position in the fireplace. With luck, it would last several days. Another student wound her clock. Another refilled the box of kindling wood in the kitchen from the supply piled on the back porch. We checked to make sure doors were tightly fastened and the food was all put away and everything was battened down for the night. Then we gathered again in the living room and stood somewhat awkwardly near the front door.

Dressed in her Sunday best, Aunt Arie often hypnotized the English classes that originated the Foxfire *magazine. No student who was involved has ever forgotten the experience.*

At that point, I witnessed the spontaneous and absolutely unprompted ritual I had watched so many times before in that same room: the students all lined up and each, in turn, grasped Aunt Arie's hands, said good-bye, smiled as she told each, in turn, that she'd be waiting for the next visit, gave her a long hug, and went out the door. The first student out groped his way to the car and turned on the headlights so the rest of us could see the way. Several waited behind while I said good-bye and then walked with me across the yard. Aunt Arie made her way to the end of the porch and stood there in the cold as we started the Bronco, turned around, and headed down the driveway. Looking back, we could still see her standing there, waving, refusing to go back inside until our lights were completely out of sight. We rode home, for the most part in silence.

That routine became something of a constant in the lives of Aunt Arie, myself, two of my staff members, and many of our students. It varied somewhat, of course. It varied on those Saturdays when we stayed most of the day and worked in her garden. It varied on the several Sundays when six or eight of us took her to church at Coweeta Baptist—or to church functions like all-day singings and dinners on the grounds—and then accompanied her back home to change into the more casual clothes we had stashed in the car and spend the afternoon. It varied when we had our annual Christmas party for her and much of the popcorn we popped got strung and put on the tree we had brought instead of into our stomachs. It varied on the occasions when I went to get her and brought her to school so she could sit in front of a whole class of young people again—as she had done for over sixty years in her Sunday School class—and talk and laugh and answer questions. It varied on the evening I went to get her and brought her to school, to a room where a number of community people had gathered to watch a film made about her—the first movie she had ever seen. And it varied on the occasion when several of us took her out to lunch at Kate's, a favorite small local restaurant with about eight tables and booths, and the first restaurant she had ever eaten in. (She was mystified by the whole experience, finally ordered hamburger steak, couldn't get used to the idea that someone else was in the kitchen fixing food for her, and, when the waitress brought it to our table, apologized for causing her so much trouble, saying: "Now, you didn't have to do that, honey. I could have done that myself.")

But what was unvarying was the way she greeted us with those two arms thrown into the air, and the way she said good-bye—the bookends of our relationship. And, of course, the love that radiated out of that tiny woman into the soul of every young person I know of that she ever met.

That relationship, though always intense, wasn't always easy. There was that long, difficult time, for example, when she tried to give *Foxfire* her land in the hope that some of us would come up there and live nearby. I knew we couldn't do that. There was never any question in my mind as to the way our accepting such a gift would alter—however subtly—the friendships we had with so many other people in the area. And it almost did. The first confirmation I had that my fears would come true arrived in the form of word through the ubiquitous small-town grapevine. The preacher of her own Coweeta Church, in whom she had confided, was already out in the neighborhood telling his parishioners that the only reason *Foxfire* had developed a friendship with Arie was so we could "get everything that poor old woman has."

For several months, whenever I was alone with her, the question of her land occupied part of our conversation. Finally it was arranged that she would sign the land over to Ruth and Nelson Cabe—Patsy's parents—in return for being able to live with them and be cared for by them in their home at their expense when the day came that she could no longer care for herself.

That day was surely coming, for gradually every task became more difficult for her. The time came when she never went upstairs where Ulysses's clothes were still washed and pressed and hanging in the back room, and where his walking sticks were still standing up against a door frame waiting for his hand. The newspapers that papered the walls and ceilings came loose and hung in tatters, mice made nests in her quilts, and she could only fret at the growing disarray she knew was up there. She could no longer open the jars of canned food. She could no longer draw water from her well. She could no longer carry in the firewood she needed, and so when people were not there to help her, she devised a system whereby she rolled wood in, a stick at a time, with her foot. Walking out beyond the garden to her little toilet became an almost impossible task.

In addition, there were medical problems that demanded attention. On one occasion, for example, I took her to see my physician, Dr. King, in Clayton, about some trouble she was having with her feet. She had also told me on numerous occasions, somewhat apprehensively, about a lump on her chest that seemed to be growing, but for which she refused treatment. Since I had her in the office of a competent doctor anyway, I forced her to allow him to examine her chest. He came out of the examining room shortly afterwards and told me that the tumor had to be removed as soon as possible. As I drove her home, we talked about it, and though I was expecting a major argument, it was almost as though her finally letting someone look her over had broken the ice, and she was not as resistant as I had feared she might be. Her major worry all this time had been that, like Ulysses, if she ever checked into a hospital, she'd never come back out; but Dr. King had helped her understand the need for the operation, and I assured her that Ruth and Nelson and I and my crew would be with her every day, and that with the operation she might have years more at home, whereas without it she might not. Finally, in her driveway, she said: "All right, sir. Trade made."

She did not actually enter the hospital, though, until the day Ruth went to check on her and found her burrowed under a pile of quilts on her bed suffering from pneumonia. She was admitted to Angel Memorial Hospital in Franklin on February 9, 1974, recovered, and while there had the operation to remove the tumor, which was benign. Ruth stayed with her almost constantly, though we were able to make arrangements to spell her on a regular enough basis that she could go home to relax. As Aunt Arie's spirits returned, she became a favorite among the nurses and doctors at the hospital.

Her days of living alone in her log house, however, had ended. When she was checked out of the hospital, she went home to Ruth's. There she stayed, surrounded by things Ruth and Nelson had brought from her home, mostly bedridden in a room they had prepared for her with a window that looked out

When Beulah Perry read in Foxfire *about the white oak baskets Aunt Arie taught us to make, she wanted to learn the art herself. We got the two of them together for a day-long session with dinner—one of the most powerful experiences we had together.*

into a flower garden, until the late summer of 1978, when she had to be admitted again to Angel Memorial. There she died of a stroke on September 10th at the age of ninety-two. She was buried beside Ulysses. She had always wanted to outlive her three brothers so she could see them buried properly. She outlived her last brother by three months.

Her home and property were sold to the Hollands, a family from Florida, that had read about her and wanted to restore her house and keep the property intact. The real estate developers that had wanted the property were turned away.

Impressions of Aunt Arie fill my days. Wherever I go, people inquire about her health. Former students who knew her return and say, "Remember when . . . ?" Photographs hang in my office. The image of Gary Warfield, a favorite student, helping her read the fan mail that came in from all over the country is indelible. As is the image of Don MacNeil helping her string beans. Or David Bush and Ray McBride shucking popcorn on her porch. Or Karen Cox and a gang of students spending the night with her when she was sick. Or Beulah Perry, a favorite contact, making a basket with her, and Aunt Arie's almost childlike wonder and delight at having sat down at the same table with a black woman in her own dining room and eaten dinner. Or one-liners that still echo in the recesses of my mind, like, "Every tub should stand on its own bottom" —a maxim she tried to follow until the bitter end, succumbing at last to the inevitability of our all being dependent upon each other, one way or another, in this life. Or the lovely attitude she assumed as she hid something special for us all to enjoy together the "next time" with the affectionate statement, "I'll put this away against the time you'll come again," and we'd grin conspiratorially.

Impressions that come flooding back whenever I see the play *Foxfire,* with Hume Cronyn and Jessica Tandy—playing on Broadway even as I write this—and I watch Jessica, who is Aunt Arie come to life again, wrestling to get the eyeballs out of a stage-prop hog's head with a knife I gave to her that Aunt Arie gave to me—a knife Ulysses made.

But the overall impression that lingers, and infuses my days, is not of specific moments like those, but rather of the uncommon decency and the humanity that characterized the entire experience of knowing such a woman. She was a good and decent human being in a complicated world.

And with it all, she had perspective. In the toughest of times, she'd grin and say what she had heard her mother say so often: "Ah well. This world and one more and a turnip patch'll do us all. . . ."

Yep.

BEW

4 5 6 7 8 9 10
11 12 13 14 15 16 17
18 19 20 21 22 23 24
25 26 27 28 29 30

Editor's Note

The transcriptions of two of the tape recordings made at Aunt Arie's have been left virtually intact. These are our very first interview and a tape made during a visit with one of her oldest acquaintances.

Some twenty other tape recordings were made, as well as a box full of notes—remedies, expressions, superstitions, exclamations uttered on those many visits which were not tape recorded—written down at the time in pencil on scraps of lined paper and the insides of match book covers and the backs of laundry slips and gasoline receipts, and transferred later to index cards in our office.

These twenty-odd tape recordings were meticulously transcribed, and copies of the transcriptions were cut apart and filed in manila folders by subject matter: cooking, farming, illness, religion, family, etc. Since most of the tapes were made by students who had not met her before, many of the same questions were asked, and many of her answers and stories were duplicated. These duplications were grouped inside the folders and blended together to create the richest possible answer to a question or version of a story. The story she tells about shooting a possum one night with Ulysses, for example, is one she told at least three times, and though the story line itself never varied, each time certain details surfaced that did not appear in the other versions. All these details were incorporated to make one full version of the tale. The original, dated transcriptions and tapes are on file in our archives, so that should someone wish to see each of the versions in its original form, these can be easily retrieved.

Once this blending process was completed, a final determination was made as to the subject groupings, and the material that was assigned to each of these groupings was ordered in what we felt was a logical sequence. In the chapter about farming and work, for example, the sequence was largely determined by the season during which each activity was most prominent (early-spring clearing, spring and summer planting, harvesting, etc.).

Then all the material that had been typed on the index cards was added if it did not duplicate anything in the manuscript. Different remedies, for example, were added to the section about illness and doctoring; different recipes and cooking instructions were added to the section on cooking. Expressions were blended into the text in places that I knew, through at least a hundred encounters with Aunt Arie, were appropriate.

Finally we began the long process of determining how we would deal with dialect and punctuation. Should the phrase "a'goin'," for example, appear as "a'goin' " or "agoin" or "agoing" or "a'going" or "goin' " or "going"? What if spelling a word the way she pronounced it created a new word that was potentially confusing? She never said "sure," for example. She always said something most closely resembling "shore." What about "was," most often pronounced "uz," as in, "They'uz goin' t'town when . . ."? That's as close as we can come to the way she said it, but doesn't "they'uz," the form we used in the version of the original interview that appeared in *The Foxfire Book,* look too extreme—too Dogpatch, if you will? To what extent do large chunks of text riddled with apostrophes and strange spellings become almost unreadable, as in the *Uncle Remus* stories?

Consider this case, for example: When Margie Bennett, one of my staff members, slid her car off Aunt Arie's driveway into the ditch beside it, she was understandably upset. Aunt Arie's description of her reaction, told to me later, on tape, went something like this: "I'uz s'sorry fer that girl. She'uz hacked t'death. I don' let nothin' hack me that bad. She'uz jus' hacked t'death." For the majority of readers, that's probably too extreme; and it runs the risk, I think, of making Aunt Arie seem like a character out of a comic strip.

With the help of our editor, Bill Whitehead, we came up with a system that approximates the dialect without going to extremes and still preserves much of the flavor of her speech. Then the text was made consistent with this scheme.

There are inconsistencies in the dialect, but they are intentional, reflecting the inconsistencies in her usage. Sometimes, for example, Aunt Arie said "you" and "to" and "of" very distinctly for emphasis, and sometimes they were abbreviated as in "y'know" and "t'walk" and "a'course." Thus a sentence like, "Now I want you t'listen to what I say," looks like someone has erred, with its two forms of "to." It has been written that way on purpose, however, to come as close as possible to capturing the actual sounds of Arie's words. Likewise, "I was eight year old," and, "I've lived here forty-five years." That's the way she said those two things. She said "my" in "myself," but shortened the pronoun in many of its other uses. She said, "I'm gonna go," but she also said, "I'm goin' t'th'store." Such variances have made this a proofreader's nightmare.

I hope it works. I think it does.

Foxfire Fund, Inc. is an educational, nonprofit organization run by high school students and its own adult staff at the Rabun County High School in northeast Georgia. For the past sixteen years students have published the quarterly magazine, *Foxfire,* that records and documents the lore and folkways of the Southern Appalachian Mountain culture. From this magazine has come the successful series of books published by Doubleday, Inc., known as *The Foxfire Book, Foxfire 2, Foxfire 3, Foxfire 4, Foxfire 5, Foxfire 6,* and *Foxfire 7* (the first to be edited by a former Foxfire student, Paul Gillespie). *Foxfire 8* is due later this year. Other divisions have been added to the overall Foxfire program which include: video tape and television, record production, Appalachian music and folklore, environmental awareness, and photography.

The newest addition to the Foxfire program is the Foxfire Press, a new publishing venture for the Foxfire staff and students. The Press will be publishing a series of books, calendars, and related items. The first two projects published by the Press and E. P. Dutton, Inc. are *Aunt Arie: A Foxfire Portrait* and the *Foxfire Calendar 1984.* Coming later this year is *The Foxfire Book of Woodstove Cookery.*

1.

"I've spent my happiest days here"

The chapter that follows is a transcription of that first tape-recorded interview Paul Gillespie and I made at Aunt Arie's. Because we did not begin to tape until we had been there several minutes and had explained who we were and had gotten permission to use the recorder, the transcription begins rather abruptly in the midst of our visit, after I had already offered to help with the hog's head and had gone to work. Aunt Arie hovered nervously nearby and assisted as she was able.

The tape recorder was unplugged and moved four times during the visit, which adds somewhat to the disjointed nature of the transcription. We began in the kitchen with the hog's head. That job finished, we all moved to the living room, and as Paul continued to ask questions I stepped outdoors to take a few photographs before the sun went down. When I returned, Aunt Arie really seemed to want us to stay for dinner. Since all of us had been alone over Thanksgiving and had not celebrated the holiday in any way, we decided to cook up a small feast for ourselves, and we moved back into the kitchen. The tape recorder continued to run all the time we were preparing the meal. We then moved to the dining room to eat, reset the recorder, and caught a portion of the conversation over dinner.

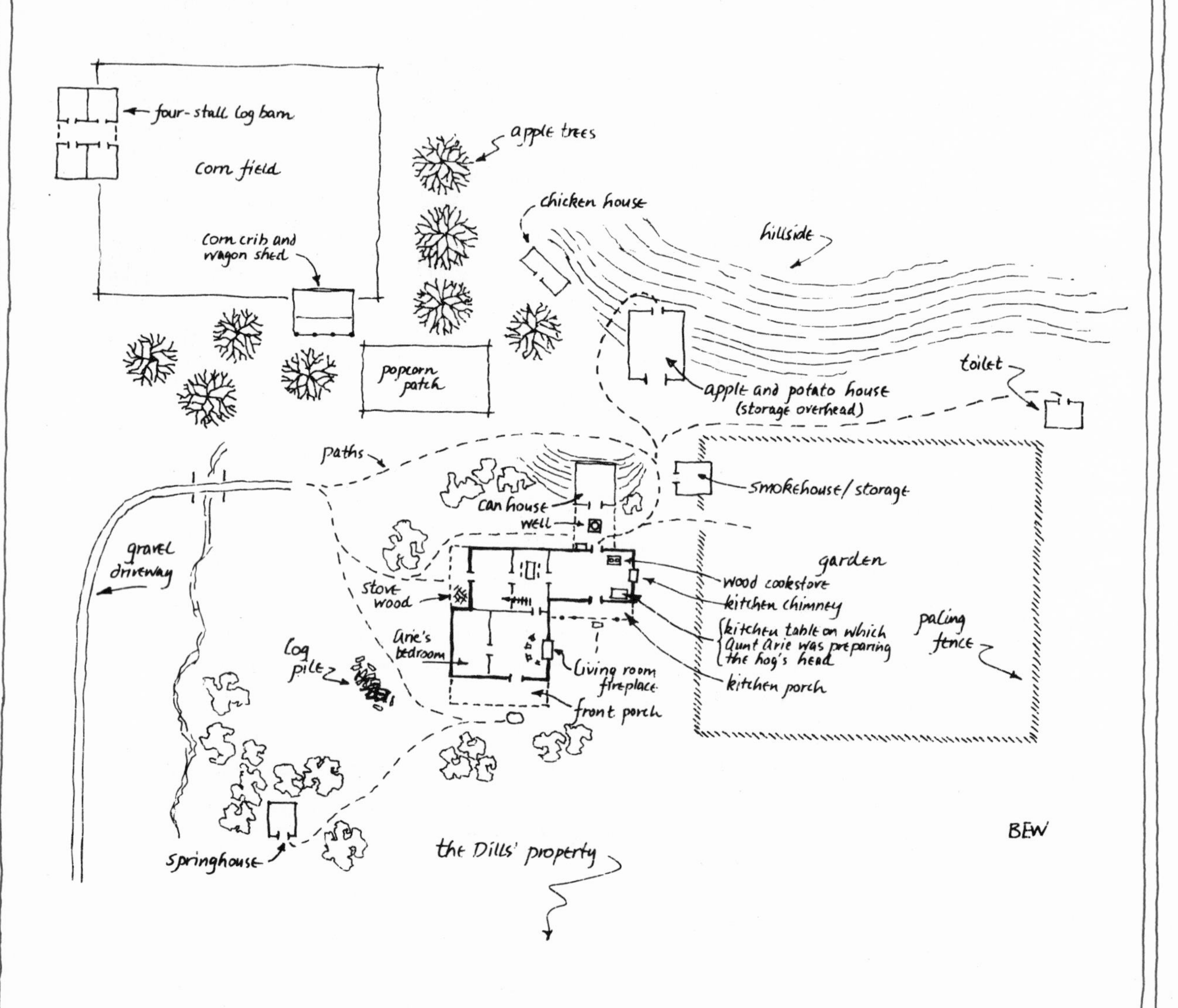

The end of Aunt Arie's house and her front porch. Behind the downstairs window was her bedroom.

The result comes as close as any tape recording we have to hinting—however imperfectly—at the wide-ranging, free-associative nature of most of our talks with her.

It was after this first interview with Aunt Arie that I knew the size of the job ahead of me in terms of understanding the language she and her peers spoke. For example, when I asked if she'd mind our coming and tape recording her again, she replied, "I don't care for it a bit more'n spit in th'fire." Where I was raised, when someone said they didn't care for something, it meant they didn't like it. Had she not indicated through a number of other things she said that she wanted us to come back soon, I might have assumed she never wanted to see us again. I'm grateful that she meant she didn't mind.

ABOVE: From the garden, looking back toward Aunt Arie's house, one could see the front porch and living room chimney on the left, the kitchen wing and chimney at the center, the long, low roof covering the well and can house to the right, and the smokehouse turned storage shed, far right, at the upper corner of the garden. The roof of the corn crib is visible beyond the kitchen chimney.

ABOVE, RIGHT: Aunt Arie's toilet was beyond the far corner of her garden.

RIGHT: From the spring house, looking up toward the front porch and kitchen wing.

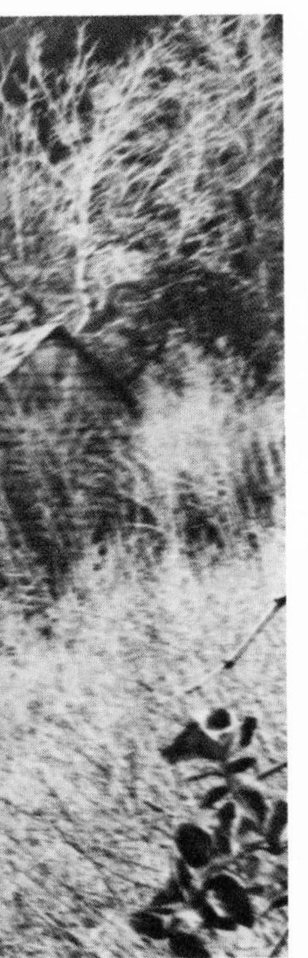

AUNT ARIE: Been in one wreck and I had m'arm broke. Been in some pretty close places, but still I've got through some way'r'nother. But now, it's not been easy. Been a lotta sufferin' in it. Yes sir, been a lotta sufferin' in it for me.

They come last night and brought m'supper. *Law,* what a supper they did bring me. It tickled me. I'd done eat and was done in th'bed and was just about ready t'go t'sleep. I thought Jenny would've knowed better'n that, but I guess she just didn't think. Y'know, she just didn't think. [Pans rattling; muffled conversation.] Do you know Mr. Dowdle?

WIG: I don't believe so.

A: He lives right over there. Boys, he's good t'me. He's Penny Dowdle's boy. Lives over yonder right in th'forks a'th'road as y'turn this way. That's where his daddy lived. [Moving the hog's head around.]

A: Now see if you can take your finger and pull that eyeball up and cut it off.

W: OK.

A: I can, if I had strength.

W: Tell me again what you're going to make with all this.

A: Souse.

W: Souse?

A: Souse meat. Boy, that's th'best stuff. I love it better'n I do sausage.

W: How do you make that?

A: Take this head now—I'll soak it till I soak ever' bit a'this blood out of it.

W: Soak all the blood out of it?

A: Yes, soak it till it's just as white in th'mornin'. That's th'reason we're gettin' it ready this evenin'. Then I'll cook it and then I'll take th'meat and grind it on th'sausage grinder. Then take th'juice that this was cooked in—part of it—and put some sage. Ain't got no sage, though. Put black pepper in it and red pepper and stir it all up till it's just as good and fine as it can be, and then put it in them little can jars and seal it. I always put it in pint jars. Then we open it along any time in th'winter and eat that. Boys, it's better'n anything in the world nearly.

W: How do you cook it? When you take it out you heat it up?

A: Well, yes, if y'want to. If y'don't, just cut it out and eat it cold. Lotta people eats it cold. I fix mine in this pan and then pack it in jars, and then process it just a little while so it'll save. I have t'go down there and get someone t'help me seal th'cans unless somebody happens in like you did. Lotsa times they do. They happen in, and I get ashamed of myself askin' people ever' time they come. I went and fixed th'bed today—cleaned all out from under there and put some kerosene oil on it and then I couldn't lift it back. Mr. Philps was here earlier today and I mentioned it, and they went in there and lifted it back. I said if I'd knowed they were goin' t'do that, I wouldn't a'said a word.

W: Now, what do I have to do to this eye now?

A: Let me see one more time. I don't believe I can because a'this hand. I'll break m'knife. If I was stout enough I could pull that out, but I can't. I don't know how t'get it out.

W: OK. Let me keep trying.

A: Well, I know your hand is stouter than mine.

W: [Laughs.] Is the other side like this too?

A: Yeah. It's th'same.

W: It's got the eye in it too?

A: Yeah, I guess it has. I've done already trimmed that hair all off. They didn't half fix it. I don't know who done it, but they didn't do it good. But they're good neighbors. Now she brought that plateful. Had a piece a'turkey that big on it. I said, "I've done eat supper."

That knife's been t'breakfast, I think. It's as dull as a froe. [Laughter.] You ever use a froe?

W: Sure.

A: I've helped do it. We use t'make boards at Poppy's lots. Since I've been here, we've made lots of'em. Are you doin' any good at it?

W: Oh, a little bit. Doesn't this bother you? Pulling eyes out of things like this and all that?

A: No, I don't care for it a bit more'n spit in th'fire. Oh, I've just done everthing in m'life till I just don't care for nothin' that way. I don't, I just don't. Nothin' don't never bother me. I mean don't make me sick. Y'know, some people, when th'blood comes s'bad and s'bad and s'bad, they just run off and leave it. They can't stand it, and I don't pay it a bit'a 'tention in th'world. Me and Ulyss', that's m'husband, Ulyss' Carpenter, we sat down one night after supper in there and counted how many people that I'd been to in sickness, and waited on'em and dressed'em and washed'em and closed their eyes and all, and I got thirty-two and he got

In summer, grape vines covered the kitchen chimney.

thirty-three. That's how many people I've done. Do you know Tom?

W: No.

A: He's dead now. He use t'be our doctor, and he wanted Mommy t'let me be a trained nurse. Law, Mommy wouldn't let me be a trained nurse. Why, she'd a'went into a fit sure'nough if I did. She said that was disgraceful. That's th'way Mommy looked at it. So I never got t'be. I always did love t'wait on sickness, though. Law, I just loved t'wait on sickness.

W: What are you going to do with this eye when you get it out?

A: Throw it away. Y'know, I went to a place up on Coweeta one day at th'schoolhouse up there, and they had a hog's head cooked, and they wanted me t'eat some of it. I eat some a'th'hog's head with that eye cooked in it and I didn't know it and after I eat it—you couldn't a'hired me t'eat it with th'eye in it. I wouldn't a'eat a bit of it, but I didn't know it. . . .

Now, he's havin' a hard time with that head [talking to Paul about Wig].

W: Well, I can tell you one thing for sure. It's the first time I've ever been to visit somebody and they've asked me to cut a hog's eye out. I don't reckon it'll ever happen again in my whole life. [Laughter.]

A: Might not. Might not. Can't never tell. Here lately seems like everthing in th'world happens. That's hateful, ain't it? [Wig laughs.] Wish I had somethin' to. . . .

PAUL GILLESPIE: Mean hog.

A: One thing, that knife's too dull. I don't think I've got nary 'nother one that's any sharper. These is all good knives. Homemade. They last a lifetime, nearly. But they're wore plumb out now. Poppy made that'n. Poppy and Mount t'gether made these two here. This is th'one I always use t'peel apples with when I was a'dryin'em. Dried twenty bushel a'apples once. I reckon back then y'couldn't buy knives like these in a store. If they did *we* never did have none of'em. Poppy just always made ours. I reckon Poppy always had a bought pocket knife, though. They always bought their pocket knives.

W: How did they make these knives?

A: Back then they used crosscut saw blades for th'knife blades—old crosscut saw blades that'd went t'th'bad. T'make holes in th'metal [for the brads that held the handle on] they'd get that iron hot and lay it down on somethin' solid and take nails and a hammer and hammer that nail through th'metal, turnin' it over back'erds and forwards and th'first thing y'know, a hole goes through. Yes sir. Y'made th'blade just however long y'wanted. Y'see, some of'em was shorter'n th'others. Some of'em was

real long. Then get th'blade hot again and lay it on somethin' solid again and take th'hammer and beat th'edge down and then take a file and file'em off good.

Then t'make th'handles, we just got a piece a'wood and whittled it out with a knife. Poppy always used white oak t'make his knife handles. He used white oak for everthing he done.

These knives are wore out now, though. Course th'crosscut saw blades was wore out t'begin with. I don't know how long I've had 'em. They've belonged t'three families, y'see. No wonder they're wore out!

Well, I've a good notion t'go get th'hand saw and let you saw that in two right through here and let you get that out. If it takes s'long t'get that other'n out as it did this'n you'll be wore t'death!

The first photograph we ever took of Aunt Arie. She was about to peel, then wash and fry, Irish potatoes for our dinner, and her expression summarized the confusion she felt at having a tape recorder and camera present on what would otherwise have been a straightforward visit with "strangers."

[While she goes to find a saw, there is a whispered conversation between Wig and Paul about how sickening the hog's head is. Aunt Arie returns.]

A: I guess this saw's over a hundred years old. Lonzo Knight said that was th'best hand saw he'd ever see'd in his life. He sharpens it. I take it over there and he sharpens it. I ain't took it over there since Ulyss' died. You reckon you can saw it and get it out any better?

W: I think I've about got it.

A: Well, all right then. I don't reckon bones'd hurt a hand saw any worse'n wood.

W: If I had something sharp. . . .

A: I wish we'd had somethin' sharp t'get it out. That knife use t'be a goodun. It ain't been used in a while. I don't know. . . . Let me reach my fingers down in there and see if I can pull it out. You take that knife out and let me see if I can pull it up till you can. . . . [Arie works at it.] Why, that knife won't cut nothin'. Wish I could get this'n down in there. It's s'near out y'hate t'saw it in two, don't y'?

W: Yep.

A: I don't want t'cut that eyeball if I can help it, cause th'black stuff'll run all-l-l over everthing.

W: Let me see if I can get it.

A: Y'need a good pulley. . . . Oh Lord [laughing], see if you can pull it out a little further. Oh goodness alive! [Laughing.]

W: I can feel what's holding it.

A: I wish I was stout like I use t'be. I've been awful little all a'my life. My hands never has been nothin', but boys, they've done lotsa hard work. I wish I could. . . . Ah, they ain't no sense in wishin' no such as that t'call back twenty-five years ago when I could work. That's silly. I think, honestly, I worked and done th'best I could; and t'wish you could go over your life again, I think that's silly in a way.

P: Well, I don't know.

A: Well, y'ain't never gonna get it?

W: Yep. I got it.

A: Good! You let me have it and I'm gonna take it and throw it away. Now what about—there's another'n here just th'same way.

W: OK. There you are. [Hands her the eyeball.]

A: I don't know who helped'em, but I don't see why in th'world they didn't fix it like they did that'n last year.

[Arie goes to the kitchen door to throw the eyeball away. Paul watches her and suddenly starts laughing as the eyeball hits the tin roof of the adjacent can house, rolls off, and hangs on the clothesline. Paul tells Wig, and they are laughing when Arie returns. She realizes what they are laughing at, and she starts laughing with them.]

A: Oh goodness alive!

W: Well, Aunt Arie, you're a pistol!

The first hog eyeball rolled off the can house roof and snagged on the clothesline.

[Arie proceeds to worry about the next eyeball while Paul and Wig continue to be hysterical.]

A: Don't y'think it'd be easier t'saw that down through that and then cut it out that way?

W: [Still laughing.] Well, let's take a look at it and see.

A: Ah, it's just like that other'n.

W: I believe he's got it shut on us, don't you? [Laughter.] What was that? [Pointing to a hole in the side of the head.] What was that right there?

A: That's where his ear was. His wife made him cut them out. I give'em t'them, and I never thought a breath a'these eyes or I would a'asked him t'get them out too.

W: What do you do with the ears?

A: Lotsa people eats'em. I wouldn't eat one for nothin' I ever see'd.

W: Well, how would you eat something like an ear?

A: Ah, you'd have t'clean that ol' hair off of it and scrape it all-l-l off good and cook it. It's as good and clean as any of it, but I don't want none of it. [Laughter.] Which would you rather do? Saw it down with that, or. . . . [Laughing.] Now I ain't got that'n trimmed out. See, I cleaned this'n out before you come. Trimmed all that ol' hair off.

W: Let me do some trimming here. What do I have to do?

A: Shave that hair off over there.

W: Do you take the skin off too?

A: Yeah. Over here where this is.

W: You start here and peel that whole piece of skin off?

A: No. No, just this that's got hair on it.

W: Just right here, huh?

A: The skin's what makes it good. I cook that skin. Looky there. [Looking inside the mouth at the tongue.] I never see'd as much meat left on nothin' in all my life. I want you'uns to looky there. Did you ever see as much meat left on a hog's tongue in your life?

W: That's a lot, isn't it?

A: Yeah, it is. Don't look like they'd want t'give such as that away. But they wouldn't take a cent for it. No sir. Well, they come up here a while back, and I got lotsa old junk here and yander and round about upstairs, downstairs, and in ol' boxes and bureau drawers, and everthing else that could be thought of, and I know I give'em one ring that costed thirty-eight dollars. I know that. And them other rings, I don't know what they cost. Anyhow, I told her last night she better take some pay for this hog's head, and she said, "I'm not a'gonna do it." She said, "You give me them rings and I didn't pay for them." I said, "I *give* you them." She said, "I'm givin' you this."

W: So she just gave this head to you?

A: Yeah. She just gave it to me. She did last year, too. They're good neighbors. Law, what good neighbors they are.

W: Is that okay, or did I not take enough of that or too much or what?

A: If you got all th'hairs off it's all right. It gags me when I get a hair in m'mouth. I'll just gag and keep on and on. Ulyss' use t'just laugh at me. He use t'just die laughin' at me. I'd get up and go out front and not eat nary'nother bite. He was always laughin' at me for doin' that. I don't know why I do it, but I do do it. [Pause.] Law, how I do love t'fix somethin' t'eat. Yes. That's what we live on, ain't it? Yes sir. You'll always remember what you done today when you come back, won't y'?

W: Yeah, I sure will!

A: Where do you live at?

W: I live down at Rabun Gap—Betty's Creek Road.

A: Yeah, I know where Betty's Creek's at. You know Harvey Cabe?

W: Sure. Works with the telephone company?

A: Yeah. I was there not too long ago. That's my brother's boy.

W: You know, one of our favorite people is Harley Carpenter.

A: Yeah.

W: He's kin to them, isn't he?

A: Yeah. He's kin t'th'Carpenters, Harley is. Well, do you know Nelson Cabe?

W: Yeah.

A: He works at that factory up yonder all th'time. His wife drives a school bus and cooks at th'schoolhouse. You know Patsy down here? You'uns first come with her? She's finishin' school this year, and Dennis [her brother] is in college. They just got th'two children.

W: You know, another thing we wanted to ask you about was, back then when you slaughtered a hog, how did you cure up the rest of the meat? Did you smoke it?

A: I don't want no ol' smoked meat. You might, but I don't. See that little house right out there? Well, that's th'smokehouse. Now we'd kill as high as four big hogs at one time.

W: How many?

A: Four. We have killed four big hogs at one time. Take and cut'em all up. Just like this is. We always salted ours th'day that we cut'em up. Some people waits till th'next day, but I don't like that. Take and spread th'hams and shoulders and middlin's out on th'bench. Ulyss' made benches in there, and spread it all out. Then take salt and black pepper—not too much black pepper—and mix it all up in a pan, we always did, and pour that over th'meat. We'd always let it lay out there till it got cured. Then, see, that black pepper keeps th'flies off of it, and that salt preserves it. We never did freeze no meat.

W: And you never smoked it?

A: No sir. Well, now, if th'flies comes. . . . If y'kill it too soon [while the weather's still warm and they're alive] and they smell fresh meat, they'll come and they'll brew in it. You know, they'll lay eggs there and they'll make worms. Well now, you'll hear'em when they come. We've got a ol' Dutch oven that we use t'bake bread in. We'd put coals down in it and take red pepper and put down on them coals and set it down under th'meat t'run th'flies off.

W: You mean you put red coals underneath the meat?

A: In th'oven, cause th'oven's iron, y'know, and it's on legs and it won't burn th'floor. I wonder where that ol' iron oven is? I was studyin' about it th'other day. I've got some upstairs.

W: And you'd build a fire inside that oven?

A: No. Build it in th'fireplace and put th'coals in th'oven out here.

W: How big was it?

A: Maybe th'top of it was as big as a skillet. Not hardly as big as that. I've got two of'em. Got one with a handle to it. I call it a fryin' pan. They're upstairs. Go upstairs if you'uns can get up there. There's so much nastiness up there, I don't know whether you can get up there or not. I do hate t'have my things that way, but I can't help it.

[To Wig, who is still working with the hog's head.] Y'doin' any good?

W: You think we ought to try with this saw?

A: Saw right down through it. It has t'be cut up anyhow. It won't hurt it.

W: I'm worried about the saw.

A: Ah, it won't hurt it. If it does, let it holler. It's spent its days.

W: If it does, let it holler? [Laughing.]

A: Yeah. [Laughing.] Yes sir, it's spent its days. That's my husband's daddy's saw. [Pause while Wig saws.] Don't you hit th'eyeball if you can help it!

W: What'll happen if I hit it?

A: Oh, that ol' black stuff'll just run out all over you. [Laughter.] I don't want t'see it. It ain't a bit nasty in th'world, but I just don't want t'see it.

P: Get it all over everything.

A: That's right, too. [To Wig.] That's just about as hard as th'other way, ain't it? Boys, Miss Dills, if she were here I'd let her take that out. She's took out hundreds of 'em. I never did try t'take out nary'n before. This is th'first one I ever tried. What about bein' eighty-four years old and helped with th'cookin' and everthing all m'life, and never done this? Y'see, at my house, they was four boys and one girl and I was th'oldest girl, and they always done all such as'at. And Mommy wouldn't let me cut a stick a'wood, no sir. I wanted t'cook many times, but if she heard that ax hit one lick'r two licks on th'wood pile: "Lay that ax down!" That was when I knowed t'do it. She'd a'whupped me all over.

I wish I did have a good sharp knife.

W: That saw's not going to help much.

A: It ain't? I can't sharpen knives'r do nothin'! I use t'have a good grindstone put up there at th'crib shed, and use t'grind them knives. Ulyss'd hold th'knives and I'd turn th'grinder. But I ain't got nobody t'do that no more. I hope you boys never has t'live by yourselves. In one way it's a joy. In another way, it's lonesome. Uneasy. Uneasy many times. Nobody t'help you. Don't make no difference how bad sick y'get, there's nobody t'hand you a dose a'medicine nor t'do a thing in th'world. Boys, it's not s'good, I can tell y'that now. They's families that want t'come here and live. They's one family from Rabun Gap wanted t'come here and live.

W: Up here on this place?

A: Yeah.

W: There you are! [Hands her the second eye.]

A: Done a little better, didn't it? They wanted t'come here and live, but they've got a whole gang a'younguns and they'd be in school. I'd have t'wait on'em, and I said I didn't want t'do that. I just don't want t'do that. [Pause.] Now that's all I want you t'do. That's a whole lot. I just couldn't do that myself. Two heads are better'n one, even if one *is* a sheep's head!

W: You know, you've still got a lot of hairs left on here.

A: I got th'fire in th'stove. I'll either cut'em off or singe'em off, or scald'em off. See, I done got m'water on. Put it on th'fire just a while ago. But that's all I'm gonna do with that for now. I'll pour cold water over that and in th'mornin' it'll be just as white, and then I'll put it in my cooker, I call it.

W: That's where the ear is attached, right there?

A: Yes. That's right.

W: See those little hairs right there?

A: Yeah. You never got it all out, did y'?

W: I don't believe you want that in there.

A: No. I don't. [She goes across the kitchen to throw the second eye away, and comes back.] I trot myself to death.

W: Trot yourself to death?

A: Yeah. Ulyss' use t'go on about me trottin' so much. He'd ask me what'd I make s'many steps for! [Pause, then laughs.] Now if I live, and you'uns live, and you'uns come t'eat with me any time next winter, I'll open a can a'souse.

W: I don't know whether I want to see it again any more or not. [Laughter.]

A: [Laughter.] Oh, it's good, souse is. It's good, that is if it's cooked good and cleaned good. Do y'love th'tongue of a hog?

W: Yeah, it's all right. Can you fix the tongue some way special and not grind it up?

A: I don't never grind it up.

W: How do you fix the tongue?

A: I just cook it in with th'head. Cook it in t'gether and then th'tongue is good and tender. Then, peel off that ol'—I don't know what it is but it ain't no skin. It ain't got no hair on it. But peel that off and eat th'tongue. I like that. And I love th'feet. You love th'hog's foot?

W: Never have had any.

A: Law, how good they are. But it takes a awful lot t'clean'em till they're fit t'eat. Well, till you're better paid someday, I might do like Uncle Bud said, my mother's brother. He wasn't all here, y'know what I mean now. And when you'd do anything, he'd say, "Now I thank you," and he said, "I'll return th'compliment someday." Well, you can't never tell.

W: Sure.

A: No, you can't never tell. I never did think that I'd see you'uns again this quick. I told Mrs. Philps about you'uns comin', and she already knowed it.

W: She did?

A: Yeah. She said, "We got one of th'best magazines in Georgia [in *Foxfire*]. Did you know that?" I said, "Yeah, that boy told me."

I think I'm gonna wash that salt off.

W: Now what are you going to do with those teeth?

A: Oh. They'll stay in there till it cooks. Then I'll throw'em out.

W: Oh. I see.

A: Yeah. See, all that meat will come off a'that jawbone. Well now, I'll tell you another thing y'might need sometime. When y'boil these jawbones, take all th'meat off and get th'marrow out a'them jawbones, and for th'sore throat it's just as good as it can be.

W: What do you do with the marrow? You put that on the outside?

Every March, fresh soil filled the fruit and V-8 cans lined up on her front porch railing for spring and summer flowers.

A: Just put it on th'outside; and what we always used—now you may laugh, and if y'do it's all right—but take a ol' stockin'—a woman's stockin', y'know—and pin it around your neck and that will cure most any sore throat.

W: Is that right?

A: Just put th'whole stockin' around and pin it back here. Put th'marrow, I call it, on that stockin' and put it pretty tight around th'neck and pin it back there and let it stay all night and th'next mornin' your throat'll be well nine times out a'ten.

W: Do you cook that marrow before you do that or do you put it on raw?

A: Cook it.

W: Cook it?

A: Yeah. Y'see, when y'cook th'head, then ever' bit a'th'meat'll come off a' th'bone. Well, then, you take th'bone and get that marrow out of it.

W: Could you save the marrow for later on in the winter?

A: Well, I don't know now. Y'might. Y'might take one a'them bones and put it up somewhere's, and then when y'need it, y'might bust it and get th'marrow out of it and use it. I don't know that. I just don't know. Could try it. Guesswork's as good as any, if it hits.

W: Can I wash my hands?

A: Yeah! Can't stand m'hands with grease on'em hardly. Gotta get some hot water. I have t'get somethin' t'hold that kettle with. It's hot as floojens. [Pause.] I hate t'see winter's dark days come. I wish it never would come. I know better'n t'wish such as'at cause I *know* it'll come. It always has. Y'know, dark days has always come. [Pause—washing hands.] Boys, I had a good Thanksgivin' dinner all by m'self. I cooked a chicken. A big chicken. I thought somebody'd come for dinner, but they didn't. I had beans and other stuff cooked, but I never eat nary a bite a'nothin' but th'chicken.

W: Nobody else came, huh?

A: I just ate that chicken. I'd rather have chicken any time than turkey. Yes sir.

I sure had. I love chicken. I'm silly about chicken. I just love it. [Laughter.]

[Pointing out the wooden stand the washbasin sits on as we wash.] My husband was blind in one eye. He fixed that t'set this washpan on. Y'see how straight he sawed that? I wouldn't take nothin' for it, t'wash on. It's just right t'wash on. If I had plenty a'money, I'd put me a short sink right here so I wouldn't have t'trot out th'door ever' time t'pour th'water out. That's hard on y'.

W: Yeah, you have to go to the well every time you need water, don't you?

A: Yes. But I guess I've got just about what I'll have when I'm took away from here. Looks like th'porch out there is gonna have t'be fixed, and they want me t'sell this place *so* bad. Y'know, they're after this place all th'time.

W: Who's after it?

A: I can get lotsa money for this place and I know it. I've already been offered a lot for it and I wouldn't take it. Offered five hundred dollars a acre for forty acres—th'backside a'this mountain. See, now this land goes over across this mountain and plumb down on th'other side, and th'government land comes up against it and they want that. I said, "I don't want t'sell it." They just looked up at me s'funny. They's sixty-eight acres of it in all, and they said they'd give twenty thousand dollars for forty acres and then they'd give a thousand dollars a acre for th'rest of it. I said, "What would I do with that money?" They looked at me s'funny. I don't care nothin' about money much. I have t'have it, y'know. You have t'have money t'live, but. . . . Well, y'want t'go in yonder t'th'livin' room now?

W: Yeah, that would be fine.

A: My feet's a'gettin' sorta cold. [We go into the living room.] Bought two yards a'cloth and made me some underclothes, and I made Mommy some underclothes and made th'rest of it into blankets. I'm still usin' them blankets. Course they're wore out, but, law, they've got th'heat in'em just th'same. I've got one doubled up and I put it on m'feet at night. Bring

rm it by th'fire and put m'feet in it, and m'feet stay good
e of'em said, "You'll freeze."
it tickled at our little ol' preacher. He's a goodun. He just
aid, "Why don't you and Mr. Ulyss' sleep in here where
er said a word. I thought t'myself, "Me and Ulyss' hadn't
twenty some years." Ever since I been struck with paral-
uldn't sleep with me. He'd take them fits in his sleep and
a'th'cover off and pile'em out on th'floor, and so he never
th me any more. Afraid he would hurt me, and he would
ot in that bed in yonder. Anyhow, I said t'myself, "Now
didn't know now." Course, I didn't tell him. I never let on.
e. He didn't know what he was a'talkin' about and I did,
it go at that.

Under a tin roof, between the kitchen and the can house, stood the well, and in front of it, attached to the wall, was a counter on which she washed her dishes in shallow pans.

We've got a good little ol' preacher, though. He's just as good as he can be. He's good t'come and see me, and he was awful good while I was sick. I had a sick spell a right smart two year ago, I reckon, and he was awful good t'run and get in clothes or just do whatever they was t'do. He'd do that. He just didn't care. Y'know, lotta preachers wouldn't do that t'save your life, but he does.

[We settle ourselves in the living room in front of the fire in the fireplace. Wig mentions he may step outside in a few minutes to take several pictures before it gets dark.]

A: Do just whatever you want t'do. That's what t'do. Y'know, whatever's right t'do, well, that's what t'do.

P: Could you tell us a little bit about how it was back when you were young and you were growing up? You know, how things went? Would you rather be back then, or are you glad that it's. . . .

A: Lord, I'd rather be here now. [Laughter.] Now I use t'live on Hickory Knoll. I was born and raised on Hickory Knoll till I was eight year old. Grandma Cabe lived right out from me, and that was th'joy a'my life runnin' out there t'see Grandma. And she'd come out there and see me. I can see her walkin' till today. Yeah. I lived there till I was eight year old and then we moved from over there in wagons. Do you know where J.R. lives?

P: No ma'am. I don't think I do.

A: Well, anyhow, we moved from there and I lived there till I was married. Then when I married, I moved from there t'over here and I've lived here forty-five years. Law, I'd rather have th'things like they are now. Course we had a good time there at Grandma Cabe's, us younguns did. It was hard livin', though.

W: That's one of the things we wanted to know about most of all. We're still pretty young, and we have a hard time imagining how you survived. How did you get your food, and how did you build your houses, and how did you get your clothes and all that kind of thing? How did you make it?

A: Well, I tell you, I don't know how Poppy made it. Mommy never see'd a well day in her life. She was poor as a whippoorwill, and she was born with somethin' th'matter with her head, and one side a'her head run from th'time she was born till she died. Poppy had a awful hard time. His daddy died way'fore he was born and so he had a hard time t'begin with. Then after he was married, he had a worse time, I'll say, with all that sickness and everthing on him. And Mommy didn't love wheat bread. Y'know, there's not many people that don't love wheat bread in place a'cornbread. So he'd go off and he worked for John Smith for a peck a'corn a day so he could get Mommy cornbread t'eat. Why, he was as good t'Mommy as a baby. Now, you won't believe this, and I don't care whether y'do or not. Y'know, if I tell anybody anything, they can believe it, all right—and if they don't believe it, well, that's all right too. I don't care if they do or not. But I never heared Poppy give Mommy a ill word in my life.

W: An ill word?

A: Uh huh. I never heared Poppy give Mommy a ill word in my life. But now I can't say that about Mommy, cause she was sick and anything worried her t'death. We had some hogs. They use t'have a stock lot in here and they let th'hogs run all on th'outside. And one a'our hogs went over th'highway over there where th'ol' academy schoolhouse use t'stand and got in Jeff Ramey's corn patch and eat some of his corn. He come after Poppy and told him t'come get his hog, and he charged Poppy two dollars for what th'hog damaged. Boys, Poppy was so mad he didn't know what t'do. He come back and that was th'maddest I ever seen Poppy in my life. And Mommy—he called her "Dink," that was her nickname—now she said somethin' t'Poppy and he says, "Now, Dink, don't you say a word *to* me while I'm mad," and that was everthing that was ever said about that. She hushed, a'course, and he never said nary'nother word. Now that was th'illest word ever I heared Poppy tell Mommy in my life. Ulyss' said he didn't believe it, and I said, "I don't care whether you do 'r not. Don't make no difference t'me."

W: Go ahead and tell Paul all that and I'll get some pictures and be back in just a minute.

A: All right. My dad could cure th'thrash. Do you know what kinda person it takes t'cure th'thrash?

P: No ma'am. I've talked to some, but I don't know what kind of person. . . .

A: Poppy could cure th'thrash because he never see'd his daddy.

P: Is that what it takes?

A: Poppy was born after Grandpa Cabe [his father] died, so he never see'd his daddy. Now I've seen him cure hundreds a'children. I've see'd them fight him like a wildcat. They'd bring their little younguns t'him and he'd take both hands and hold their mouth open and blow in it three times. He'd blow in their mouth three times and that'd always cure th'thrash. Never do another thing. I've see'd th'mammy—and th'daddy too—bring'em t'Poppy t'keep him from havin' t'walk t'them. Didn't have no way t'go then *but* t'walk, y'know.

But we had it rough. His parents divided up th'land on Coweeta and Poppy got his part of it, and that's where we lived on up till Mommy died. Then he sold out and went t'Georgia and never had nothin' n'more. He was throwed about like a dog, and that's th'reason I give you good advice. Don't you never do nothin' like that while you live. If your parents leave you with somethin' like that property, you stick t'what you have.

Poppy went and stayed with my brothers in Georgia until all a'th'money he got out a'th'place was gone and he got t'where he couldn't work. So then their wives run him off, and back up here he came. Course, now, I was just as glad that he come back up here as I could be; but still, t'run him off. . . . Your wife will be different t'your folks than you. You remember that. That year he come and died here, me and Ulyss' t'gether paid all th'doctor bills and all th'buryin' outfit. We paid ever' bit of it, and now, there ain't been a one in th'family that's ever said nary a word to me from that day t'this about that. I lived just th'same. I ain't went hungry and I ain't went much cold. Another thing I'll tell you: where there's a will, there's a way.

P: But you think you'd lots rather live today than back then?

A: Oh, yeah. It's a whole lot easier. I've hoed corn a many a day for a quarter. Many a day. Many a day. Y'see, when we were all at home, my oldest brother, Lindsey, bought up a lot a'cattle and brought in there, and we had t'make a livin' for them while he worked away on a job. Well, we fed them cattle and tended t'them cattle. Then we use t'pick huckleberries, me and another brother did, and take t'George Dillard and swap'em for two gallons a'syrup. Had t'do somethin' t'make a livin'. Mommy wasn't able t'help Poppy do nothin', and Poppy just had so much *to* do. There was four boys, but course my baby brother died when he was nearly four year old. Th'rest of us are still livin' except Lindsey. Lindsey Cabe died two'r'three year ago. So my oldest brother's dead and my baby brother's dead. I'm between'em. I was th' only girl.

P: Well, you made it all right, though, back then, didn't you? You had your food?

A: Yeah, we made it all right. We always had plenty t'eat. That's one thing. We've always had plenty a'what we had. Y'know what I mean. We didn't have no great stuff that cost a lot. We never did buy much. We just didn't have nothin' t'pay for it, and we always tried t'pay as we went. Y'know, if y'get t'goin' in debt, y'can't pay it t'save your life. I'm scared t'death a'debts. I owe for this road now. It worries me t'death some nights if I go t'bed and get t'studyin' about it. But no, I think I'd *way* rather live now than then. You *can* have a little money now. Use t'be I didn't have enough money t'mail a letter with. You know how much candy I bought in my life before I was married? I was thirty-eight years old before I married, and I had bought one nickel's worth a'candy in my life. I just didn't have nothin' t'buy with. Mommy was sick and we had t'hire so much help done. Poppy hired a girl till I got big enough t'do th'work. And you know how much he'd have t'pay? Seventy-five cents a week.

But we picked strawberries 'r blackberries and always had somethin' t'eat. Always had somethin' t'eat. Pickled beans. Why, we pickled beans in a twenty-gallon barrel. Don't do that n'more. Ain't got nary a bean this year. First year I've missed in a long time. Groundhogs ate m'beans up and I never had nary one t'pick. I always had plenty a'leather breeches [beans]. Always raised plenty a'stuff t'eat. Raised as high as seventy-five bushel a'Irish taters over in that field over there. We got a big field over there. Good land. It'll go t'th'bad now, I guess, with nobody tendin' it. I just wonder about that.

P: When you were young, though, did you enjoy working with your brothers?

A: All th'time. Lord, yes, that was th'joy a'my life—workin' with them younguns.

P: Bringing in the food and all?

A: Yes sir. That's true. And we didn't have no fights and rackets like they do nowadays. Y'know I've taught Sunday School over here s'long. A man I know who also teaches Sunday School said, " 'Bout all I can get done is t'keep'em from fightin'." Well, I'll tell y' what happened in my Sunday School class one day. Sorta scared me. I never did have much trouble, but one Sunday two brothers in my Sunday School class got mad at one another and they got out their knives. I was a'watchin'em. I always watch my Sunday School class cause little younguns'll do anything lotsa times. But, boys, I kept watchin'em and I looked for that one boy t'stab his brother any minute, but he never. I was already aware a'th'family and knew they was mean. I picked beans for th'family a many a day.

I used t'pick beans everwhere. I went clear t'th'other side a'Highlands and everwhere else and picked beans t'make money. And we was pickin' beans one day and one a'those little ol' boys got his sister down and kicked her. Why, I thought he was gonna kill her, and I wouldn't a'said a word if he had. I was afraid t'speak t'him—afraid he'd knock me down. I'll bet his daddy give him a goodun when he got back if they told it, and I'll bet they did. Their father was as mean as he could be. He'd insult Jesus Christ. He had that born and bred in th'bone and it never got out a'th'flesh. But he was as good t'me as a baby. He never give me a ill word, and he was just as kind t'me as anybody ever could be. I reckon his wife left him. Them boys, I don't know where they are now. It's a wonder they ain't been killed if they is still as mean as they was. May have been. I don't know. I ain't heared nothin' about'em in a long time.

P: If you had one thing that you could say was your most valuable possession —something that you couldn't get along without—what would it be?

A: I just don't hardly know. I don't hardly remember anything that I needed that I didn't get. Poppy would've got me anything. My daddy was just as good t'me as he could be. T'tell th'truth, I was th'joy of my daddy's life. Everthing that he went t'do, I was right into it a'helpin' out. Didn't make no difference what it was. He even made me a old washboard. I had all that family t'wash for, so he made me a washboard long enough t'go down in th'tub out a'a piece a'timber. He sawed it down, and sawed th'grooves, and I washed on that washboard till I was married. Yes sir. And used that ol' homemade lye soap. I made many a pot a'soap. Used good oak ashes and homemade lard till I finally got t'where I bought Red Devil lye. T'make it get hard, y'put a little more lye or a little more grease, whichever one y'thought y'needed. If y'used a little more grease in it, when it got cold th'lye would rise up in it. You can tell when th'lye is comin' up cause it starts gettin' colored. After y'made it y'cut it out in bars if it got hard enough. Sometimes it wouldn't get hard enough because I didn't put enough grease in it.

P: You used lye soap and a washboard all those years?

A: Yeah. I've got a glass washboard now in yonder. I reckon it's still there. Ulyss' got me a glass washboard before we finally at last got th'washin' machine. That's a good thing t'wash on is a glass washboard.

P: This house, do you know how old it is?

A: Uh huh. We built it. Me and Ulyss' built everthing that's here except th'kitchen chimney. It's been built twice. One day we was in yonder eatin' dinner. Calvin Carpenter and his wife was here, and *down* went th'chimney. Scared us all t'death. We was eatin' dinner, or they was. I hadn't got t'th'table yet. But Poppy and my brother built it back.

P: How many years old would you say this place is?

A: I just don't know. Just can't remember.

P: But you and your husband built it?

A: Uh huh. Built everthing that's here. We worked awful hard. Ulyss' was a good worker. Law, he was a good saver, too. He wasn't stingy. He wanted everbody t'eat everthing in this world, and I'm just th'same way. I want everbody t'eat all they want. He wasn't stingy, but he was savin'. His mother was a Ledford, and if y'know any a'th'Ledfords, they're savin'.

P: Well, did you make your own clothes?

A: Yeah. About everthing I've ever had in my life has been homemade. I ordered two undercoats th'other day. I said, "I'm eighty-four year old and that's th'second undercoat I ever bought in my life." Now, that's th'truth. They good and warm, though. They're part wool. But, boys, I paid enough for 'em. I paid seven dollars for two of'em, and I thought that was terrible. When you go t'buy stuff ready made, you have t'have a pocketful a'money if you get anywhere nowadays. But I've done a lotta sewin'. Lord, I sure have. Self brag's half scandal, but I've done a lotta good sewin', cardin', and spinnin' and knittin'. I can knit with four needles yet. I've knit many a pair a'wool socks. And I crochet lots, too. I never set here and do nothin'. Mrs. Philps wanted t'know what in th'world was I doin' when she come in earlier. I was crochetin'. . . . I laid it down over there. I guess it'll get tangled up. Sometimes this hand draws up and I can't do nothin' with it. Well, then I want t'get up and go somewheres else. It just gets all over me, y'know. I can't stand it. But I have t'finish what I'm workin' on now. That's a Christmas present. I give away lots a'Christmas presents. Law, I give away lots of'em, and I'm glad of it. I'm glad I can. But that's her Christmas present if I get it done. I hope I do. If I work at it like I have today, I'll not get nothin' done, though.

P: You still like to keep working, don't you?

A: I just *can't* set here and do nothin'. I just can't.

P: Do you still fix your food like your mom taught you?

A: Yeah. I got my sweet taters put up under there. Did you ever put up any sweet taters?

P: No ma'am.

A: Well, now them's *my* first done this new way. I'm gonna tell you how and then you can do'em after this. Dig your taters and sun'em till they gets th'least bit swivaled [shriveled], I call it, and put'em in pasteboard boxes and cover'em up. I got that big ol' linsey quilt from upstairs and covered 'em up, and, law, not a one of'em's rotted yet.

Now that's what I can't hardly stand. [Pointing to her hand, which is drawing up.] Y'see how that does? Y'know how I use t'get my taters peeled for me? Get me taters like these, and Ulyss'd be down there in th'field a'plowin'. I'd take my taters and my knife and pan where he was a'plowin'r hoein' corn and get him t'peel'em; come back and cook 'em. Where there's a will, there's a way. You can do anything. Yeah, boys, you live as long as I have, you'll find it out.

P: You can always find a way to do something, can't you?

A: Yes sir. Mommy always told me, "Where there's a will, there's a way," and since I've been like I am, I've found it out.

P: How long do you leave those sweet potatoes in boxes?

A: Till you eat'em up. Just take'em out a'there as y'eat'em up. Miss Dills learnt me that. I know one woman that use t'do that, but I never knowed how she done it. Now I've learned. I put my sweet taters up in that ol'cellar up yonder last year and th'rats eat th'last one of'em up. I never got none of'em. Eat my Irish taters up, too. This year I put'em in this can house and so I got plenty. I love sweet taters.

P: You tend to that garden all by yourself, don't you?

A: I hire somebody t'come here and plow it in th'spring, and then I sometimes get somebody t'lay it off. I can't hardly lay off ground. It's hard on m'shoulder. But from that, I do th'rest of it. Sometimes I get somebody t'come and help plant. I always get somebody t'come help me plant th'Irish taters. I could do it, I reckon, and I *do* do part of it. ——— came and helped me this year. Had it all planted but two rows. You know him?

P: No ma'am.

A: He's one a'them mean gang. He's so mean he'd fight a steam sawmill. He's good t'me, though. He's just as good t'me as he can be. I'll tell what he said that day. It's sorta ugly, but I'll tell y'. Now I didn't know what t'do, and I didn't know what t'say, and so I didn't do nothin'. Just stood there and didn't do nothin'. My neighbor has a big white horse in that pasture down there, and when ——— came that mornin', I had all th'Irish taters planted that I was gonna plant but two rows. I had already planted seven rows myself. He come up there and he layed th'last two rows off about that deep. I wondered why in th'world he was layin' off Irish tater rows so deep. I never see'd nobody lay off Irish tater rows that deep in all my life. Well, I was down below him a'coverin' th'ones that I had planted, and he said, "Goddamn that horse!"

Well, I felt like goin' through th'ground. I never felt s'quare in my life. And I looked up t'see what th'horse was doin'. Poor ol' horse was just standin' there and wadn't doin' a thing. I never opened my mouth. He knowed I hate cussin'. I hate cussin' worse'n anything that ever come my road. He knows it. He never said nary a word. I stood there and I looked at him t'see what he meant. He never said nary'nother word, and I never said nary a word.

I went on and covered that row and he picked up a sack a'fertilizer he brought with him, and says, "This is th'way I put in fertilizer." And he put in fifty pounds a'fertilizer in them two short rows a'taters —and y'can see what they made, too. They wadn't no good. And I said: "Well, that's all I'm gonna plant. Let's go t'dinner." And he said, "No," he'd already eat dinner. I knowed he hadn't. I told him t'come on in there, and he come on in and sat down. I got some cake and stuff and he eat that. What made him ever say that for I don't know, but I never felt as bad in my life. Now, that's th'truth. As mean as he was and all, I didn't know what he might say next. He never said nothin'. Always, fierce words needs mendin'. You'll learn that, boys, when y'go out through life. Did you ever meet ———?

P: No ma'am.

A: Well, you ain't lost nothin' by it. She wasn't no *manner* a'count. She cussed like a sea horse. I don't like t'hear a man cuss and I *sure* don't like t'hear a woman cuss. Now what is your given name?

P: Gillespie.

A: Gillespie.

P: Yes ma'am.

A: I'll try my best t'remember that. And what do they call y'?

P: Paul.

A: Paul. Yeah, you told me that a while ago. Paul Gillespie. I can't remember names. I wish I could.

P: I can't either.

A: I can't remember names like I ought to. And I've got a brother that remembers ever' face he ever see'd in his life. I can't do that. I don't remember faces too good. You'uns'll stay for supper, won't y'? I reckon we should start fixin'. I'm sorta hungry! [We move into the kitchen.] Reckon how many taters we'll eat? We don't want t'cook too many. I got plenty of'em, but. . . .

P: Don't want t'waste them, do you?

A: Y'know, Irish taters ain't fit t'eat warmed over. I don't warm Irish taters over much unless I make'em into tater biscuits.

P: How do you make those?

A: Take Irish taters and cook'em good and done. Mash'em up just as fine as they can be and put some pepper in'em, and egg if y'want to. I ain't got no eggs. Ain't got no chickens. Fox got ever' chicken I had. I had twenty-two and he catched ever' one of'em. Anyway, put'em in a pan a'lard'r gravy —whatever y'got—and fry'em. Boys, they good.

P: Lard?

A: Yeah, lard'r gravy. Whichever y'have.

P: And after you put them in that, you just fry them?

A: Yeah. Just put'em in there and fry'em good and brown, and how *good* they are. I already got beans cooked and I got rice cooked.

P: You gave *Foxfire* a remedy when Mike and Andrea were here not too long ago.

Something about some cinnamon put in some hot water? How'd that go?

A: That there's for th'dysentery. Take th'cinnamon and put it in a cup 'r whatever y'want to. Pour hot water on it and let it stand there a little while. Just give th'patient a little sup at a time, and nine times out a'ten, y'never have t'repeat that. Now I know that. I've tried it on myself.

P: Put a tablespoon in a glass of hot water?

A: About a teaspoon. [Builds a fire in the wood cookstove while she is talking.]

I wonder what that is a'burnin'? Maybe somethin' on th'bottom a'some a'them pans. I could a'left that on a little long. Whew. That's somethin' I rarely do. [Continues peeling potatoes and rinsing them in a pan of cold water.]

P: Want me to do that for you?

A: No. When I put that hand in cold water, it nearly kills me. I don't do it hardly ever. I did then, but I could've got me some warm.

P: I guess back when you were young you didn't have many doctors and you just had to make your own remedies?

A: That's beans a'burnin'! You smell'em?

P: Yes ma'am.

A: Yeah. Well, I'm goin' t'set that pan off.

P: I guess you just have to make your own remedies?

A: Yes. Do you know boneset? It's th'best thing for a bad cold that ever I've see'd in my life. It's so bitter it'll almost kill y', but it's th'best thing for a bad cold that there ever was in th'world.

P: You make a tea out of it, too?

A: Uh huh. It grows on th'branch banks all around 'bout so high. Took a many a teacup full of it.

[Drops a potato.] Come back here! I bet you never see'd nobody peel Irish taters without washin'em, did y'?

P: Yes ma'am, I have.

A: Well, I do. Then I wash'em good thisaway. Now, worse'n anything I do need is a little ol' sink right here. Shew! How cold that water is!

I do love t'cook, though. I'd rather cook as t'do anything. Ulyss' always said I'd rather cook as t'eat. I said, "I had!" I'd rather cook than do anything I've ever done.

P: You cook it just like you were taught?

A: Yeah. I've cooked ever since way 'fore I was eight year old. Mommy was always sick and lotsa times y'couldn't get nobody t'stay with her. Use to, didn't have no meal chest like we have now. Put th'meal up in a sack and I'd climb up in a chair and sift th'meal and put on bread for Mommy. I remember that just like it was yesterday.

P: Do you have any old favorite recipes?

A: No. I can't think a'nary one right now.

P: You just make it as you go, huh?

A: Yeah. [Pause.] I cut a many a meal a'vittles on this piece a'plank, though, I tell you.

[Wig returns.]

W: We're going to have Irish potatoes, huh?

A: I was tellin' him a while ago how I use t'get my taters peeled. I can't hardly peel taters now t'save my life. I use t'get my taters in a pan and take'em t'th'field where Ulyss' was, and we'd peel'em and then I'd come back t'th'house and cook'em. I've done it a many a time.

W: How did you keep potatoes in the winter?

A: We had a big ol' tater house up yonder we use t'keep'em in. Now, either one a'you remember th'day they had that walkin' business [a fund-raising walkathon] from Clayton t'Franklin?

W: Yeah.

A: That day, th'side a'that tater house fell out. Ulyss' went over t'th'road t'see 'em walkin', and I went t'get taters and there was th'biggest light in th'house, and I said, "What in th'world's th'matter with th'tater house?" There it was, th'side of it fell out. I went t'get Roy Moffit. Ulyss' started and he couldn't walk. There's a way out across here over th'mountain that you can walk and get there twice as quick. I went over there t'get

SOUTHLAND

Roy Moffit t'come. When he come, we was goin' t'tear that'n down and build it back. He said, "Let's don't do it," and we said, "All right." That's what we done. I wouldn't take a thousand dollars for it right now t'do without it. I certainly wouldn't.

W: Did you used to bury those potatoes and put hay over them or dirt over them?

A: Put'em in a cellar and cover'em up with dirt 'r else—tell y' th'truth, we covered up th'sweet taters but. . . . [Pauses, busy with cooking.] That's th'only thing in th'world that I do.

W: What's that?

A: Let th'fire go out in th'stove and have t'build a new one. I never kept a fire in th'stove in my life. My brother always kept th'fire in th'stove. He helped me with th'cookin'. He did. I've cooked all these many years since I've been married and I still let th'fire go out. I don't know what makes me do it. I don't like t'do it, but then I do it just th'same. Now I'll have t'wash my hands again. Wash'em in that water. B-r-r-r. How cold that is! But law, cookin' is th'joy a'my life. That's a fact. I love t'cook. I'd a heap rather cook as t'eat. That's th'truth.

[Kitten comes into the kitchen and distracts everyone momentarily.] I've got me a big long stick with a rag tied on th'end of it that I use t'play with that cat. Had me plenty a'laughs playin' with that cat with that stick. Mommy didn't want no cats. She said they'd get in th'bed at night when you was asleep and suck your breath. Made me sorta uneasy about'em when I was little. And she said if you handled'em, you'd get worms. That's why I don't let this'n get in my lap much. I just pine blank can't hardly stand it. But that cat's all th'pastime I got, if y'call that pastime. I get m'supper, and nobody here but me, and I've set here and played with that cat and just set here and died laughin' at it. Just love t'do that.

W: You don't mind living up here by yourself?

A: Well, it's mighty lonesome. 'Specially days like when it comes storms and things like that. That's not s'good. And still I don't mind it a bit in th'world. I never have been afraid a'nothin' in my life. There's only one thing that I'm afraid of and that's snakes. When that big'n came in that big pile a'kindlin' wood out there on th'back porch here a while back, it scared th'life out a'me, just about it. I like t'have never got over it. I ain't like this poor ol' Florida woman that lived over here one time, though. She was afraid of a bear, and carried her ax ever' time she come over here. Tickled me. She carried that ax with her ever' time she come over here. A little ol' hand ax. I said, "What are you gonna do with that?" She said, "Kill a bear with it." I said, "I've never see'd a bear in my life." Poor ol' thing's gone back t'Florida now. I ain't heard from her since she's been gone. Boy, she was a good neighbor, though.

W: What did you used to do for coffee when you couldn't buy it in a store?

A: I'll tell y'what we used now, and you'll agree with me. Y'might have t'use it some time. Parched wheat. But wheat's just about scarce now, ain't it? Yeah, it is. And lotsa ol' people use t'use rye. Mommy use t'use that sometimes. But t'fix wheat, y'take the coffle out of it and wash that wheat good and put it in a pan and put it in th'stove and parch it. Keep it stirred till it's good and brown and put it in a old-timey coffee mill. Grind that wheat up and it makes a awful pretty coffee. Or y'put it in a Dutch oven and parch it on th'fireplace. That's th'way we always parched coffee beans.

W: What is the coffle?

A: Well, it's ol' rot, I reckon y'call it. It'll stripe some places in th'wheat and it'll just ruin th'wheat.

W: Is it like a mold or mildew?

A: Yeah. It's like a mold. It's not like wheat but it's in there. Now I'll tell you what'll cure that. Poppy use t'store wheat. You know bluestone. A little ol' hard blue stone. Now y'take th'wheat and put it in a tub. Y'have t'put it in a wooden tub 'r a wooden vessel cause th'bluestone'll eat metal all up. Put so much bluestone in a bushel a'wheat and keep that stirred up.

That's th'way I learned that bluestone is another homemade remedy. I'd stir that in with my hand, and it'd cure ever' sore that you had on your hand.

W: Bluestone will cure all the sores on your hand?

A: Yes sir. I'm goin' t'tell you'uns this now, too. I ain't goin' t'tell you'uns to *do* it—you just do what you please about that. My Grandma Cabe died older'n me, and she never had t'wear no specks. Y'see, I don't wear specks neither. She'd use th'least piece a'that bluestone and drop it down in a teacup a'water and let that stay there a minute and take that out and bathe her eyes in that water, and she could see when she died and didn't have t'wear specks. I do my eyes that way now.

W: You just take a little bit of bluestone? About as much as the end of your little finger?

A: Yes, and don't let it stay in there till it all melts. Just drop it down in there and take it out. Y'know, it'll turn th'water blue in just a little bit. [Stirs food.]

W: You know what? I didn't have any Thanksgiving dinner yesterday, and Paul didn't either. His parents are away. So we'll just have our Thanksgiving dinner today.

A: I hope it'll be good.

W: It'll be better than what we had yesterday!

A: Well, I just set down by myself yesterday and I eat ever' bite a'chicken I could hold. It was s'good, and tender as it could be. Course I had beans.

[Somehow the conversation turns to tin cans]. Y'know, I scared a groundhog away with a gang a'them things last spring. See, the groundhog dug a hole and had a den in th'garden. I had two bushel baskets fulla cans. I took'em out there and poured'em in that groundhog hole and I took a stick and beat'em in and y'know, that groundhog left and never did come back. Them rattlin' cans—he just couldn't bear it.

W: You used to make your own lard, didn't you?

A: Yes, ever' bit of it.

W: How did you get your lard, and what did you keep it in when you got it?

A: In big ol' four-gallon jars.

W: And how did you get it?

A: Took th'lard out a'th'hog and cut it up, ground it up.

W: It's just fat, isn't it?

A: Yeah, just fat. Leaf lard. And I always saved th'gut fat but nobody else did.

W: Gut fat?

A: Come off th'guts on th'inside a'th'hog. Not many people do it without tearin' th'guts. That just ruins it, y'know. Y'have t'be awful careful. Y'have t'know how t'do things so it can be used. I'll say it that way.

[Long pause. Sounds of food cooking.] I wonder what you'uns'd think if I set th'things on th'table and just eat out a'th'pans.

W: That'd be all right.

A: You'uns ever do that?

W: Sure!

A: Boys, I do too. Long as it don't discomfit you, that's what we'll do. [Pause —more cooking.]

W: You say you wouldn't want to leave here or move out?

A: No, I don't. That's th'truth. I just don't want t'move out a'here. I may. . . . I may have to.

W: Why do you want to stay? I think I know why you want to, but I want you to say it in your own words.

A: Well, it's just home. That's all. It's just home, and I've stayed here s' long. Spent my happiest days here. And I'll tell you th'truth, I'm not bothered by one single thing in this world here. That groundhog was th'only thing in th'world that bothered me—and the foxes. They won't let me have a chicken. They catched th'last one of'em. I wanted t'get some more, but Ulyss' said there wadn't no use, so I ain't.

W: Who built all these outbuildings around here?

A: Ulyss' built th'last one of'em.

W: I think I saw a hen house up there, didn't I?

A: Yes. Law, we've sold a many a egg. We've made a good livin'. If y'want t'know th'truth, we made a livin' and made lotsa money here. But now we've put in lots a'time. Many and many a night I've been workin' when two o'clock come in th'mornin', cardin' and spinnin'. Ulyss' quarreled. I never paid it no 'tention. What I wanted t'do, I just went ahead and done th'best I could with it and went on. I had a good spinnin' wheel. I sold it th'other day. [Making a pan of bread.]

W: You make up a batch of batter to last you a couple of days? Is that the way you do it?

A: Yeah. See, I ain't got no milk. Have t'use this ol' bought stuff [dried milk]. It ain't no 'count, but it does. It answers.

W: It answers?

A: Yeah, it answers and that's all.

W: Is that just flour and milk?

A: Lard.

W: Flour and lard?

A: Lard and flour, and milk—that ol' powdered milk that y'buy. Do you know ______?

W: No, I don't know him.

A: He makes bread when he comes. He's a good hand t'make bread. I make out like he ain't no 'count for nothin', but he can handle that bread. I just do that for devilment. [Laughing, and rattling bread pans.] He's good t'me. He ain't what he ought t'be, but I don't guess I'm what I ought t'be. You might not be just what *you* ought t'be, and he might not be just what *he* ought t'be. He gets t'where he drinks liquor. Ain't nobody that drinks liquor that's just what they oughta be. But he comes down here and helps me cook. And he'll make up bread or die. Boys, he think's he's th'best bread maker. He *is* a good bread maker, but I won't let on.

One day he made up th'bread and he never washed his hands and I didn't like it. Th'next time he come, I didn't let him get into it. I try t'be clean. I ain't goin' t'eat nothin' nasty if I know it. No sir. And you cook with hands not washed and that's nasty. Yes sir. That's what I call nasty. I read in th'paper that unwashed hands carry more germs'n anything else. I believe it. So I don't have my hands in nothin' unless I wash'em.

[Begins to mix powdered milk with water for bread.] Can't hardly lift that dipper a'water with this hand. Boys, if it gets t'where I can't do nothin', I'll have t'get someone t'come live with me 'r go somewheres else t'stay, one [or the other]. I lived here in this house with'em for forty-three years, and I hope you never have t'live in a house with nobody else. Half a dozen families mixed up t'gether. Lived here off and on while we boarded folks—teachers and family and such. I hope you never have t'live in a house with nobody else. You'll never be at home. Now, if you ever have t'live with anybody else you remember that, boys, cause I tried it forty-three years, and I think by that time I learned it. Aunt Avie, for example. Aunt Avie was Ulyss's stepmother. She lived here. Now she went crazy as a bedbug.

W: Crazy as a bedbug?

A: Yeah. Now, that's a sayin', ain't it?

W: Yeah. [Paul gets some water for her.]

A: Now I'm goin' t'go do somethin' now I never had t'do while Ulyss' was here.

W: What's that?

A: Set th'table. He was a good cook. He cooked better cakes'n me. And he always set th'table. [Paul draws more water.] That's another thing that I can't hardly do. Done without water for two days a while back cause I couldn't draw a bucket a'water t'save my life.

[Pouring food into bowls.] If that pan was t'burn me right bad, I'd drop it. That's th'way I do things. Ulyss' use t'laugh at me. Law, how he use t'laugh at me. Anything get a little too hot and I'd drop it. Now this is what I couldn't do for years—what I'm a'doin' now. [Putting food into serving dishes and bowls.] I'd cook th'rations, and Ulyss'd come take'em up. I couldn't. See, this hand wouldn't stand th'weight. [Getting bread out of stove.]

W: Mmm. Boy, that bread looks good.

A: Bread baked like that is good. [Shakes pan and bangs it against side of stove.]

W: That's how you tell when it's done, huh? Shake the pan?

A: It comes loose, y'see. There. Now that's just as good as wheat t'th'mill!

[With food on table, we sit down to eat.] Will either one a'you ask th'blessin'?

W: Would you like me to?

A: Yeah. I never set down at th'table but what I want th'blessin' asked. Been raised that way. [Wig says blessing.]

Now y'see what they is here. Just help yourself. I can't wait on th'table like I use to. I can't wait on th'table like my mother did, either. This is what Ulyss' didn't like—me a'leavin' my bread that way. He didn't like me leavin' my bread wrong side outwards [upside down on the dish].

W: He wanted the top up, huh?

A: Boys, he turned it over ever' time he come in. [Pause.] I ain't had no Irish taters cooked in two'r three days. I'm awful 'bout Irish taters. [Passing bowls of food around; people helping themselves.]

P: Remember the last time I was here? You were telling me something about nobody would ever sleep here because they thought the house was haunted. Is that right?

A: Yeah, Bill Carpenter, he won't sleep here atall. 'Fraid it's hainted.

W: Well, who's it haunted by?

A: *Nobody.* Why, he just got scared. It was ———. She was dreamin' or somethin', and she was sleepin' in that room in yonder. He was sittin' up in this room with Aunt Avie. And ——— took climbin' fits, I call it, in her sleep. Tremors or somethin'. They got scared in there and got out a'huntin' t'see what th'noise was. I knowed already what it was. I never told him no better—and I ain't till yet—cause if that's what they wanted t'believe, I don't care. He don't stay all night n'more, though. He ain't been here t'stay all night since I don't know when. But ain't no haints here no bigger'n myself.

Now when we was little we believed in'em, but they never was nothin'. I remember once when Lindsey was sick, Poppy planted a big ol' cane patch right over from th'house and put me and Lindsey over

RIDDLES

Out of the dead there came the living.
Six there were and seven to be.
Tell me this riddle and I'll set you free.

ANSWER: *A bird built a nest in a dead horse's skull. Laid seven eggs and six hatched.*

Big at the middle
Little at the top
Something in the middle
Goes flippity flop

ANSWER: *Churn.*

First it's white, then it's red,
two days old and then it's dead.
Tho' it's of short duration
it clothes the world and feeds the nation.

ANSWER: *Cotton.*

there t'work it and thin it out and he went t'town. Well, comin' light, we got t'playin' about and wadn't tryin' t'do nothin', and somethin' commenced right down below us. They was a big branch right down below us way bigger'n this'n. You ever hear a bullfrog holler? You know th'big ol' coarse racket some of'em makes. Well, it commenced and scared me and Lindsey just about t'death, and we went t'work just as hard as we could go. Thought somethin' was comin' at us cause we wadn't workin'! I'll never forget that while I live. Scared plumb t'death. Yes sir. Now we got that cane patch weeded out 'fore Poppy come back! Now that's th'first time I can ever remember bein' scared.

W: Well, did the people back then believe in ghosts and that kind of thing?

A: Why, Lord, yes. Mommy did.

W: Did she?

A: Oh yeah. She was afraid, Mommy was. Was afraid a'anything in this world. She wouldn't a bit more come here and stay all night by herself for nothin'. You couldn't hire her t'stay here with just me by ourselves. Cynthia, that was Ulyss's stepmother, said ever' night when they'd go t'bed here, y'could hear th'cups a'rattlin'. They said then when you lit th'lamp, everthing'd be just as still as it could be. Cynthia didn't pay it no 'tention, but Mommy was scared t'death of it.

I'll tell you another place they say's hainted now. Y'know this big ol' white house right down here? On this bridge right down here, they say you never can cross that bridge with a light without th'light goin' out, but that's not so cause I've crossed it hundreds a'times. I've carried a light over it a many a time by myself. I use t'go from here t'Coweeta Church t'th'preachin' by myself at night. I had t'cross that bridge on th'way t'church, and I never had *my* light t'go out. I've been up and down there for forty-three years and *I've* never see'd nary a haint.

W: Never seen nary a haint?

A: No sir!

W: What do you suppose one would look like if there are such things?

A: Ain't see'd no haint bigger'n myself.

W: You suppose they'd look like people, though, if there were some?

A: Why, no. All haints ever is is just somebody scarin' somebody, usually.

W: Did they have any kind of ways to protect themselves from that kind of thing?

A: No, no. I don't reckon we did. Now they use t'say that Grandpa Carpenter made whiskey. Made it all his life, I reckon. That was my husband's grandpa—Uncle Dave. They kept tryin' t'get him t'stop, and he just *kept* makin' whiskey. One night he had a awful run a'liquor ready t'run off, and th'devil got after him. Chains commenced t'rattlin' all around th'stillhouse, goin' round and round. I reckon he went out t'find out what it was, but course he never found nothin'. Now that was what they called a haint. Boys, he stopped right that minute makin' liquor and never made another drop while he was livin'. Poured out whatever he had and quit that night. He said th'devil was after him. He said th'devil was appearin' t'him and showed him that night never t'make n'more liquor—that it was wrong t'make liquor—so he never made n'more. Not till he died. It scared grandpa t'death. Scared him that bad!

Now there's some that'll finally quit makin' liquor, but there's some that never quits it. Ulyss' and me never made th'stuff, but it's been made on our place right over there. Ulyss' went across that holler right over there and found a still, and took th'mattock that was there and cut it all t'pieces. I don't know how many barrels he cut up. We found out whose it was way after that. We didn't know then, but we found out later. He use t'live right over there, and they'd have frolics there and get drunk and cut up. God didn't put up with him makin' whiskey long, and He took him away from here. Y'know God don't put up with people that does meanness on and on and on. He takes'em out a'here. He gives'em time t'repent, though. Y'know God is good. God is a merciful God, and He gives'em all th'time they need t'repent. Then, if He knows they ain't gonna repent, He takes'em out a'here. Yes sir. Now I've watched that for th'last eighty-odd years, and I've seen it done over and over and over.

I don't know what anybody in th'world would have a taste for that ol' strong stuff for. I have took it out a'a teaspoon. Mommy's sister, Aunt Mag, give it t'me. Now, she would drink liquor. Her old man drunk it all th'time. They'd get drunk in a thought, but I wadn't a'gonna fool with it. I sure didn't like th'taste of it. I didn't like th'fix of it on th'people, neither. When liquor's in, sense is out. We lived right on this side a'th' road that goes up and down Coweeta. You don't know'at th'dickens I've heared and th'hollerin' I've heared and th'shootin' I've heared and all such things like that caused by liquor.

I slept upstairs by that winder that faced th'road up there. I done it a'purpose so that when a racket commenced, I could get up and go t'th'winder t'see who it was and what th'racket was 'r who was bein' killed 'r what they was doin'. I got up a many a time. I always found out what happened t'ever' one but one, and that was some woman that screamed her eyes just about plumb out. I raised th'winder up—even went out on th'porch and set in th'winder—and y'know, from that day t'this, I'll never know who that woman was. She screamed her eyes out. No tellin' who it was 'r what they was doin'. Not a bit. I've heared'em cussin' and shoutin' up and down that road a many a night. And th'screams I heared on Coweeta, it's a wonder I've got a bit a'sense. Shew! It's a thousand wonders that I slept atall. You just didn't know who was killed 'r what they was doin'. No tellin' what they done. They fit and scratched all th'time. Fightin's bad for old clothes [Laughs.]

But ever since I've been knee high to a duck's egg, they've made liquor up on Coweeta. Folks always made liquor up there. Don't know if they make it now 'r not. ——— made liquor up there all his life, I reckon. He wadn't worth a cuss, and he raised a shabby family. Ever' one a'them's gone t'th'bad. I just didn't like none a'that man. Anyhow, th'law was after him all th'time. Course he always had somebody out a'watchin'. Once he got his still out a'th'stillhouse and set it up right over there in th'meadow out from our house. Th'neighbors come on over here and wanted me and Mommy t'go over there and look at that still. It was hid in a ditch over there in that meadow. "Well," Mommy said, "I'm not a'goin'." Course, I didn't have no better sense or I'd a'went I guess. I wadn't thinkin' about th'law catchin' *me.* Mommy said if th'law had come along and caught us foolin' around with that stillhouse, they'd a'got *us.*

Finally it got so you could see th'light in th'stillhouse and they started cussin' us out for goin' through that trail in th'meadow. Some men went through there one night a'huntin' and see'd that light and next thing y'know, th'law got'em. I'd see'd'em be mean enough *to* report'em, but *I* never done it. If you report'em they might get mad at you. Long as you was good t'them, they'd be good t'you. They never did bother us none except they burned up everthing I had once. I reckon that was a botherment.

Oh, they's been lotsa meanness done on Coweeta. I don't know how many men's been killed up there. God don't put up with such as that. Now, I believe that just as much as anything. Tell th'truth, I've watched lots of it, and God always has His way. And sooner or later He'll do it. And I can't help but be proud of it. I'm mighty proud a'what God does. I am. You may not agree with all I say, but that's all right. I believe it just th'same. Yes sir.

[Talking about dinner, and passing butter, salt, honey, etc.] I don't like honey much. It's nasty. Honey's th'nastiest thing you ever eat in your life.

W: Is it?

A: Oh, honey's th'nastiest thing I ever see'd in my life. Now, they had seventy-five stands a'bees when I first come here. All that was bees up there, and all this here down here was bees. I worked them bees and that honey, and it was th'nastiest stuff anybody ever eat. And they make out like it's as pure as it can be. I know better'n that. I tried it out. I know.

W: What makes it nasty? What do you mean?

A: It's just nasty. That's all. Those ol' bees is as nasty as they can be. Finally ever' one died. They stung me all over. One day everbody went off t'work and a hive swarmed, and I had on wool stockin's. I put them bees up and they 'bout stung me t'death. Now I *knowed* that was one prayer that I prayed that was answered. I prayed for God t'destroy th'last bee they was up here and he did. Never left nary *one.* No sir. They was a lot a'money in'em, but Lord, th'trouble they was.

W: What kind of hives did they keep them in?

A: Just ol' homemade gums.

W: Those are hollow sections of tree trunks, aren't they?

A: Yeah.

W: Are there any of those left any more?

A: I don't think they's a single gum around here nowheres. Now, some of'em was made out a'lumber—y'know, made square, and some of'em was holler trees. I don't believe they's nary'n up in the grainery, though. If they is, I don't remember it. This old junk man comes here and takes everthing I got. He's give us many a dollar, though.

W: Where's the junk man from?

A: I believe he lives at Canton. He's been here lots. Got so he comes after dark, and I don't like that. Takes a whole lotta things that I don't know he takes. I can't keep up with him. Course he's got several dollars worth a'stuff. We had them big high lamps, y'know. Had five'r'six of'em. He kept wantin'em and I finally at last let him have that'un out a'th'bedroom. I let him have it for two dollars. I oughtn't a'done that. And he never paid me for it. He said he did, but I know he never done it. And I said t'myself, that's th'last thing he'll ever get here. He wants that corded bedstead in there that you'uns was takin' a picture of. He's just a'dyin' for that. Said he'd give me thirty dollars cash money for that and another bedstead. I said, "I ain't gonna let you have it."

W: Don't do it. Don't let him have it.

A: I'm not.

W: What kinds of things has he bought here? What have you sold him?

A: Anything and everthing in this world could be thought of. Baskets, and ol' boxes, and scaldin' barrels, and anything in this world he could pick up. He'd go upstairs and get all that he wanted up there, come down, and go off with it. But th'last time he come, I know he took that lamp, and he ain't come back n'more. Him and his wife's parted. He come one evenin' and it come a storm, and he got his stuff and carried it out there, and then he come out there at th'well and got down on his knees on one side a'th'well. I can't get down on my knees, so I just had t'stand there. Ulyss' got down on his knees with him and you never heared such a prayer come out a'nobody in your life as come out a'that man. I was standin' there, about t'faint a'standin' there s'long. I'd been runnin' all day and was tired t'death anyhow. I told Ulyss' I was glad when he got done. He prayed a good prayer, though. He just prayed a real good prayer. He's eat here, I don't know how many times. He comes in about th'time we get dinner ready, and he comes and eats.

W: Do you ever feel he doesn't give you a fair price?

A: Lotsa times I have. Yeah. He's cheated me and I know it. I said when anybody cheats me, I don't want t'have another thing t'do with'em. If I want t'give you a dollar, I'll give you a dollar, and I don't expect you t'pay me for it. I don't expect you t'give me another dollar. If I *give* anybody anything, that's what I mean t'do. When Jenny give me all that meat in there, and I give her them rings out a'th'bureau, I didn't charge her nothin' for'em, and that's th'reason she wouldn't charge me for that meat. Now *that's* all right. That was all right. I don't mind that. But when I say, "I'll take a nickel for it," I expect t'get a nickel, and if I don't ask nothin' I don't expect t'get nothin'. But I asked two dollars for that lamp, and he never give it to me. I know he didn't. Said he did, but I know he didn't. Well, love many and trust few and always paddle your own canoe. [Laughing.] That's what Mommy said.

W: You know, if you went to his place and saw what he charged for those things. . . .

A: Yes, I know.

W: . . . I bet you'd be surprised.

A: Now that cupboard there, he just wants that s'bad he just don't know what t'do.

W: Don't.

A: I ain't goin' t'let him have it. That's my mother's cupboard and I'm not. I bought it and paid for it when we moved over here, but he'll never get it. This'n in here is one that Ulyss's papa made. Poppy made ever' one a'th'younguns a cupboard, and that's one Poppy had when he was first married. Him and Uncle John Fletcher made it. And I said, "You're not goin' t'get that cupboard." He begged for it, though. Someone said I could get four hundred dollars for that cupboard.

W: But he wouldn't give you that much for it, I don't guess.

A: Oh no. Not t'save your life. He's a cheap guy. He is. He's a cheap guy. Still, he's been lotsa help t'us.

My brother in Georgia is th'one that's been a lotta help t'me. He give us that stove in there and he give us that battery radio, and ever' month a'his life he brought us a car fulla rations. He lived in Toccoie and we never had t'tell him t'bring'em. He come up here th'other day. He don't come now like he did, though. He has t'work, and he don't have a chance t'come, I don't reckon. I told him th'other day, I said, "Th'first thousand dollars this place brings if it's sold goes t'you." Stood there sorta grinnin' and never said a word. And I never said n'more. He never said nary a word about it. Good ol' boy. He was here last Sunday.

W: I just hate to think of somebody coming up here and buying things from you and not giving you what they're worth.

A: Well, they do, though. Willard said for me t'quit it. He said last Sunday if he was me, he'd quit lettin'em come in here and take my stuff that way. They have took a lot a'stuff. And I know they've took lotsa stuff from here that they've never paid for. [Pause.] Ain't no use t'grieve after spilt milk.

[Talk about dinner]. Now Ulyss' wouldn't a'had all this [clutter of dishes and pans and pots] on th'table. Ever' time we ate, I'd have t'move all that in there on th'meal chest, and I got tired of it. Finally I said, "They can eat with it on th'table." It don't bother a thing in th'world. Not a thing. I use t'keep boarders, and I tell you, I didn't do th'boarders like I have you'uns—just put you'uns down at a messy table.

W: Ah, we like it this way. This is nice.

A: It makes it easier all around, don't it?

W: Yeah.

A: Yes sir. It sure does. . . .

2.

"He married me, and he died with me"

I was borned and raised in Macon County, eight miles this side a'Franklin, between there and Dillard, Georgia. I lived there all m'life.

My daddy was borned on Hickory Knoll, and all of us younguns was borned up there. We use t'live on Grandma Cabe's place over there in a little ol' log cabin where Fred Taylor now lives. Lived there till I was eight year old. Then we moved t'Coweeta, and I lived there till I was thirty-eight year old.

I was th'only girl in th'family. I was raised with four brothers and Poppy. That was five men. Then when I come here after me and Ulyss' married, they was three men lived here: Uncle Bud, Poppy, and Ulyss'. So I've been raised with men all m'life. Knowed nothin' else. I always been good t'men and men's always been good t'me and I never thought nothin' about it.

I never worked nowheres only sometimes go somewheres and stay where there was sickness'r somethin' like that. Mommy and Poppy just couldn't do without me. See, Mommy was sickly and she wasn't able t'do nothin'. They just couldn't live without I was there t'cook and do all th'washin' and quilt and everthing like that. What about a little ol' bitty gal havin' t'do all th'washin' by myself with *my* hands. Everbody always went on about m'hands bein' s'little. That's cause they was worked t'death. And Mommy washed me t'death when I was a baby. They said if she didn't quit washin' me I'd never amount to nothin'.

Now Mommy never see'd a well day in her life. She took medicine ever' day. They was somethin' in her head wrong when she was born. Ol' stuff would run out'a her head and drip on her shoulders as long as she lived. And she never complained. She was born that way and couldn't help it. She put up with it. Just put up with it. Y'know people wouldn't do that now. They'd quarrel all th'time. But, boys, Mommy never. And she had them—I don't know what she had. She had somethin'r'nother that'd cramp her arm'r'leg and you'd have t'break that loose. Course th'ol'doctors, if they ever said what it was, I didn't know. I was little then. But I've see'd her cramped in th'winter t'where it'd take a many a hard rub t'break that cramp loose. We always kept it from her heart, though. Th'doctors told us t'always keep it from gettin' t'th'heart. Now you'uns remember that, if y'ever have to. If anybody ever takes a bad cramp, always put somethin' hot here, between it and th'heart. Now I'll tell you how I done. Course you could do whatever you want t'do. We had a ol'-fashion' kettle, y'know. I'd set that kettle right by th'fire, get th'water hot, and I'd put a hand towel in th'hot water and wring that out and put it on Mommy till I'd have her wet all over. That'd break that cramp loose. I blistered my hands s'many times a'wringin' that out in that hot water, but th'doctor, Doc Nevilles, he said that was what t'do, too. And that's what we always done.

I went t'one month a'school in my life without missin' a day because a'Mommy bein' sick all th'time. About ever' week I'd have t'stay home a day'r two t'look after her, so I didn't get t'go learn too much. I did go some, though. When I could go, I went t'th'old schoolhouse up there on Coweeta. It had one room with a fireplace. We never did go to a two-teacher school. Always had just one teacher. We had arithmetic and spellin', readin', and ol' grammar. I never did like grammar. And geography, I loved geography. And they was another'n —what was th'other'n? Yeah, history! I always liked history.

We took our dinner with us—anything in th'world that we had fixed for dinner th'night before like roastin' ears, sweet taters, and pies and cookies. We never went without somethin' fixed, and Mommy never would let us go t'school without baked pies, and tarts. Then after dinner we'd get t'play. Now I really enjoyed that because t'tell you th'truth, I didn't get t'play much at home at all when I was little. They was too much t'do, and times was too hard. I don't know what made'em s'hard, but they was. We was just born in hard times. I never had a bought doll in my life. I had an ol' rag doll when I was a little girl. They put one under the Christmas tree for me. It's still a'layin' in there on th'bed now, if someone ain't picked it up and took it off. And I've never been to a dance in my life. I've *seen* one 'r two people dance in my life, but I never went t'nary dance. I never went to a party in my life neither.

We got t'play at school, though. We'd play ball with one a'them balls made out a'yarn. Divide th'gang up into two teams, one on each side a'th'schoolhouse. One team would throw th'ball over th'house and th'other team had t'catch it and throw it back over. You couldn't pick it up off th'ground and then throw it over th'house. You had t'catch it. If you didn't catch it and had t'pick it up off th'ground, you couldn't throw it back over th'house t'th'other side, but you had t'run it back around th'house t'th'other team. We'd just keep a'doin' that for hours at a time. Round and round. We'd run our legs off runnin' round that big ol' house!

And we use t'always have maypole marches. We had a big high maypole, and they marched round and round that maypole, and I can remember them hands a'goin' up just as well as if it was yesterday. There was a song we always sang with that. I went t'bed here one night not too long ago and somethin'r 'nother—I don't know. Sometimes I can't sleep. Sometimes I hear a racket that I don't understand and it kinda undoes me till I get up and see what it is, you know what I mean. Now I ain't afraid, but I still want t'know what it is. And that maypole song come t'me just as plain. Eighty-odd years since I heard it. [Sings.]:

Quinine, ginseng, pink root, poke root,
little obedilldock, and pennyroyal tea!

They held their hands up till th'end a'th'song. What about that, me as little as I was, rememberin' that? I'm amazed at myself! I don't see how I remember that song and remember that motion just as well as if it was yesterday. [Long pause.] Well, anyhow, I didn't get much in th'schoolin' business. I just learned all my learnin' from ever' Dick, Tom, and Harry that come round. I've always had plenty a'company, and I've always paid 'tention t'what they said and what they done. Yes, that's human nature. I knowed I couldn't go t'school much, so it was either learn that way 'r know nothin'.

Now if Mommy had a'lived, I'd be there yet. I never would a'married if my mother'd lived because I was goin' t'take care of her. I waited on my mother day and night. That's th'truth. That's th'reason I never got t'play none much at home. Many a night I was up waitin' on m'mother when everbody else was in th'bed asleep. But I said, after all, I guess I done just as well.

But that's th'reason I never did marry while she was alive. Mommy never did want me t'marry, and if she'd lived t'this day I wouldn't have married. I took care of her till she died. She was fifty-eight years old when she died, and I took care of her for over thirty years. Y'understand, though, that I don't regret one single minute of it. I waited on m'Mommy and I'm proud of it. I rejoice t'God for givin' me good strength. Whatever you do for your mother, don't ever regret it cause she's th'best friend you'll ever have. I don't care what kind of friends you have in this world, you'll never have one that'll ever come up to your mother. And when she's gone, you'll rejoice that you took care a'her, and God'll certainly bless you for it. God will repay you for all that. Now you younguns remember that. I have, and I'm almost eighty-eight year old.

So that's why I never married till I was thirty-eight year old. Now if I

Poppy, Arie's father

would a'went ahead and married and had a family of m'own, I would a'had somebody t'help me out now. I'd a'married a little sooner and then I'd a'had someone t'stay here with me instead a'sittin' here by myself. So it was sorta hard on me, but still I don't regret one single minute.

Poppy farmed and worked awful hard. He was a strong man, and he was a good worker. He just worked on farms here and yonder. We raised what we eat. We got a place up on Coweeta and we use t'tend all that land down there. Had a hard way of makin' a livin', but we made a good honest livin'. Finally, when the railroad come through here, Poppy worked on th'railroad. He helped build th'track. I remember th'first day th'railroad come in here as well as if it was yesterday. They come in here a'celebratin' and goin' on and everthing. Everbody was s'proud of it. They called it a good asset t'th'Macon County township. We was all proud t'death of it. I never will forget that.

See, there wasn't no transportation hardly goin' in or out a'th'county, so our little train was a great help t'Macon County. It gave people a lot a'work. It was a lot a'help t'us because Poppy worked on it, and then my brother Randy, he was eighteen year old and when he went t'work on it, they like t'not have let him work but they did. He helped them put down them crossties. I'll never forget th'day they had a explosion of some kind and one of th'boys that worked on th'railroad got killed and my brother was scared t'death. He come runnin' t'th'house.

I rode on that little ol' train several times—rode up t'Franklin t'where it went back'erds t'turn round, and then get off th'train and walk maybe a mile t'where we'd spend th'night, and then come back on th'train th'next day. I didn't like ridin' on it much, though. It was all strange for me. Th'last time I rode on it, I cried all th'way home. I had a box t'put on and course I couldn't lift it and do like I'd like t'have. Th'conductor thought I could, I reckon, I don't know, but he didn't treat me right and I cried. I'm bad for that. Anybody mistreats me, I cry and I never can get over it. I just keep on, and on, and on. Folks tried t'get me t'report him and I said: "No sir! I just hope I never see him again as long as I live." He really didn't do me no harm, but he just acted s'hateful, and that's th'last time I ever been on a train. I said I'd never ride that train again as long as I lived, and I never have. That's been about forty-five years ago, I guess. I said I'd walk before I ever got on that train anymore. But that was after Poppy had died, so he wasn't workin' on it.

Anyhow, while Poppy was alive, he always kept plenty. We never went hungry in our lives. Even when times was hard. And he was good t'Mommy, too. If she ever wanted for anythin' in her life and never got it I didn't know it. He'd work for twenty-five cents a day t'get her exactly what she wanted—'r anyhow, what she needed. I'll say it thataway. She may not have always got what she wanted, but she got what she needed. And he never got out a'heart, either. I don't know why he never got out a'heart. Sometimes Mommy got ill-tempered but he never said a word. Y'know anybody who's sick all th'time ain't got th'patience a'them that are well. They just ain't got it, and can't help it. But I never see'd Poppy mad but once 'r twice in my life.

Whatever Mommy wanted—it didn't make no difference what it cost—that's what she got if he could do it. I remember one time Doc Brabson told Poppy t'get Mommy some homemade whiskey and put somethin' in it for medicine. I forget what they said t'put in it, but that's th'only thing that would do her any good. Well, y'know what he done? He got on ol' Sam—that was our horse—and he went clear t'Persimmon in Georgia t'get that whiskey. Whatever they prescribed for Mommy, that's what Poppy done.

And she just didn't want wheat bread, so I've knowed Poppy t'work for a peck a'corn a day t'get her cornbread. I'd love t'see a man do that now. I bet they ain't one under twenty-five year old in Macon County that'd do that now. They just don't care like they use to.

He was good. He was th'best man in th'world. I loved my daddy. I believe I loved m'daddy better'n I did Mommy. Poppy was good t'me. He was as good t'me as a baby. Loved me. And I loved him. When he got old, he sold some land and give me fifty dollars t'bury him with; and when he died, it still lacked fifty dollars a'bein' enough. I never said a word. No sir. Went right on and paid it.

Y'know, some people fights their mommy and daddy. I never. I never cussed'em, neither. And I wouldn't a'struck my daddy and mommy—I'd a'died before I'd struck'em a lick. If they'd a'killed me, I wouldn't a'struck'em.

Now Ulyss' never had parents like mine. Never been a human bein' in this world that ever had as hard a time as Ulyss' Carpenter had. Ulyss's mother died when he was five year old, and he never walked till he was five year old. His daddy, Uncle Bud, took him t'live with his sister Liddy. One day Uncle Bud went t'see Ulyss', and when he got there Aunt Liddy was out gettin' wood and it was spittin' snow, and Ulyss' was settin' there on th'porch a'cryin' with a little dress on and th'snow a'blowin' in on him. He had a big ol' line put down between his legs and tied round his waist and t'th'house t'hold him t'keep him on th'porch. It made Uncle Bud mad, and he picked him up and he took him

Ulysses

Ada Garland, Ulysses' first wife

t'Aunt Marie's, and Ulyss' never had t'go over there and stay n'more. Y'know, he never did get over that, though. Aunt Liddy treated him like that, and cause she treated him that way in th'cold and th'snow, he never did get over it. Never. He wasn't but five year old, neither. Yes sir. Boys, he made up for bein' tied in th'long run. Oh, he could outwalk a mule. Yes sir.

Me and Ulyss' use t'go t'gether even before him and his first wife was married. We'd go t'church t'gether and come back, and I would get dinner and then we sat for th'rest of th'day. We would stay in th'house, and if we didn't stay in th'house we stayed on th'porch. We had a ol' pump organ but I couldn't play it and neither could Ulyss', so we just sat and talked. Then he got in with Ada and married her, and they went off t'th'state a'Washington. Mommy had died then, and so I had several other boyfriends. I had s'many boyfriends I couldn't tell you who they all were! I went with one man—I guess he's still livin' —and his mother lived right down th'road, and she said he had a apron fulla money and she wanted me t'marry him. I said I wadn't goin' t'marry anybody for their money. If you children marry, be sure you marry someone you love and somebody that'll be good to you. If y'marry someone for their money, ever'bit of it has wings and will fly away. You girls remember that. His mother wanted me t'marry him, but I said, "No sir." I went with many a boy, though.

After Ada died, Ulyss' come back here and th'first thing he done, a' course, was t'come up there where I was at. I was still single, and th'next thing y'know we was married. It just happened. I had cared for him for such a long time, though.

We went t'Georgia t'be married. Got married there at Dillard. I was wearin' blue serge. I always heard if y'marry in brown, you'll live in a frown; if y'marry in gray, you'll go far away; if y'marry in yellow, you're ashamed of your fellow; if y'marry in green, you're ashamed t'be seen; if y'marry in white, you've chosen all right; if y'marry in blue, you'll always be true. People believed in all that. Why, you couldn't hire some people t'marry in yellow t'save your life. I reckon I believed all that, too, cause I was married in blue. After we married, we went back t'my home on our weddin' night and then moved here t'Ulyss's home and we stayed here since th'first day that we came up here. Then Ulyss' died and left me by myself. He married me, and he died with me. Just as happy as he could be. He was. Just as happy as he could be. Th'twenty-ninth day of December is my birthday. I was thirty-eight year old on a Saturday and married th'next day, and we moved here on New Year's Day, and I've been livin' here ever since. I just moved three times in my life. Lived in three different houses.

Folks want me t'sell this house and build another'n, but I said, "I ain't a'gonna build nary'nother house!" I helped build two houses and th'barns that went with'em already, and I said, "I've built my last." Gettin' too old t'be way up there on top a'them things.

Ulysses and Arie

Ulysses and Arie with Patsy Cabe Kelly and Dennis Cabe. Patsy is now a mother—she, as a friend of Andrea Burrell (who was a Foxfire student), told Andrea about Aunt Arie.

At m'first home, I helped build ever' bit a'that one—barn and all. Ever' bit a'it. I'll tell y'what happened one day. It was funny t'me. I ought t'be ashamed t'tell this but I'm goin' to. [Laughter.] I was on a big ledge puttin' a board on th'lower end a'th'kitchen. The house—it was high on th'hillside. Poppy was puttin' th'last weather-boardin' on up at th'top when th'scaffel fell. It was awful high and it fell right down. I didn't happen t'be up there at th'time, but Poppy was on it and he went straight down with it. Poppy just looked up, laughed, and said, "Well, sir, I'm sittin' here just like I was up there!" Boys, that just tickled us younguns t'death! [Laughter.] I never will forget that. It *did* scare me, though.

Now this house here has been built thirty-two years [in 1975], and me

Left to right: Dorothy Cabe, Arie's niece; Mount Cabe, Arie's brother; Grady Cabe, Arie's nephew; Cecil Cabe, another nephew; and Poppy, Arie's father. Aunt Arie and Ulysses are in the foreground.

and Ulyss' built everthing here except th'kitchen chimney. We was married a little over four years before we built it. Before, we lived in a little ol' log house that was here. We slept in th'dinin' room and then we had a bed upstairs, too. The way we got that house was from Uncle Bud and Aunt Avie, Ulyss's father and stepmother. They'd lived here on this place for fifty'r sixty years before I come here—ever since they'd been married. Well, after me and Ulyss' married, they willed this place to Ulyss' and we just come here and moved into that little log house. It served, except th'kitchen was about plumb down, so Ulyss' tore it down and built another kitchen. It still wasn't no house much, though.

I kept beggin' Ulyss' t'build a house, so finally he tore down th'ol' log house and we built this'n. The neighbors made a raisin' and put it up. T'make a house-raisin', y'go t'th'woods wherever your timbers are at, and cut th'logs and take'em down t'th'place you're gonna build th'house, and then ask all your neighbors t'come on a certain date. You'd need four men with good axes, and they'd have t'know what t'do. Each one took a corner a'th'house, and th'others stood on th'ground and got th'logs ready and rolled'em up there where they notched'em and put'em down. Next thing y'know, they'd got up th'square a'th'house. And somebody'd lay them rafters off a certain way and cut th' notches in th'rafters and nail'em t'gether at th'top and put'em up. They'd raise a house in one day if it was a good gang a'men.

Then me and Ulyss' did all th'rest. I helped on all a'this and that that I could. I even helped a little bit on th'chimneys. We built them out a'rock and mud. We hauled th'rocks on a sled back when we had a team a'mules. We'd put th'mules t'th'sled and drive'em up yonder on th'mountain and get out th'rock and put'em on th'sled, and then me and Ulyss'd get on that sled and ride t'th'house.

Then we'd go to a certain place and get th'kinda mud that's sticky. We got th'mud for this livin' room chimney out a'th'bank right up yonder at th'chicken house. Made th'mud up right there. We'd make a hole and put water in it and put that red dirt from th'chicken house in there and mix it up—not too awful thin. If y'have it too awful thin it'll squash all out when y'put th'heavy rocks on it. We'd work it up till it didn't have no more water in it much and then it'll glue th'rock t'gether. Look at that chimney. That's been there since we built this house and it's still standin' there yet like when it was built. Yes sir. Not a thing in th'world there but water and dirt! And they ain't a better fireplace in Macon County than that.

Course they're not all that good. One a'th'chimneys here's been built twice. It fell down once and we got Poppy t'build it back. They was a whole crowd a'folks at th'house eatin' dinner one day and just ever' little ol' youngun in th'world was there. Th'younguns was in th'house, not out in th'yard a'playin'. Just as I got all th'dinner nearly set out on th'table, I went out on th'kitchen porch t'do somethin'. Well sir, that big ol' house chimney out there, th'front-room chimney, it fell down! Boys, you never heared such a racket in all th'days a'your life. It fell right past th'dinin' room winder [laughter] and th'front end a'th'garden. Well, that was th'scariest I've been, and I've been scared just about t'death. Nora Bell Carpenter said she thought th'world was comin' t'an end! [Laughter.] We was all scared and run out t'see about it. Use t'be, we always had lots a' little ol' younguns out there playin', but it just had happened that not one a'them younguns was out there playin' then. I'll say it this way, "God does all things well!" But th'chimney fell down t'th'mantel, so we had t'do without for a while.

And chimney sweepers builds nests in'em ever' year. Heared one in there th'other day. Scared me sorta. I can't hardly tell whether it's snakes or chimney sweepers. But at least I've *got* chimneys. Don't have t'do without like this poor ol' woman down here. She done all th'work *she* could do t'build it, but her husband wouldn't pay her no 'tention. He died and left it.

Ulyss' wouldn't never do me that way. He was good t'me and I was good t'him. Y'know what I miss? Me and Ulyss' would sit right here at this table for hours at a time and talk just th'way we're doin' now. I love t'set at th'table and talk. Ain't that funny? You got a place t'lay your hands and all. [Laughing.] I enjoy it. I do, I just enjoy it. [Laughing, and glancing at one of the students.] You never heared such a talker as I am, have you, honey? You'll remember me forever, won't you! [Laughing.] Oh, goodness alive!

And we always had lotsa company, just like this. They'd gang up at our house and we'd sit up and talk and sing till one and two o'clock in th'mornin'. We just had good singin's now. That's all they was to it. I use t'know lotsa songs. Y'want me t'sing y'one? [Laughing.] I don't know whether I can sing today or not! I'll try it, but I may not sing it good.

The cuckoo is a pretty bird.
She sings as she flies.
She brings us glad tidings,
And she tells us no lies.

AUNT ARIE

She sucks all the sweet flowers,
For to make her voice clear.
And she never says "cuckoo,"
Till the spring of the year.

Meeting is a pleasure.
Parting is a grief.
The false-hearted true love
Is worse than a thief.

A thief he will rob you,
Take all that you have.
A false-hearted true love
Will bring you to the grave.

The grave it will mold you,
And mold you to dust.
There's not a man in a thousand
That a poor girl can trust.

They will hug you, they will kiss you,
Young girls to deceive.
There's not a man in a thousand
That a poor girl can believe.

Come, all ye fair ladies,
Take warning from me.
Never place your affections
On a green growing tree.

The top it will yellow.
The roots also die.
If I am forsaken
I know not for why.

Do you like that song, honey? I do. [Pause.] Yeah, had lotsa good times. Sometimes it was hard—'specially when we had all our folks livin' with us. I can't tell you 'r nobody else what a hard time I had all them years. See, there was Uncle Bud, Aunt Avie, and Dovie, Ulyss's girl by his first wife, that moved in with us. Th'next thing y'know, here Poppy come. Well, there all of'em was for me t'wait on. Th'third day a'March, Aunt Avie died. Th'twenty-eighth a' March, Uncle Bud died—only twenty-five days' difference in their death. And then th'sixth day a'September, Dovie married. All that happened in one year. Boys, that was a burden off a'me, I'll tell you, t'have three off a'me I'd had t'wait on day and night. I cried my eyes out nearly, I was s'lonesome and all, but you

Aunt Avie and Uncle Bud Carpenter (Ulysses' parents)

don't know what a burden all that'd been t'have somebody on us all th'time like that. It kept us busy. Ulyss' had t'go all over this whole country and work.

But he was a good worker, and I enjoyed ever' bit a'my married life t'Ulyss' Carpenter. Now that's th'truth. I tell you, children, if you marry somebody that's had a hard time, be good to'em and you'll be repaid for it, because I was just as good t'Ulyss' as if he was a baby, and I was repaid fourfold—a hundredfold. They was a many a day when he was young that Ulyss' wanted for somethin' t'eat, and I knowed it, and that's th'exact reason I never let him go without a meal. If he told me what he wanted, and we had it, then I went and got it. I never let him go without what he wanted.

And Ulyss' was good t'me as a baby. He never give me no lick as long as he lived, and he never got no ill words out a'me. He had a temper, though. He'd fight. He'd fight, oh Lord, like everthing. Fight like a wildcat. Ulyss'd get mad in a minute. If you said a word to him that he didn't like, he would slap your head plum off, and in two minutes. Then he'd be just like he was. I'm not that way. That's th'Cabe in me.

They's times I wish I had said somethin', but then I know it wouldn't a' done no good. Like th'time these ol' house-painter men come here. Now that's th'worst ever I was hurt in my life. They come and took three hundred and fifty dollars away from here. They come here and got in with Ulyss' and out-talked him. I was afraid t'say anything, t'tell th'truth. Ulyss'd cut'em all t'pieces and I knowed it, and t'save any trouble and any fightin' and scratchin'. . . . I knowed what he'd do. I've see'd him. So I never said anything. I let'em take that money off and I never opened my mouth. Three hundred and fifty dollars and you couldn't tell they ever done anything when they was done. But I stood there and got'em a good dinner—blistered m'heels before ever I got dinner ready—and they went down th'road t'th'bank and got th'money out, and Ulyss' went with 'em, and they went off down th'road with that money. I just wanted that money s'bad I didn't know what t'do. But I was afraid t'say anything, afraid Ulyss'd cut'em all t'pieces. He was as quick as lightnin'. He could walk around me a dozen times. I'm slow. I know I'm slow. But they painted this house with that ol' stuff that's on it. I never did get it all off upstairs and it never has been got off th'winders. And Ulyss' was so ashamed of that, Eliot, he wouldn't go t'church for a year. Said he was ashamed for anyone t'see him.

But he was a good ol' boy. He never did feel well all th'time we was married. He was that way when we married, and course he died that way. He was ruptured, and then he had one eye knocked out. That little black pupil that's in there in th'middle a'your eye? It was way down nearly t'th'eyelid down here. I see'd a many a time for him. I followed that man wherever he went. I was afraid he'd get—and finally *did* get—snakebit. He had t'run t'th'doctor as quick as he could go. Y'know that followed him t'his grave. He was bit th'fourth day a'July in th'corn crib. He was in there shuckin' corn and it come a awful storm that day, and we had cows t'milk, and milk t'churn, and then butter t'make. I was in th'kitchen a'churnin' and he come t'th'house and said he was snakebit. It was a copperhead. I said, "You'll have t'go t'th'doctor," and I picked up my churn right quick. *"Now,"* I said, "let's go." He said, "I guess I better," and I said, "Yes, you're goin' t'th'doctor." Jerry Dills lived in this house right down here and he had a car. I went down t'th'road down here and Jerry come by and I hollered and asked Jerry—*told him*—t'take Ulyss' t'th'doctor. Ed Angel was th'doctor then. When they got there Dr. Angel didn't know what t'do. He had t'go and read about snakebites before he could ever find out th'right medicine t'give Ulyss'. But y'know, Dr. Angel cured him. Ulyss' layed around here two 'r three days, and course he never tried t'do nothin'. He scared me t'death nearly, and I been scared a'snakes ever since. Wadn't a minute I wadn't afraid t'put m'feet down. I was afraid I'd put'em on a snake.

They's lotsa them around here, too. We killed as high as seventeen snakes here in one summer. That's th'truth. We counted'em. I never killed'em all. David Cabe, Mount's boy, come up here and helped me dig Irish taters, and he dug up a bed a'snakes. With what he killed and what we killed, we killed seventeen in one summer. I'll kill ever' snake I can find. I just keep on till I kill'em all. Marie got rattlesnake bit last year, and they was a hour gettin' her t'th'doctor in Toccoie [Toccoa, Georgia] and they said she was about dead. That got me

Lee Garland (Lee was Ulysses' first wife's brother, killed in the State of Washington—brought back to Georgia and buried in Tom's Creek)

An unidentified shot, including Ulysses, fifth from the left

Left to right: Bill Garland, Ulysses' first wife's father; Tom Garland, Bill's son; Ulysses; Ada Garland, Ulysses' first wife; Bess Shaw, Tom's wife

scareder'n ever. I can't help it t'save my life. They keep sayin', "You be careful, you be careful, you be careful." And I do watch. I do. I know they're dangerous.

So I watch, but sometimes I don't watch good enough. Here not too long ago, I went through th'kitchen and see'd somethin' layin' down on th'floor and reached down t'pick it up, and when I got ahold of it, a'course it was a snake, and I tell you, I let that thing loose! [Laughter.] I reckon th'cats had brought it in dead. I reckon they had. But it sure scared me when I picked it up, I can tell you! He was dead, but I didn't know he was dead. Didn't know he was a'livin' neither. [Laughs.] For a while after that, I'll tell th'truth, I got afraid t'go t'bed. 'Fraid I'd put my foot down on a cold snake. Now that's th'truth. But I'm not so afraid of'em that I'm afraid t'kill'em like some people I know. Why, you kill'em, they done with you then. Don't bother you n'more. I kill ever'one I can kill.

Some people are so afraid, they won't. Like one time we was gettin' dinner one day, and we didn't use t'have no kind of a house. Cracks in th'floor that big. Myrtle Knight, she lived right below me. She was a good neighbor. Whenever I had any work t'do she'd come up and help me. Well, th'kinda house we lived in, we used scraps and all such as this and that t'build it. That's all we had, and that's what we used. We couldn't buy th'good stuff, so that's what Ulyss' used. And th'floor wadn't double then. They was cracks in it like these here. So one day Myrtle and me was a'cannin' in th'kitchen, and a snake come up right next t'th'stove. Pretty good-size snake, too. Myrtle went out th'lower kitchen door a'screamin' and a'hollerin' about that snake. She went just a' screamin' like she was goin' into a fit and her not near that snake. She wasn't even *near* th'snake. Course I didn't have nary thing in th'world in there t'kill it with, so I took my foot and done it that way a time 'r two [stomping on the floor to show how] and give it a roll under m'foot and killed it.

Myrtle like t'died. She was scared t'death, poor ol' thing. I never heared nobody carry on so in my life. She wouldn't a'killed that snake for nothin' in this world. Why, you just put your foot on it like this and rub right hard and they can't move. [Laughter.] But I sure did laugh at Myrtle! She was scareder'n

Mommy was a'snakes. One come up through th'floor at home one time, and Mommy jumped up on th'middle a'th'table. She was scared t'death. She was worse'n me. Why, I never was that scared of a snake. I was scared of'em, but I ain't *that* scared. No sir. If Mommy had walked on a thousand snakes she wouldn't a'killed nary one. She wouldn't. She wouldn't even look at'em hardly. She'd run from'em.

But now when I get on one and don't see it, I'm about like Myrtle 'r Mommy. One time we was plantin' my garden. Eliot was helpin' me here. He brought two more boys with him and laid th'lower side a'th'garden off, and me and Eliot was a'droppin' th'corn and th'boys was a'layin' it off and was gonna put th'fertilizer in. Well, when they brought th'fertilizer in here with'em, I had'em unload it on that front porch up there so we wouldn't have s'far t'go. I use t'unload it up there at th'crib, but then I'd have t'trip all th'way up t'th'crib and my leg got t'where it wouldn't trip up there, so I wanted'em t'put it on th'porch so I wouldn't have t'go s'far. Eliot come with me t'th'porch after th'fertilizer, and I had th'stove wood piled up out yonder on th'porch too, and he catched hold a'me and give me a push.

Well, I didn't know him. Eliot was a stranger t'me then. Now I don't have no idea that he'd hurt me for nothin' in this world—I ain't a bit afraid a'him—but when he took ahold a'me and give me a push, I didn't know what. . . . He said, "You're a'steppin' on a snake," and he pushed me off of it. There was a snake right down there in th'stove wood. Oh-h-h, that shivered me all over. It scared me s'bad it give me th'weak jerks. I said, "That snake'll get me tonight."

Well, them two boys got that corn covered, and we come on back in here, and then they went out there and they stayed and they stayed and they stayed. I said, "Eliot, what's them boys a'doin'?" They'd moved ever' stick a'that stove wood and killed that snake. Boys, how glad I was, and I thanked'em and thanked'em and thanked'em forever and forever, and said, "I won't be afraid a'that snake a'gettin' me tonight!"

And I have let'em get away from me. I let that one get away one time. I don't know *what* was th'matter with me. Just afraid. I just stood there. Just couldn't move. I let that snake go crawlin' off down th'hill. [Laughter.] It'd come a hard rain that day, on up in th'day sorta. I had a fire that day. Not many days but what I don't have a fire. Now that's th'truth. Well, I got up for somethin' and walked out in th'yard. The sun was shinin' s'pretty and bright. I looked down and there laid a snake, and I never see'd such a snake in my life. I walked as close as from you t'me before I see'd it. It was piled up in th'weeds this high. It scared me t'death nearly. I thought when I first walked up on it it was Mrs. Dills' ol' big cat—that's th'biggest cat I've ever see'd. Scared me t'death when I found out it was a snake.

I never moved. Just kept a'standin' there lookin' at it. I never moved. Never said a word. Next thing I knowed that snake crawled in a ol' pile a'lumber under th'porch. I said, "Lord, what a snake!" I run into th'house and got th'DDT and sprayed it all-l-l over t'run it out from in under there. Then I went into th'house and set down by th'fire. After a while I said, "I have t'go back and look at m'snake." I went out yonder where I keep m'hoe first, and I got m'hoe t'kill it with. But I'd stayed in th'house a little too long. When I got back out there, that snake'd crawled out from under th'floor and was goin' down th'road t'th'garden. I just stood there. It dumbfounded me. I stood right there and looked at that snake go down t'th'garden. Never struck it nary lick with th'hoe it scared me s'bad. I let that snake crawl off and leave me with a hoe in my hand! It scared me s'bad it went t'my heart. Now that's what was th'matter with me. I was just scared too bad. I just couldn't help it. That was th'first time that I ever let a snake get away from me in my life.

But at least that DDT did run it off. Y'know what else'll run'em off? Burn ol' shoes.

My brother's boy, he was stationed in Japan durin' World War Two, and they told him if y'want t'run snakes off from around your house t'burn old shoes. People wonders why I save ol' shoes. That's why. I've got ol' shoes in th'smokehouse now, and I want'em t'stay there till I need'em. Anybody can fix that. Put some trash down in th'bottom of a ol' tin tub or somethin', and put th'shoes on top and put a little kerosene oil over it, and then set it afire and cover it up with a piece a'tin and Lord, it smokes good. I reckon it does. Now, I've tried it and I know from experience that it works. I did it this year. When I fell on that big'n in th'garden th'other day I smoked it out. I went and got some a' Ulyss's ol' shoes and a washtub that had a hole in it and put'em down in it, and got me some coals and put down in there and set it afire, and it stayed there and smoked till I never seen that snake back here n'more.

Now if I was t'get bit, I don't know what I'd do here by myself. This preacher was out on th'mountain and he set down on a log. Now I heared him tell this myself. He set down on a log and this rattlesnake and blacksnake commenced t'fightin', and he watched'em, and he said that blacksnake would run up and give that rattlesnake a lick, then run back t'this certain weed and eat some of it and come back and fight s'more, till that blacksnake finally killed that rattlesnake. And he knowed what kinda weed it was, and he said it could cure anybody that had th'snakebite, but I don't know what it was. . . .

Another thing I'm scared t'death of is a mad dog. You would be too if you'd see'd what I have. Uncle Joe Beasley lived up on th'hill just a little above us. He got mad dog bit comin' from Coweeta, and *he* went mad. They put him in a room and locked him up and he gnawed his shoulders all off. Gnawed his flesh. They couldn't kill him. Didn't want to—y'know what I mean—cause that was their daddy and they was just younguns. So they put him in that room t'keep him from a'bitin' anybody else. He finally died. I forget just how long it did take for him t'die, but I can see him today. That's th'kind a'impression he made on me, now. Oh, how bad that was. That's th'only madman ever I see'd thataway, and I was scared t'death a'him. 'Fraid he'd get out some way'r 'nother. He stayed stout for a long time. A mad person—or whatever's mad—is stout as a mule, 'r appears t'be as stout as can be. Poor ol' feller. I reckon everbody was sorry for him just like they'd be if you was t'get mad dog bit or scratched. They tell me if y'get scratched by a cat you go mad. I don't know. But just think about gettin' mad dog bit or somethin' and then go 'bout and eat your flesh all off! Y'know when they go mad they want t'bite 'r scratch somethin' 'r somebody all th'time.

That's why I never loved dogs much. Ulyss' did but I never. I love'em out somewhere up yonder but I don't want'em here. I'm afraid of'em. I have plenty a'dogs come here. They come here ever' day nearly, but I don't play with'em. I stay away.

Ulyss' use t'have t'shoot dogs in th'yard t'keep'em from comin' in th'house. I never been as scared s'bad in my life as one time. My daddy was here then. He was old and couldn't get about. One Sunday evenin'—it was a day like this kinda, only worse—it just poured th'rain after dinner, and after it sorta slacked up, me and Ulyss' left Poppy settin' here on th'porch and we went off up there below th'cribs where th'syrup mill use t'be. Me and Ulyss' walked up there, and Ulyss' started a'playin' with a pretty little ol' dog, and goodness gracious alive, that dog took a fit and started runnin' just as hard as it could run towards th'cove over there. Use t'be a shed road there, and it went on that trail toward th'woods, and then here it come back. We hollered, "Poppy, get in th'house, get in th'house!" Course me and Ulyss' both run t'th'house as quick as we could, and Ulyss' got th'gun, and when he come back th'dog was still havin' a fit. He stayed there a right smart little bit, and Ulyss' finally shot him right out there. A mad dog scares me t'death.

And they say mad cats are worse'n dogs. They climb th'walls. They just do any whichaway. Let them in th'house and they scare th'life out a'me. You get a mad cat in th'house and they realize they're fastened and they'll climb th'wall and do anything else, and they'll scratch you, too. Lord, they scare me t'death. I'm afraid a'snakes too, but you can get out a'th'way a'snakes. I'd love t'see you get out a'th'way of a mad dog 'r cat. A cat'll take a runnin' fit and run right over th'top a'you. They'll scare y't'death. That's all they is to it.

A neighbor brought me a great big ol' black cat and it went mad and took a fit. Use t'be a chimney in this other room up there, and it laid down behind that chimney and took a fit. I'd started t'get some water or somethin' and walked right over that cat and it havin' a fit. I said how dangerous that was when it could a'bit me. Ulyss' killed it just as quick as he come home. He was gone somewheres, and when he come back I told him that cat had a fit and was layin' out there. It got so bad off it couldn't get up, so he killed it.

You'uns would a'liked Ulyss'. I wish you'd see'd me and him. It'd tickle you'uns t'death. Ulyss' wore a hat too much, and it took all th'hair off his head and made a big bald spot up there. I found out he didn't want me t'do it, so ever' time I passed him settin' there or anywhere, I'd reach down and kiss him on top a'th'head, then walk right on by and never say a word. He didn't either, not nary word. I done that a'purpose for his funny looks. I done part of it for meanness cause he looked up at me *so* funny. I'd do that t'see his funny looks. And really t'see if he ever would say a word about it. I done that for years, honey, and he died and never said nothin', and *I* never. I'm a'tellin' this t'you younguns, but I sure never said nothin' t'*him.* Do you think I'm pretty mean? [Laughter.] Why, he enjoyed th'last bit of it! Yeah, he did, just as well as I did! He died and never said nothin'. No, Ulyss' wouldn't. No sir. [Laughing.]

Yeah, we worked hard. Made a good life. Why, you just had t'work 'r starve, one. [Laughs.] Pays a body t'work more'n it does t'starve! I enjoyed it. I enjoy work. Hard work never hurt nobody. Never hurt me. Made me tired many a time, but it paid out. Ulyss' enjoyed work, too. He'd always come in of a night and tell me everthing that happened durin' th'day. He'd tell me all he'd see'd and heared that day, and I told him all who'd come here that day and everthing that was done here. Well, then we would go t'bed, and whatever I'd heared that I hadn't told Ulyss', I told him after we went t'bed. We talked till midnight many a night. Yes sir. That was silly, but that's what we done whenever he was gone all day and I was left here by myself. In th'middle a'th'night I still catch myself talkin' t'him yet. I raise my head up and start t'tell him somethin'. What about that, him bein' gone as long as he has?

We'd been married forty-three years when he died. That's a long time. Now I'll tell you th'last word Ulyss' said t'me before he went t'th'hospital. They wanted him t'go t'th'hospital, but I didn't want him t'go. I *knowed* when they got him t'that hospital, he wouldn't come back here n'more. I knowed better'n they did how bad off he was, but still I didn't want him t'go. He'd lay on th'lounge ever' day. Just stayed in there. I finally said: "Ulyss', do you want t'go t'th'hospi-

"My custard eater's gone."

tal? If you want t'go t'th'hospital, you go on. I'm not a'goin' t'*tell* you t'go. You *know* I'm not goin' t'say, 'You go out a'here.' " Well, he decided t'go. When they was takin' him, they got as far as th'door, and he turned and looked back at me and said, "Now Arie, you take care a'yourself." That's th'last word he ever told me t'do. That's th'reason I'm tryin' t'take care a'my *own* self. He told me to, and that's th'reason I'm not gonna let nobody run over me. He told me not to. I'm just goin' t'do my best t'do just what he wants me to. Yes sir. I believe God requires me t'do just what he asked me t'do.

3.

"Pays a body t'work more'n it does t'starve"

Before I was eight year old I was workin' in th'field. Mommy couldn't help much since she'd fell and tore her leg out a'place, and they was four boys, but they wasn't never at home. They was always out workin' on a public job somewheres. So I had t'help Poppy take care a'things. By th'time I married, I'd done everthing 'cept ditch and plow. I've helped *cover* ditches, but I never have ditched. Mommy never would let me on account a'my side. I'd throw that dirt over th'ditches and cover'em up, though. And she never would let me cut wood. No sir, she never would let me cut wood. When I picked up th'ax and Mommy heared it, she'd say, "Lay that ax down!" Lord, I knowed t'do it 'r she'd be out there with a switch switchin' me. But I carried plenty of it. Still do, even though it hurts me pretty bad t'carry in wood nowadays.

So I did some a'just about everthing they was t'be done. I use t'tend cows.

Nary one of'em on that hill could milk, not nary one of'em. Mommy never was able t'milk. She never went t'get milk like other people, so I had t'be there at milkin' time twice a day. Four cows was as many as we had at a time. You milk four cows and tend t'four little calves and see if you ain't give out. I'll tell you younguns how I use t'do calves. I had a hard time with calves. Had a big ol' barn out from th'house and they was a lot right behind th'barn. A good fence on this side and a good fence on that. Well, I'd go milk th'cows and then take'em t'th'pasture. Then I'd have t'do somethin' with th'calves. I'd turn'em out and they'd outrun me, a'course. They was wild as they could be. You'uns ever see anybody walk calves? You'd die laughin' if you could see me a'walkin' a calf. I'd half run th'little ol' calves t'th'end a'th'branch with whatever I could. Then I'd catch a little ol' calf by th'hind leg and make it walk on three legs t'th'pen. [Laughter.] I done a many a one that way. They was as stout as I was, y'know, but you take a calf on three legs, they can't do much. That's th'only way I could manage'em. Had t'do that 'r they'd get away from me. One outdone me one time in th'rain—got away from me—and went clear out t'Charlie McClure's. Ulyss' had t'go after her. Course Charlie kept her for us till Ulyss' got there.

And I know what it is t'churn. Some days I had t'churn twice a day. Course I don't eat butter. I ain't eat a bite a'butter in seventy years. We had a ol' cow—her name was Lige—she was black-and-white-spotted. Well, she got sick and got down in th'mud, and I worked with that ol' cow and raised her up out a'th'mud till I got turned against milk and butter and I never eat another bite in my life. Ain't yet. Never even put my tongue to it again in seventy-odd years.

And ever' year I was there I helped my father in th'fields and th'gardens. Early in th'year they'd clear new ground. They took axes and chopped th'trees down, and they'd keep part a'that timber and burn th'rest of it up in log heaps. Y'know what a log heap is, don't you? Y'know they're long. You set'em afire and that big oak timber'll burn two'r three days. It'll just keep a'burnin' and keep a'burnin'. We'd have t'get up at night and look whether they was a fire had got out, and set anything else afire.

I don't know what in th'world they burnt th'timber that come off that cleared land for, but they done it, and th'next thing y'know they'd be needin' timber. They wadn't savin' about timber like they are now. Nowadays y' couldn't find a log heap afire anywhere.

Anyways, then we always cleaned off th'garden and fixed it and burnt all th'trash. We use t'have a big garden and we always had horses. My grandma Cabe give my daddy a horse when he got married. The horse's name was Sam. I reckon he's dead now. I use t'ride that horse t'work on th'farm on yon side a'th'river up and down below Grandma's. Well, after we got th'garden cleaned off, we'd clean out th'barns and scatter that manure all over th'garden. Haul it out there with a one-horse sled. Then we'd take all our ashes that we'd burned durin' th'year and put them on th'garden. After Ulyss' and I married, we done th'same thing I do now. I've got a tub full a'ashes now. I was goin' t'carry'em out this mornin', but I said, "I can't carry that tub out." I forgot it last week, it was s'heavy, and that's hard on me. I can't hardly lift it.

After we got th'manure and ashes spread, then ol' Sam always plowed our garden and mixed it all up, and it always made a good garden. Sam was th'best ol' horse, law-w-w. We kept him till he was twenty-two year old. Then Poppy sold him t'somebody. I did hate that he sold that horse. I wish we'd kept him, y'know, cause three'r four a'us little ol' younguns, just as many as could, would ride on that poor ol' horse's back. He never throwed nobody off, though. He was raised that way, yes sir.

I got me a many a good laugh with stock. I've handled stock all my life. I use t'could run like a turkey. Now that's th'truth. I could outrun a mule. I could just almost fly. That's all they was to it. But I had t'learn that. We had a big mule barn where Lindsey had two big mules, and course I had t'tend'em. I'd have t'put'em in that barn. They'd be out in a big ol' lot around th'barn, and when I'd go t'put'em up, around that barn they'd go, round and round. I've run'em till I wished they wadn't a mule in th'world! I'd be so tired. They'd run this way a while and run that way a while. Well, I couldn't be but only in one place. And Mommy wouldn't help me run'em t'save your life. So I *had* t'learn t'outrun'em. [Laughing.]

After Ulyss' and I married, we had a team a'mules we plowed with till we got rid of'em. After that we dug th'garden up by hand for years and years. We got tired a'that, though. You dig up a big enough patch t'make seventy-five bushel a'Irish taters and you get tired of it! It's not th'right thing t'do nohow. That's horse's work. That ain't human's work. So after that we'd pay a neighbor fifteen dollars t'bring his tractor and have it done thataway.

But pretty soon, then, after everthing was plowed, we'd plant. We always planted our Irish taters on th'dark moon in February. If you want Irish taters t'do good now, you'uns can remember that. Plant'em on th'dark moon in February and they'll make good Irish taters. And if y'want'em t'make bigger taters, just keep coverin'em with more dirt as they come up. That makes'em harder t'dig because they're deeper, but they're bigger and better.

We always planted onions real early too. I still always plant mine in early March. If you plant'em too late, they won't make nothin'. I've tried that. I got out a'seed a'little white onions last year, and finally I got Marie t'go up there t'th'feed store and get me onions, and I planted'em, and boys, they didn't make nothin'. It was too late. When y'plant onions too late, they just will not make. It gets too hot on'em. Same way about cabbage. You can set out cabbage when th'sun's too hot, and it'll cook'em and they don't do no good; so I always set out cabbage soon and I never do fail t'have early cabbage. Now I buy th'plants. I don't wait till I raise'em. We use t'buy seed, but I don't now. I buy th'cabbage plants cause it don't take as many as it use to, y'know. Just as soon as you can get th'garden fixed, set out your cabbage. Frost don't hurt cabbage much. Set out early cabbage and it makes awful good chow chow.

Now th'next thing was corn and beans. This is what Mommy always done, now. She always argued if you'd plant corn on th'seventeenth day a' March, it'd not get frostbit. And that's when she always planted corn. And she always planted beans in March, too. But I can't do that now. Th'seasons has changed. They ain't like they use t'be. They're later. So now I plant corn 'long about th'first a'April. I want t'be sure t'have corn cause I sure love roastin' ears. Yes I do. And I plant beans th'first a'April, too, cause any bit a'frost comes on

Every year Foxfire students helped Aunt Arie in her garden. Here Gary Warfield and Laurie Brunson walk with her through the new plants.

th'beans and it ruins'em; they just ain't no 'count. And I don't care how good you work'em, they take th' "stand stills," I call it. They just stand there so high, and they never have a mess a'beans on'em. I know it. I tried that. And now you boys, you may not nary one agree with me. If y'do, all right, and if y'don't, all right. I don't plant beans on a Wednesday. Now I've tried it twice and I know. If y'plant beans on a Wednesday, 'specially if it's on th'old a'th'moon, they'll be s'tough you can't hardly cook'em t'save your life. I don't know why. Can't understand that, and still it's that way. And y'don't never plant nothin' when th'Amber Days is here. Now you'uns remember that.

Mommy'd always plant beets th'end a'March, and I still do that, now. I'll tell you when t'plant beets. Th'twenty-sixth, twenty-seventh, and twenty-eighth a'March. If you'll sow beets on them three days you'll sure have beets. That's when I plant mine. And if I wait till after that time, they just make little bitty ol' things and they'll never do no good. But if you'll plant'em th'twenty-sixth, twenty-seventh, and twenty-eighth a'March you'll sure have beets. I have'em by th'bushel. I use t'sell lots a'beets all th'time. I don't raise beets t'sell now. I just buy a fifteen-cent package 'r twenty-five-cent package 'r whatever I want and sow it. And y'have t'weed'em good. If y'let th'weeds get ahead a'you they're hard t'raise, beets is. I love t'fool with'em th'best a'anything, cause I love pickle' beets about as good as anything I ever eat. I always can me some.

Next comes okra, and lettuce. I always sow lotsa lettuce. And 'maters. I always have lotsa 'maters. I'm th'awfullest 'mater eater in th'world. Ulyss' always said I could eat a peck a day. Lord, how I do love'em. Ulyss' always laughed at me. But I don't love canned 'maters. No sir, I don't.

Now, th'tenth a'May is a pretty good time t'plant, too. I always plant my watermelon seed and cucumber seed and mushmelon seed th'tenth day a'May. That was Mommy's time t'plant it, and she learnt it t'me, and I've always done that. And then in late June I plant beans and cabbage again for late stuff. Lotsa times I have planted a little *too* late and th'frost would get'em and I wouldn't have neither one. But if y'have a good chance and don't plant'em too late, they'll make th'best eatin' beans they ever was.

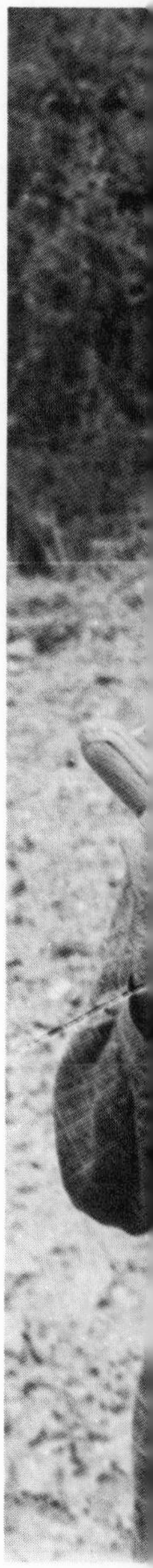

Sometimes a day in Aunt Arie's garden resulted in more conversation than work. Here Dicki Chastain listens as Aunt Arie tells another story.

Now if I have any watermelons and popcorn this year, you'uns must all come and help me eat it! [Laughter.] Oh, law mercy. Popcorn, that's somethin' I forgot t'mention. All my life I've had popcorn. Never missed a year in my life, before Ulyss' died, a'havin' popcorn. Poppy always planted popcorn. Well, after we married, Ulyss' always planted popcorn. And not just a little bit. We raised it by the bushel, and shucked it out and all through th'winter in that fireplace, we parched popcorn. Put it on th'fire in that old corn kapper [popper]. It's just about wore out now. But we never missed a meal without parchin' or kappin' —ever what y'want t'call it—popcorn. Wadn't much trouble, y'know. And I just miss doin' that s'bad since Ulyss' is gone. Sit there and eat that right down t'th'shot [unpopped kernels]. This year I said, "If I live, I'm *gonna* plant me some." Went on t'town with Miss Dills and we went into a store down there where I never been use t'goin', and I can't see nothin' like I use to and can't hear nothin'—can't hear thunder hardly. Anyways, I got a package a'popcorn t'*plant.* At least that's what I thought I did. And when I went t'plant it, it was popcorn t'*parch.* There I was and I didn't know what in th'world t'do. I said, "Plant it anyhow!" That's th'first time I had ever *bought* any popcorn in my life. It had a little package in it—somethin' y'put on it t'kap it with. Now you children may know about such as'at, a'course, but I don't. I said, "I'll plant it anyhow; it may come up." Well, it did! It come up just as good as any.

And this year I got me a package a'watermelon seed and a package a'mushmelon seed, and when I opened th'package a'watermelon seed, they wasn't that big. I don't know what was th'matter with'em. "Well," I said, "I'll just plant you'uns and be done with it." Didn't many of'em come up. Not too many. They never did all th'mushmelon seed ever come up neither. Cantaloupes, they come up good. I got'em hoed out a while ago. Nearly past twelve o'clock when I come down. Wo-o-o boys, I was so hot! I dug'em s'hard. You dig up a patch as big as that is up there, without a sign of a plow, and as hard as th'ground is now, and see if you don't get hot! [Laughing.]

But now, children, if we have any luck, we'll soon have melons t'eat, and this winter we'll have popcorn t'parch. That is, if th'deers and such'll leave it alone. They ain't no fence round that garden now much atall. I looked at it yesterday and right out there another place has fell down since last week. Reckon you'uns can help me fix that? We might get it built back. We need to. Last summer a deer come in there and eat up my roastin' ears. I went in there and there it had pulled my roastin' ears all down and eat'em, and wasted'em. "Well," I said, "I don't know what in th'world is goin' t'happen t'me next!" And squirrels'll eat your roastin' ears up in th'fall a'th'year. That is, they'll nibble'em out here and ruin th'rest of'em. Course a fence won't stop that. Or rabbits, hardly. Rabbits'll eat up ever sweet tater vine that's put out if you don't spray th'last one of'em. I have t'spray my sweet taters on account of'em. I don't want t'be without sweet taters. Ebbie Cabe said if y'ate lotsa sweet taters, you'd never have pellegra. But anyhow I have t'spray about everthing now cause they's all kind a'beetles and bugs and everthing else that gets on your beans now, and y'have t'keep'em sprayed. Y'wouldn't have a bean if y'didn't spray'em. Even th'cucumbers has those, so y'have t'spray them too. I keep mine sprayed pretty good, though.

And then th'Dills' guineas comes up ever 'day. They eat lotsa bugs out a'that garden. They bug it all th'time, and that's a big help. And law, they're fun t'watch. They're good company, them guineas is.

We use t'never be bothered with beetles and bugs like we are now. I don't know how come them t'be in this country now like they is. Never use t'have a bug when we kept th'fields burned off. I reckon that fire kept'em killed out. But course we still had th'deers and squirrels and such as'at t'worry 'bout. And cows. *Had* t'keep th'gardens fenced on account a'th'cows. They'll just ruin your garden. Boys, if y'ever felt like cryin', when they get up in your garden and eat up everthing, your heart just aches.

Well, then, if y'make it past th'storms and th'bugs and th'cows, then comes gatherin' time. Time t'gather everthing in and put it up and dry it and can it and pickle it and preserve it and make jelly and all such as'at for th'winter.

One of the many things she taught us how to make, while she was still able, was white oak split baskets. The sixteen-year-old hand beside Aunt Arie's, trying to help, belongs to Jan Brown. Because of the dry, tough condition of the splits, the loss of strength in Aunt Arie's hands, and the inexperience of the students who assisted, the finished basket was embarrassingly crude by her standards; but she claims she was as proud of it as anything she ever made.

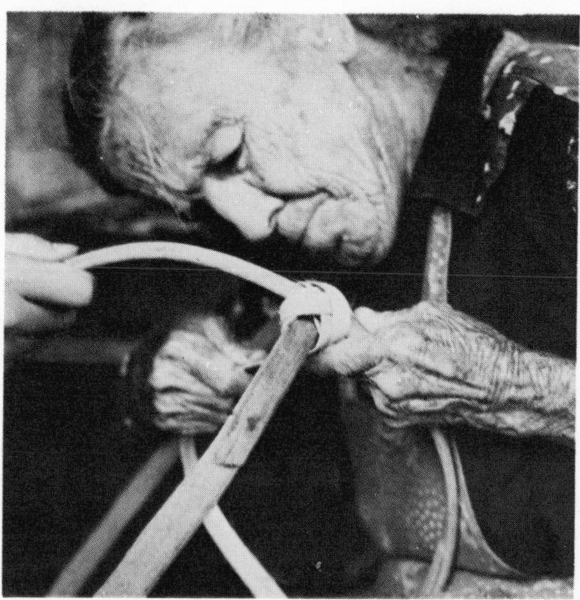

Put up th'pie plant [rhubarb] and corn and beans and all that. That's th'time I like best is fall, cause you're puttin' up everthing t'eat. I just like that. And even when I was little I was a big help. I use t'love t'pull fodder th'best. I sure did. But I didn't love t'cut th'tops. My arms is too short. Th'high corn hurts me s'bad I just didn't love t'cut tops. I love t'pull fodder, though. Poppy said I had pulled more fodder than anyone he'd ever see'd in his life. Cause I was down little, y'know; I could just go a'flyin'.

After Ulyss' and I married and moved up here, we really farmed. We sold lotsa stuff off a'this place and now it ain't got nothin' t'sell. But I had a good worker. Ulyss' was a good worker and loved t'do anything so's he could get th'money for it. He was a money lover, and he made money, too, Ulyss' did.

One year we raised seventy-five bushel a'sweet pepper right down there and sold it. I don't raise s'much sweet pepper now as we use to, but I still raise strong pepper. My garden wouldn't be a garden if I didn't have a bushel a'strong pepper in it. Lotsa people still comes here t'get my strong pepper t'put on their meat.

And now we've raised hundreds a'dollars worth a'tobaccer on this place. I always loved t'raise tobaccer. And apples. One year they was three hundred bushel a'apples took away from here. We sold one hundred bushel and give th'rest away. That's th'way we done. They was Sweet Buffs. If you know anything about apples, you know what good apples they was.

One fall I picked fifty-two bushel a'ol' field peas. You can believe that 'r not. [Laughing.] I picked'em over in that holler and I couldn't carry'em home here, and Ulyss' had a great big ol' horse—a good ol' horse. He put him t'th'sled. I'd put them peas in tow sacks, we always called'em. You know what I'm talkin' about. Put'em in there and we fenced in th'whole end a'that porch there. Whenever we'd get that porch full, we'd thrash'em out. And when we got'em all thrashed out, why, that merchant out at town'd come out here and get'em and weigh'em that day. Then we'd fill th'porch up and do it again. Finally at last they weighed out fifty-two bushel and I got a hundred and four dollars for'em. Boys, I was tickled t'death a'that.

I picked beans and picked peas and everthing in th'world. I've set down and cried many a time with my back, it hurt s'bad. And as long as Ulyss' lived I stacked ever' stack a'roastin' ears we had with my hands th'way they are, and we raised as many as two hundred bushel a'corn here in one year. One time we had a wreck with th'sled with a load a'corn on it. Ol' Nick was th'horse, and he come round that curve up there and made too sharp a turn, and th'sled turned over and I went down th'holler rollin', and Ulyss' screamed. Boys, he was scared t'death. 'Fraid I'd got killed. I rolled out from under it and it never hurt me nary bit. I just looked for him t'turn over that sled thataway and get killed, but he never. Ulyss' was quick as he could be. He couldn't see but he was quick-witted.

You could get hurt easy if y'didn't watch. Another time I was helpin' t'stack one stack right across th'hill there, and them stalks was as slick as they could be. When y'get t'where you have t'walk on one leg, you won't walk as good as y'will with two, I can tell y'that now. And I stepped on a stalk with frost on it and fell down and hurt myself pretty bad. It scared Ulyss'. He said, "Get back t'that house!" I said, "All right." I went back t'th'house and doctored where I skint m'leg up, and went back down t'stack that load. Boys, he like t'had a fit when I went back down t'stack that load a'roastin' ears. But I stacked it. Toted ever' bit of it and stacked ever' bit of it up.

We went after a man that lived right down there one time t'come and help us stack roastin' ears t'keep us from havin' t'do so much, cause I didn't think I could with my arm th'way it was. He said he couldn't come. I said, "I'll stack it myself!" I went on back and I said, "I never will go back and ask him t'do nothin' else." I have, though. I went not long ago and asked him t'come and help lay off m'garden. Just as certain as you say you *won't* do a thing, that's just what you're likely t'do! You remember that. [Laughs.] I tried that, too. Yeah-h-h! [Laughing.]

When I was little, Poppy'd raise a big crop a'corn—maybe two hundred bushel—and put it in a crib shed. On a certain day they'd have a corn shuckin' and get all th'neighbors from everwheres t'come in here. If we had'em like we use to, we'd have ever' one a'you younguns come down here and we'd have th'best time.

They'd always come at dinnertime—some of'em before dinner. Well, they'd set down t'eat, and then they'd go on t'shuckin'. Sometimes they'd shuck till twelve at night before they'd ever get up, and sing and holler and whoop and all th'devil! And they'd take th'shucks and hide people in'em and do everthing. Why they had ever' kinda fun in th'world. That made people love t'go to'em. If you'd been contrary or hateful, wouldn't a'been nobody'd wanted t'go.

When they got th'corn shucked, they'd put th'man a'th'house on a rail and carry him t'th'house and set'im down and comb his head—comb th'lice off his head down on th'floor and stomp'em with their feet. Y'know, that wasn't so, but they just done that for th'devilment and fun!

And we've picked as high as twenty-five gallon a'huckleberries out there on that ridge and sold'em. Use t'be a huckleberry ridge right out there. It was in pines, and they cut th'pines down and sold'em, and that give th'huckleberries room t'grow. Me and Ulyss' picked twenty-five gallon there one time. I'd rather go huckleberry pickin' and strawberry pickin' as t'eat.

And blackberries. Ulyss' was plumb blind in one eye and just about blind in th'other'n. He finally decided he was goin' t'th'eye specialist, and we was goin' t'get him t'fix his eye. You know how we paid for it? Me and him got out there and picked blackberries for forty cent a gallon. We picked blackberries and he carried'em on his back t'Franklin t'pay for that doctor bill. Boys, it was hard on you, too. You'd always have t'go durin' th'heat a'th'day t'get back home before dark. If you had a load a'corn'r taters 'r whatever you had t'trade, when you'd walk up there and back in th'heat a'th'day, you was just about give out when y'got back t'th'house.

Did chestnuts th'same way. That pickin' up chestnuts, that's th'way I use t'get money for m'shoes. Back up there in Devil's Cove and all th'places up in there, that's where we picked up chestnuts. Yeah, they all got blight and died, though. Ain't a chestnut tree left nowhere that I know of.

Through guiding students, Gary Ramey and Roy Dickerson,
Aunt Arie taught us all how to bottom a chair with white oak splits.

Course in th'wintertime I always carded and spun and pieced quilts. Mommy taught me how t'do all such as'at. Mommy was a good quilter.

Now one thing I never did learn how t'do was weave. Poppy's sisters—they ever' one wove. And they wove on Mommy's side. It come on both sides of me. But Mommy never did weave none. She wadn't able. And Poppy was gonna buy me a loom, but we didn't have nothin' t'buy with, so I never got me no loom. Spent money for Mommy's medicine all th'time, so we just did th'best we could.

But Poppy had lotsa sheep, and when Poppy and them sheared'em, I'd take th'wool and wash it out good, and then in th'winter I'd card it and spin it and use that t'knit all th'boys' socks and knit all my stockin's. Many, many times I'd card and spin till two'r three o'clock in th'mornin'. They'd holler at me, "Git in that bed!" Or they'd make me go upstairs and spin so it wouldn't bother'em. [Laughs.] That tickled you'uns. I see you'uns laughin'! But I loved t'do that. I'd work till I give teetotally plumb out! I loved t'work. Loved t'watch wool thread roll up on that shuck [bobbin]. Had a good spinnin' wheel. It was made for Mommy. I let somebody talk me out of it here a while back for five dollars. I shouldn't a'done that, I reckon, but I'll never spin n'more. That spinnin' wheel'll not do me one bit a'good n'more.

One winter I carded and spun enough wool t'make forty-two yards a'cloth. I took it to Otsie Bates and got her t'weave it for me. Ol' Otsie was a good ol' Otsie. She's dead now. I've been in with that family ever since we attended school back there in th'woods. They lived right near Otto. I been good friends with that family all this many years. And boys, they was good, too. You didn't go over there t'eat without you got a table full. I eat there a many a time. They'd come here, 'r I went there. I'd go t'church and I'd go home with'em. They'd come t'church and they'd come home with me. We use t'eat there often, and I miss'em so bad.

Anyways, she wove forty-two yards a'cloth out a'that wool thread. We had twenty-seven geese, and I picked them geese and made a featherbed for ever' one a'th'younguns and for me and Mommy and Poppy; and then I took

"Ain't nothin'
in th'world like
good homemade
pleasure."

that wool cloth Otsie wove and made blankets for ever' one a'th'beds and made two slips for Mommy and two slips for me. That's been nearly sixty year ago, and I'm still wearin' them slips yet, believe that 'r not. They're as thin as vanity, but boys, they just last you forever and ever. And y'know how they was washed, don't y'? Out there where th'branch is. Had a wash place fixed out there, and I washed all our clothes there. Boiled'em in a black washpot with homemade lye soap and battled'em and renched'em in that branch. But I've still got them clothes. Patched some a'them blankets th'other day. They's still good wool about 'em. Boys, you can tell th'difference when you put one a'them on th'bed, too. They better'n cotton ones today. What about anything lastin' that long? Don't look like it would, does it? But it does. It's homemade. Homemade lasts a lot longer. Lasts longer'n anything made today.

Even after I married Ulyss', I never bought no clothes ready-made. Made all my clothes. Y'know, I've made suits and suit coats. I made my daddy's pants. You wouldn't think I could sew that good, would y'? And y'know, they use t'have little coat suits for women? I've made'em and sold'em. Can't do that now. Can't see good enough. See, I had a ol'-fashion' sewin' machine by then. Th'first sewin' machine ever come into Macon County, I had it. I was offered two hundred dollars for that sewin' machine and wouldn't take it. It don't work any more. There's something misfixed down in there some way. But still, I won't sell it. I love t'sew. Wish I had a dollar for ever' suit a'clothes I've made.

And quilts, I wish I'd kept a count a'how many quilts I've pieced. Now I never sold none of'em. What I didn't keep, I give away. Three winters ago I pieced twenty-four and I give th'last one of'em away. I didn't keep nary one. I don't know why I didn't keep one, but I didn't do it. I've always done that, though. Winter before last I pieced twenty-three and give them away. Last winter I didn't piece nary one. This hand got where I can't cut th'scraps out. Can't use th'scissors t'cut. This hand just won't do it. I've quilted my part now. That aggravates me, sorta. Ah, that ain't no use. . . .

Y'know how I got lots a'th'scraps I made them quilts out of? [Pointing to a quilt on the lounge nearby.] Them's made out a'a neighbor's scraps. That's her old dresses. I never had no such dresses as'at. I wadn't able. Just wadn't

Aunt Arie's method of removing rust marks from clothes:

Take the piece of cloth and spread it out on a solid surface in the hot sunshine. Sprinkle salt on the stain, and then squeeze lemon juice on it and let it sit until the stain fades away. "Now I've tried that over and over and I know that by experience, but th'sun has t'be hot for that t'work."

able t'have it. So she'd bring me th'scraps and piece her one and me one. She'd get her half and I'd get my half. Yes sir. All a'them overall quilts upstairs, I done th'same thing. That's how come me t'have s'many quilts. I wouldn't a'had it otherwise. I never had no such cloth as'at. Lord, that was th'joy a'my life, workin' with all'at. Get your cloth and get your design. Then ever' little piece. . . .

I enjoyed that, and th'people I give'em to appreciated it and I appreciated givin' it to'em. Yeah. If anybody gets their house burned up, I give'em a quilt cause their house got burned up. And Joanne got her quilt burned up a'puttin' out a fire on th'stove, and I give her one. And I give her father a quilt. They got their house burned up. People are good t'me, and I appreciate it.

Then we'd make friendship quilts for weddin' presents. All th'women'd use th'same pattern and ever'one made one star and put their name on it. Then they'd send all them here and I'd put'em together and quilt'em. One time they sent out one star pattern around for us t'make a friendship quilt, and I'd say one third of'em, anyhow, come back pieced wrong. They was cut out right, but they'd put'em t'gether wrong. Well, I set down, took th'scissors, unsewed'em—ever' one of'em—cut'em apart, layed'em down and put'em back t'gether. Ulyss' said, "What're you doin' that for?" I said, "I ain't a'gonna let this leave here and it done wrong."

Well, they never knowed it, and I never told'em. What y'don't know never does hurt you.

I have one a'them quilts they done for me when I was first married. They done it for a weddin' present and, law, I wouldn't take nothin' in th'world for that quilt. That's silly, but I just wouldn't do it.

4.

"I'd a heap rather cook as t'eat"

I was a good cook and I sure have cooked enough. Now I've cooked for forty-one people and up, at one time. That's when we kept boarders here. Sawmill hands and teachers. That's th'reason I don't mind cookin'. And they didn't *play* with your rations. They *eat* your rations!

I commenced cookin' ever since I was big enough t'do anything. We had a meal chest up on a bench, and I'd get me a chair, put it beside th'chest and stand on it, and sift my meal like that in a ol' sifter. And I'd cook standin' on a chair. Mommy'd be in th'bed and she'd tell me what t'do, or show me what t'do. So I've cooked ever since before I was big enough t'do anything, and I *ought* t'be a good cook. Cooked eighty-odd years. If y'ever learnt t'do *anything,* you'll learn in that time! Yes sir. And I love t'cook. I do. I love t'cook more'n anything I've done ever in my life. Ulyss' always said I loved t'cook as good as t'eat. I said,

"I do." Yes sir. I cooked for Ulyss' forty-three years, and I've never cooked a thing in my life but what Ulyss'd eat it. That's th'truth.

Now, they's lotsa people that won't do that. No sir. Like Tom was. One time I made two'r three blackberry pies and huckleberry pies. Tom come in about th'time I had supper ready. I said, "Tom, they's some blackberry pie and some huckleberry." He said, "I don't want no berry pie!" Well, I never said a word. It sorta hurt me. I got that for Tom and he didn't want none a'that pie. Course I didn't blame him if he didn't want it, but then he could've been a little better about it. But I never said a word.

Now they's lotsa things I can't eat either, but I'll try'em. I don't eat a bite a'cheese. This woman down here had some, and I had never eat a bite a'cheese before in my life. She made a sandwich, and I said, "What y'got in it?" She said, "Cheese." I says, "I never eat a bite a'cheese in my life, but I'll try this." I made myself eat it. I didn't want it, but I eat it. It wadn't too bad. But I ain't eat none since. I don't eat butter 'r milk either, and anybody that can't eat butter 'r milk, they can't hardly eat cheese. I guess you *should* eat such as'at if you're workin', but I ain't workin' now. Just fiddlin'. Don't work like I use to. [Laughing.]

Yeah, I use t'be a pretty good cook whenever I had anything *to* cook. I don't have nothin' much t'cook now like I use to. And I always cooked on a fireplace. We had a sweet tater house and we kept sweet taters from one year over. Why, we raised enough sweet taters t'do us and everbody else, and we'd eat'em ever' day a'our lives for breakfast. Had a Dutch oven like that'n in yonder, and baked our sweet taters for breakfast ever' mornin' a'our lives on th'fireplace. Y'know it takes good wood t'cook on a fireplace, but I love t'do it. I do. It's good. Course now I've got a wood cookstove, and stove cookin's all right. I like it. And it's *so* much easier.

But you've got t'watch about a fire. I use lotsa lard—always have. And I had th'awfullest time one day here this week. I forget what day. I get th'days mixed up. But I got eight pound a'lard here a while back. Y'know eight pound a'lard'll do one a long time. Anyhow, it was too hard and I couldn't get some out t'go into th'dough I'd made up, and I walked in here and held it before th'fire.

Th'next thing I knowed, that bucket busted open and, o-h-h, th'lard was a'goin' everwhere! And I said: "Oh my, a' *ol' plastic bucket!* I never knowed'em t'put lard in a ol' plastic bucket before. That's my first one. It melted cause I helt it there too long. I see'd it had busted a hole in it, so I grabbed th'bucket up and grabbed me a paper and put it on th'paper there t'keep from spillin' th'grease all over. I can't hardly get up grease t'save my life. Went on in and I said, "What else are they gonna make t'cheat a body with?" I hadn't thought about'em ever makin' a plastic lard bucket. But they did. It was my first one.

We always rendered our own lard out and kept it in crocks 'r churn jars. That's one thing we always had was hogs. Use t'have lotsa hogs. Had'em on th'mountain. We've killed as high as four big hogs and put in there in th'meat house in one year and eat th'last bite a'th'meat except th'hams. We always sold our hams and bought more hogs back. Yeah, that's what we done. Ate lotsa meat. I never in my life remember goin' without meat a day in my life. Now that's th'truth. I'm a meat eater. They said that's th'reason I'm s'stout—because I eat s'much meat. I eat it ever' day. I don't know what I *would* do without meat. I wouldn't want t'go t'th'table if I didn't have it.

Aunt Mary up at th'Gap, she brought me a piece a'sausage down here th'other day. I believe it was that big. I was just as happy as I could be. It was frozen and I didn't know how in th'world I'd fry it, and I studied me out a plan. I laid it down on a piece a'paper, laid a piece a'plank under it, laid that sausage down, and took my hammer and pounded my knife through it.

Then I put it in a pan a'flour, rolled it over and over, put it in a pan a'grease, and fried it in a pan already hot with pure lard. When I got it fried and got ready t'take it out, I poured some water in that pan a'grease and made some gravy. Boys, that was th'best stuff I ever eat.

I'm silly about hog meat. Whenever they killed th'hogs, they fixed'em up and cut'em up, and salted'em th'first day. Ulyss' always had a certain place t'put ever' bit a'th'meat. He put th'meat in one place, th'hams in one place, and th'shoulders in one place. And cracklin's, we always called it, th'backbone and ribs and th'liver. Then Ulyss'd take a chunk a'salt and black pepper and mix it

When cooking dinner, the top of her wood stove was always filled with pans of food.

t'gether. We always had a pretty big-size panful, and he done that all with his hands. Then he'd salt that meat down. In th'spring, I'll just tell th'truth, we never did smoke meat much. I don't want no ol' smoked meat.

But if th'flies did come in, we put a ol' Dutch oven in there in th'meat house and put some coals in it and put some red pepper on it and get it afire and that was th'last a'that. Used some kinda oak 'r hickory coals, either one. Ol' chestnut wouldn't last two minutes. Ulyss' always kept good wood. How I do miss all such as'at.

And talkin' about lard, I use it in all m'bread dough. I don't love loaf bread. I just don't love it. So I still make mine. Some people uses eggs but I use lard, and I use a little sody [soda] in it. I don't use bakin' powder. I don't like it. It's bitter t'me. Use t'mix all that up with m'hands, but I use a spoon now. Y'get your hands in th'dough makin' up bread and somethin' starts burnin' on th'stove, and when there ain't nobody but you, there y'are. So I've learnt better. I make it with a spoon, mix it up, pour it in a greased pan, and set it in th'oven, and in just a few minutes you've got bread. I like it better'n I do biscuits. Eat it three times a day.

Cornbread's easy t'make too. I never measure my stuff. Get me as much water as I want t'make bread. I always make mine up with a little bit a'warm water. Put m'stuff in there and stir it up. Don't have th'dough too thin. If y'have th'dough too thin, it ain't good. That bread there run too thin. It was cooked a little too long. It was good, but it still was a little bit tough. If you have buttermilk, always fold you a little buttermilk in your dough. I never have buttermilk anymore. See, I had ol' bought milk. Ain't like homemade milk.

Use t'raise corn pones too, or corn dodgers. You ever eat any corn pones that was raised? It's made out a'cornmeal. Now it's another hard job, and I love it better'n a cat loves sweet milk. I sure do. But I ain't raised none in a long time. Poppy always had me t'raise him a corn pone t'go t'Nantahaly. See, Poppy raised stock and turned'em on Nantahaly range. Whenever th'time come, he'd say, "I'm a'goin' t'Nantahaly a certain day and you raise me some corn pones." Well, that's what I done. I had a big Dutch oven a'purpose t'bake'em in. Have t'cook'em on th'fireplace. And Lester Mann, he found out I could do that, and they was so good, why, he al-l-ways when he started t'th'mountains, he'd always come and I'd raise him a corn pone. It'd be five inches thick. Y'take that corn pone and slice it and lay it in grease and fry it in a pan in th'mountains, and that was hot bread, y'see? And law, they thought that was th'greatest thing in th'world. I've raised a many a pone that's went t'Nantahaly.

And dumplin'. I've always been a fool all a'my life about chicken and dumplin'. Get you a egg and make a good stiff dough with cornmeal and use lotsa

"A wasteful woman can throw
more out th'window with a spoon
than a man can throw
in th'door with a shovel."

black pepper and sage. Ease'em into that boilin' water and ease'em back out. That's fun t'me. Eliot's gonna bring some chicken and let me make some chicken and dumplin'. Might make fried pies, too. They're good. Roll out your dough like you're gonna make a tart, and lay it down flat. Put your fruit over here on this side and take this dough side right over here and pull it over th'top a'th'fruit and take your finger and mash it down around the edges in a half-moon shape so that fruit'll stay in there, and lay it on a pan and put it in a stove. You can put a lot more grease in'em, and sorta fry'em too, you know. Fried pies are good anyhow. Took a many a one of'em t'school. All of us loved'em. Oh, they's good.

And vegetables. I've always had plenty a'shell beans and pickled beans and leather breeches beans all th'year round. I have'em ever' day. I love beans of any kind. I don't care what kind they is. T'fix leather breeches y'take good full green beans. If they're nothin' but slabs, now, they ain't fit t'eat. Break'em up like y'gonna cook'em. Always string'em up on sewin' thread. Then put'em in shade t'dry. I put mine upstairs. Don't dry'em in th'sunshine, honey, cause if y'dry'em in th'sunshine they'll be s'hard y'can't hardly cook'em. I don't know why, but that sunshine just toughens'em and y'just can't cook'em atall. Dry'em in th'shade. I take mine upstairs.

I reckon Ulyss' put that wire up there t'hang'em on. I made my own hangers out a'wires. Y'take y'a wire and bend it down. Bend it two ways [in an "S" shape] one end t'catch up there and one down here t'hang a string a'beans on. They hang there all year, and no weevils'll get in'em. Boys, I can't bear t'eat weeviled beans. I've got t'see if I ain't got another mess 'r two a'leather breeches upstairs. I've forgot'em. I'm suppose't'have. Don't know if I have 'r not. T'cook 'em take'em off that string and break'em up. Wash'em good. I always wash mine good, and then put'em in cold water and let'em soak all night long. The water'll soak out that ol' yellowish-lookin' stuff out of'em. Then in th'mornin' take'em out a'that water. Put'em in fresh cold water and put some sody in'em t'soften'em —not over a teaspoon 'r it makes'em yeller. Parboil'em about a hour. Then wash'em out a'that and put a chunk a'meat in'em, and salt'em. Cook'em a little longer and they good! Lord, they good! Just be sure not t'add cold water to'em

Every summer, Foxfire students like Don MacNeil and Carol Maney gathered on Aunt Arie's front porch to help her string the green beans picked that afternoon from her garden. Strung on sewing thread, they would be left to dry as leather breeches for winter use.

while they're cookin'. Always add hot water from your pot on th'stove 'r they'll be hard. Y'do that with all your food. Never add cold water t'what's cookin' already.

And pickle' beans are good, too. I don't know, I've got so I can't have pickle' beans like I use t'have, though. I don't know if it's me 'r if it's th'salt. I believe it's that iodized salt. I despise it. And I love pickle' beans if they *are* only pickle' beans. I love'em. Well, I love beans just anyway.

And hominy. Did you ever eat any lye hominy? Boys, that's th'best stuff.

It's better'n sody hominy. Yeah, it sure is. Did you ever eat any sody hominy? I made a many a potful. Said th'other night 'r two ago that I wished I'd a'kept my pot. It was a three-gallon pot. I'd make it full a'hominy. Course I couldn't do that now cause they's nobody t'eat it but me and it'd ruin before I'd get it eat up. But when they use t'be six and eight here, I'd make that potful a'hominy and it would do us three at a time. You'd have t'keep it heated, though, t'keep it from sourin'. Have t'heat it ever' day t'keep it from sourin'. You have t'put lye in it t'take th'husk 'r th'hide off. They call it husk, I think. Gather up th'biggest ears a'dried corn you can find so it will be good hominy. I never tried little. I don't know what it would be like. We always got those big kernels and soaked'em overnight in cold water with a handful a'sody in it. Then in th' mornin' we'd boil that—sody and all—until that hide'd slip off when y'rubbed them kernels between your hands. Sometimes we'd have t'boil it in two 'r more waters t'get all that off. I've see'd Mommy put a shovelful a'ashes in a cloth sack and drop that down in that water and that helps get that all off. Then just fry that hominy in grease when you're ready t'eat it. I always have wanted t'fix me some popcorn hominy but I never did.

I've also raised acorn squash. We washed'em good and cut'em up in pieces. Put a little sugar on'em, put'em in a pan in th'stove, and baked'em. Watch 'em good t'keep'em from burnin'. They burn easy. Then take'em out and eat'em. They're good. I don't raise none of'em much, though. I just don't love'em good enough t'raise'em and fool with. That's all they is to it.

I love salad, too. Turnip salad and mustard salad. Y'put it in th'garden and y'never have t'sow it no more. Y'always leave some of it t'come t'seed. I've had it in that garden thirty-five year and I never had t'sow it again after th'first time.

Same with wild stuff like lamb's-quarters. Y'cook lamb's-quarters like mustard. I'll show y'some next time y'come up here in daylight. I cut some this evenin'. I don't think I got it all, though. It's a hateful weed when it gets in your garden. It's hard t'get rid of, but it's th'best thing for hogs they ever was in this world t'feed'em. They just love it. There was somethin' else called mouse-ear. It grows everwhere. Now they was a family that lived right out on top a'th'hill right yonder. She got out ever' year, and got this mouse-ear and some other kind a'weed that she mixed with it; I forget what th'name of it was. She mixed that all t'gether and she said that was th'best salad they ever was. But I never did try that. T'tell you th'truth, I was always afraid of it. Afraid I'd get poisoned. She cooked it and eat it and she loved it, just loved it. Cooked it just like mustard.

But now creases, ain't nothin' in th'world no better'n creases. Some people calls it watercress. Why, I'd hunt th'fields for it. I use t'have it in th'gar-

Hominy was always fried in grease over an open eye on the wood stove.

den, but see, when they come t'plow my garden, I sorta feel ashamed t'get in there and follow'em around and around and around—'specially strangers—and they 'bout plowed it all up. But that big field over there where we use t'raise corn, we use t'have creases all over in it, and in March I'd have creases t'eat. It's hard t'gather, though. Cook it just like y'do mustard. Take creases and mustard mixed t'gether, and you've never eat nothin' no better in your life. They're 'bout six'r eight inches high when y'get'em. When it gets in bloom you can pinch th'leaves off and not eat th'stems. I have gathered it then but I don't cook th'stems. I just cook th'leaves. Put some middlin' meat on in th'mornin' and boil it about two hours till it's all good and tender. Then pour off th'grease and put in fresh water t'boil and add that meat and them greens and boil all that t'gether about thirty minutes and you've got you somethin' good. It's good when it first comes up, sure 'nough. I was wonderin' th'other day if they was any over there. I didn't go over there cause it's growed up s'bad. I wished you could've see'd this place when Ulyss' was livin'. But law, I love them creases.

Now one thing I'm not a'gonna eat is poke salad. That's th'stinkinest stuff I ever cooked in my life. [Laughter.] I can't bear it. One day Jim Bell's brother was here. He worked across th'mountain up here, and he wanted me t'cook him poke salad. "I want some poke salad, I want some poke salad," he said. But I didn't want no poke salad. I knowed I didn't. He told me how t'cook it, though, and kept on till I gathered me some. Got that ol' poke salad and put cornmeal in it, and boys, I couldn't cook that stuff t'save my life. It gagged me t'look at it. He was just proud a'that stuff, though. Loved it better'n anything in th'world. That's th'last poke salad I ever cooked. But if you want t'try it, take young poke stalks, y'know, 'bout so high, and wash'em good and cook it good and tender. Cook th'leaves and stalks and all t'gether. Put it in a pot and boil it good and tender. It don't take too long t'cook it. Doc Nevilles said I oughta eat a big potful a'poke salad ever' year. Said it was th'healthiest stuff. [Laughter.] I knowed what it'd do for me. Make me sick.

Another way t'fix it is you can take and boil that good and tender, and take it out a'that parboil water and lay it in a pan a'hot grease with some cornmeal gravy and let it fry a little while. Now I never eat none like that, but they say that's th'best way t'cook it. I never tried that. Anybody that loves that ol' poke salad says cornmeal makes it good. Stir that all in there while it's a'boilin' just like you're makin' mush, only put it in with th'salad. That's th'way Jim Bell loved it. Why, he could eat that big dishful. That man could eat anything in this world. I never see'd a thing in this world fixed but what that man wouldn't eat it. He's one a'them that says, "I don't care what you call me as long as you call me for dinner!" [Laughing.] I call him a "trash eater" cause he'll just eat anything and everthing.

AUNT ARIE'S RECIPE FOR EGG CUSTARD

(cooked on a wood stove)

Line a small pie pan with plain biscuit dough rolled thin. Then, in a separate bowl, mix up one egg (beaten well), one cup of sweet milk, a handful of flour, a teaspoon of nutmeg, and a half teacup of sugar.

Mix it all up well, pour it into the crust, and, using just a little wood so the fire won't be too hot, bake it slowly until it "sets." It will "blubber up"—or bubble—and then the bubbles will settle.

At this point, it is ready to eat. Serves four.

Peach cobbler was baked in a shallow pan in the oven.

A Sunday dinner at Aunt Arie's was a gang of students, changed out of their church clothes, and ready for food. Here Greg Strickland, Mary Garth, and Jan Brown serve themselves, and . . .

A TYPICAL SUNDAY MENU AT AUNT ARIE'S

souse and sausage
chicken and dumplings
leather breeches
hominy
cabbage cooked in a frying pan in the broth from making souse
potatoes cooked in a Dutch oven
chow chow
bread
egg custards
peach cobbler

. . . head outside to join (LEFT TO RIGHT) *Mike Cook, Craig Williams, Paul Gillespie, Laurie Brunson, Frenda Wilburn, Andrea Burrell, and George Freeman on the ground in front of her porch.*

I never did have a thing t'do with persimmons. We had lots of'em up there on th'mountain—what th'animals didn't eat up. I never did fool with'em, though. I never did gather none cause th'possums and everthing else eat'em quick as they got good. They took'em into their paws and eat'em 'r done somethin' with'em. But all up there about our house in th'cow pasture was full a'persimmons.

Now, we always had good apples. See, we had a apple orchard there at home, so we had hundreds a'bushels a'apples till it come that storm and blowed th'trees all down, and Ulyss' never did set'em back out. Ulyss' got old and crippled on both sides and couldn't dig much, and you can't hire people t'do what you want done. You just have t'do what y'can. Course, we had plenty a'apples t'do just us. Had a few trees left up there that made up more'n we used and could eat.

But before th'trees blowed down, we had done away with three hundred bushel in one year. I tell you, honey, I got s'tired a'pickin' up apples and carryin' 'em t'th'house and givin'em t'Georgia and everwhere else till I was glad they was gone! Now that's th'truth. We cooked'em, made pies, cider, apple butter—everthing you can think of. I've made gallons a'apple cider. You have t'have a cider mill t'grind up your apples most a'th'time, and then squeeze that all out. Or you can use a big ol' wooden trough. We did. We'd fix apples and put'em in that trough and take a maul 'r whatever and beat up them apples, and strain th'cider out and put it in jugs 'r whatever you're gonna keep it in. It's hard t'make thataway. I don't like apple cider much. No, I just don't like it. I ain't got a taste for it. Boys, they loved it at home, though. Shoot, we'd make it by th'gallons, and how they did love it—'specially when it was "sharp," they called it. They let it commence t'sour just a little bit, and then how they did love it!

And we always made lots a'apple butter. Use t'make it in a big ol' black iron washpot outside on three rocks, the ol'-fashion' way they had way back yonder. But now I make it in a big galvanized dishpan on th'stove. Take you all day t'make apple butter, just about it. You have t'commence t'peel your apples soon that mornin'. If y'make apple butter you want ripe apples that'll cook up as good and fine as they can be. You have t'understand that that's th'first thing you want. If y'don't get good soft apples, they'll be lumpy, and lumpy apple butter ain't good. Lotsa people don't pay that no 'tention, but I did. And never have no apple peelin's 'r apple cores in'em. You have t'put just barely a little water in'em t'cook'em. If y'don't you'll have sloppy apple butter and it takes you forever t'cook'em down. Don't never put too much water in'em. I've tried that.

When they commenced t'cookin' down, I commenced t'mashin'em and I mashed'em just as fine as they could be. The finer y'mash your apples, th'better your apple butter is. What I used was a Irish tater masher made out a'wire. Mash it good. It takes right smart a'work t'keep it from stickin' t'th'bottom a'th'pan 'r whatever you cook it in. Then put your [sorghum] syrup and your flavorin' all in there, and keep th'fire goin' just about all day. You can flavor it with cinnamon. Ground cinnamon. We hardly ever went without cinnamon. We all loved it. If we run out, we'd get another box and have it sittin' there. We bought just a peckful a'ground cinnamon. Sometimes y'couldn't get it and then I'd use lemon. It's awful good t'flavor with.

Now y'don't have t'stir th'apple butter ever' minute, but y'have t'stir it ever' little bit t'keep it from burnin'. Have t'keep th'fire moderate. Y'don't want t'burn it. I made as high as five'r six churn jars a'apple butter—held five'r six gallons apiece. Course, if I was t'make apple butter now, I'd want t'put it in small glass jars and seal'em up so I'll have it good all summer. But we had a big shelf up in th'lower kitchen. We always put them big five-gallon jars right under that big shelf and tied'em up good with a cloth and then with paper and then put'em under that shelf. Ever' time we needed one, we untied it t'get out a big glass bowl full a'apple butter, eat it, and went back and got some more.

Makin' apple butter on th'new a'th'moon is best. But then really we couldn't always do that. We just made it when we could. It's all right. One time it's a little easier'n th'other, but when y'get ready t'make it y'don't pay it much 'tention. We always made it in th'fall a'th'year before it got too cold. We use t'have a cane mill and a evaporator, too—just a ol'-fashion' boiler. It was big and

One of Aunt Arie's five-gallon stoneware food storage jars, made by a local potter. In foreground, a pan of dried red peppers from her garden.

wide and set on top a'th'furnace. And honey, we've made apple butter in *that* too—gallons at a time.

We didn't have sugar, so, y'see, we growed our own cane, had our own cane mill, and made our own syrup sorghum. Made it good and thick. That's what we made our syrup gingerbread out of. Ulyss' loved that, and so they wasn't a week went by but what we didn't have that. And we put lots a'syrup in th'apple butter; if y'don't it'll sour. If y'don't get it good and thick and boil it down good, a five-gallon jar full a'apple butter'll sour before you get it eat up. Yes sir. They loved apple butter at my house, and mercy, law, they was s'many younguns, s'many boys, and you know what boys'll do. Poppy loved it. I did eat apple butter but I never did love it like they did. I know one thing that I really like rather'n apple butter is apple preserves. They's one kind a'apple that'll cook up, just cook into mush. Th'kind that don't cook up, that stays whole, we made preserves out a'that.

You peel'em and cut'em up in little pieces. Pour your stuff up, put your cinnamon 'r whatever you want t'flavor'em with, put'em in ol' jars and tie'em up. Boys, them preserves is good! They better'n apple butter t'me. And so's punkin butter. Ever had punkin butter? Law, I've made a many a pot full a'punkin butter. Boys, it's good. Make it just like y'do apple butter, just exactly. Take your punkin and cut it up like you're goin' t'cook it, y'know, in whatever container you've got, lots 'r little, just whatever you want t'make. Cook it right down, mash it up just as fine. Put your sugar 'r syrup in and flavorin'. That's all you have t'do. We always flavored ours with cinnamon. Just keep a'cookin' it until it's just s'thick you can't stir hardly. Oh-o-o, how good it is! If y'love punkins, you'll love punkin butter. I wish I had a mess for supper. You eat it with biscuit and butter. I love punkin butter. Yes sir, I sure do. I made a many a bowl. Punkin butter was easier t'make than apple butter and, honey, we've made a hundred big bowls in one year and eat ever' bit of it before spring. We'd have t'make gallons if we had enough t'do us a year because we loved it, and cause they was s'many of us.

You can make peach butter, too, and boys, it's good. But mercy alive, we never could get enough peaches t'make much peach butter. Growed fifty-odd bushel a'peaches right over there. Had that peach orchard in that cove over there. I don't know whether they're still over there in that cove now 'r not. Wish you could come some day if you'uns would and go with me over there. I'm afraid t'go by myself. Sold forty-odd bushel a'peaches, got a dollar a bushel for'em. They'd be more'n that now. Yes sir.

Course all that was hard on you then. I didn't care. I was stout then and could do it. But after y'done s'much of it y'got tired of it. I mean, y'got give out of it, I'll say it that way. Your strength give out.

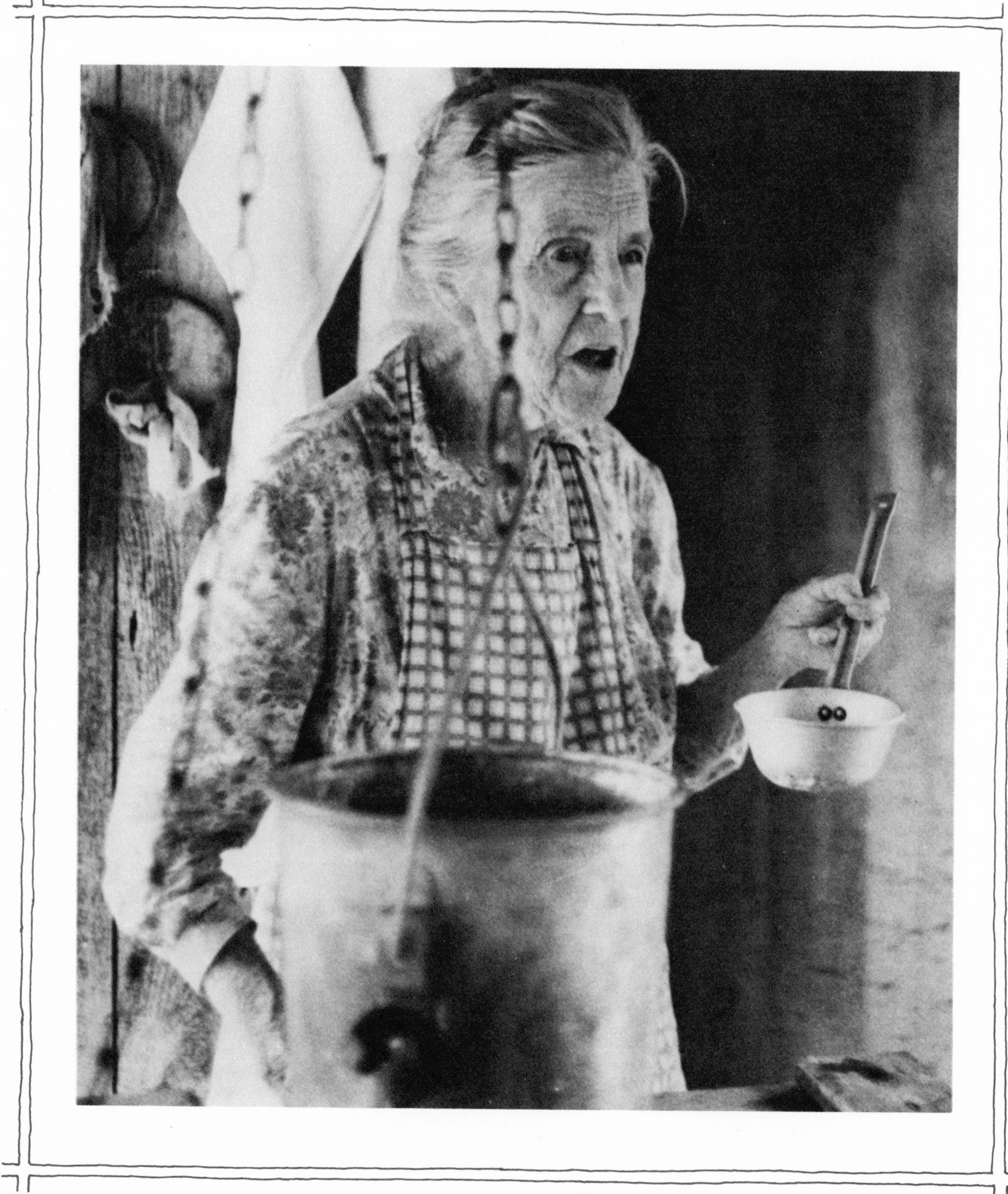

5.

"Mommy learnt me lots about th'doctorin' business"

People don't go everwhere like they use to, y'know. I use t'just go everwhere. I would again if I could. And just as sure if they was any sickness 'r somebody got bad off in th'community anywheres between Otto, way up on Coweeta, 'r plumb t'Rabun Gap, I always went as long as Ulyss' was here t'wait on Poppy and Mommy. I didn't leave my daddy by hisself, and I didn't leave Mommy by herself neither. They was somebody stayed with'em all th'time they was a'livin'. That was one thing they never done in their life was stay by theirself. Ulyss's stepmother, she cooked, and Ulyss' helped her, so when they was sickness I could go and stay a week at a time. I have done it. Done everthing, might' near it, in sickness. They'd come for me day and night. Get out a'th'bed and here I'd go. I ain't afraid a'no kind a'disease. This man's wife up here got typhoid fever and her husband wouldn't go in their house without puttin' turpentine round his mouth and everthing. He was that scared a'typhoid fever. He was s'scared he'd catch it that he'd only half take care a'her. Never bothered me a cent in this world. I've had diseases, but I ain't never died from'em!

When y'have sickness in th'family and no doctors, you sure learn t'do lotsa ways. You just have to. I can remember all th'doctor business. Yes sir. Cause I lived a long ways from th'doctor. Didn't never get t'go t'th'doctor.

I can tell you a remedy if y'ever happen t'need it, honey, that is almost a certain cure for dysentery—"bloody flux," we called it. Now I don't know whether you knowed it 'r not, but this willer that grows around th'branch banks, y'take that willer and get th'young leaves—not th'old—and make a tea out of it. And nine times out a'ten that'll cure that. There was a man just about dead with that down in Toccoie. He come into th'store where Poppy was at and he told Poppy he'd been down s'many days with that dysentery that he was about dead. Poppy said, "Law, I can cure that." He told him t'make some a'that tea and drink it, and he did, and that cured him right then and he didn't have no more trouble with it. Now you'uns can remember that. I've lived long enough t'know that, too.

And for colds, use ginger tea. Yes sir. We sure did. That's what Mommy used, too. Either ginger tea 'r red pepper tea. Now you all may not love this, but I love it better'n anything that I ever drunk in my life. Take a pod a'red pepper and lay it before th'fire on th'hearth and parch it and put it in a cup. Pour warm water on it and take syrup—we didn't have sugar like we got now, so we sweetened it with syrup—and I could drink a pint. And I just loved it. Just loved red pepper tea. It's a wonder it hadn't killed me. I've drunk it, and nine times out a'ten it's give me th'hiccups. [Laughter.] Yes sir. Y'know what cures th'hiccups? Nine sups a'water will cure th'hiccups. Take you nine sups a'water. Yes sir. I've done that. I don't know at th'times I've done that. I have th'hiccups lots. Gettin' better when y'have th'hiccups, they tell me. I'm always hearin' them younguns sayin' that. That's another sayin'. I don't know if they's anything to it 'r not.

Talkin' 'bout syrup, now you can use honey, too. Take honey and it'll cut phlegm loose.

And y'know persimmons, don't you? Now they'd get out and skin that bark, and then get yeller root off a'th'branch bank and wash that good and clean, and put it all in a jar 'r somethin'. Use t'have crocks. Put water on that and keep that skim off th'top all th'time so that wouldn't sour on you. We've drunk a many a gallon a'that. Y'*had* t'do somethin'. Done that a many a time. I ain't lately, though. I could, but I don't.

And this chestnut bark is good for somethin', but I forgot what it was good for. Does that aggravate you when y'know anything just s'good and then it just flies away? Made medicine out of it, though. And pine resin. Y'ever eat any pine resin? Boys, I've eat a many a pill of it. You don't know how t'cut a pine tree t'get it, do you? Go t'where th'pine is and cut it down thisaway and then thisaway. Cut down 'bout as high as y'want it and take that bark and sap wood all out in here and let that pine resin run down in that cut place. It'd be good and clean. It'll be just as clean where y'take that out. Y'have t'watch it t'keep it from runnin' over and wastin'. Take it t'th'house and put it in whatever y'want t'put it in. And then take you a little bit and roll it in a ball. We call it resin pills. And we use t'roll it in copper. That was for worms.

If y'got wormy, y'took one a'those copper pills and if y'had any worms in you, that got rid a'th'worms. I've took a many a dose of it. Since I been married, I pulled a worm from me [several inches] long. Right up there. I felt it. Y'know, I felt it. I reached back t'see what it was and I got ahold a'that worm and pulled it out and it was ever' bit that long. And it was as big as, I believe it was as big as my finger around. Wooo. . . . [Shivers.] I can see that ol' big worm here yet. Boys, I got rid of it. I give it a send-off. When I got rid of it, w-o-o-o. That's th'last one I ever had, I reckon, 'r th'only one I ever felt.

Mommy use t'have pin worms. She was just eat up with pin worms. Little ol' bitty ones about that sharp on th'end of'em. I never did. I never been bothered with'em and I hope I never do, cause they worry you t'death. They worry you till y'can't sleep with'em. Lord no. Now I don't know what caused

"Everything that grows
was put here for a reason,
and our job's t'find
out what it's here for."

'em. Mommy never would let nary one a'us younguns ever play with a cat. She said they would make worms in y', so I never handled no cats in my life. That's what she said, and I didn't want no worms.

And now I'll tell you boys and girls—you may have a family some day, and you may have a hard time gettin' rid a'th'thrash. That's blisters that get all round a nursin' youngun's mouth. If it gets inside their mouth and goes through a youngun, it almost kills'em. That's th'truth. Course nobody uses th'breast nowadays. Nearly always use a bottle now, and that's a help.

But Uncle Henson cured th'thrash by washin' it with so many leaves a'sage. Sometimes that'd do and sometimes it wouldn't. Th'best was t'get anyone that's born that's never see'd their daddy. Poppy never see'd his daddy, and I've see'd him cure hundreds of'em. Now Poppy used tobaccer. He never smoked like lotsa people much. He never smoked a draw a'nothin' in his life, but he chewed tobaccer. That's a Cabe for y'. I never knowed, see'd, 'r heared tell of a Cabe that didn't never use tobaccer. So whenever somebody brought a baby for him t'cure —I've watched him hundreds a'times—he'd rench out his mouth three'r four times with some good clear water cause he used tobaccer, and breathin' in them younguns' mouths might make'em sick. He'd rench out his mouth and take his two hands and open up a child's mouth—a big'n'r a little'n whichever one—hold it open and he'd blow in it. Blow one good breath one time, hold it open and blow another'n—and real easy. Can't blow too hard 'r you'll blow th'breath out of'em! He'd blow three times, and that's all that was ever done. I've see'd'em fight him like a dog and scratch him all t'pieces, but he never paid it a bit a'tention. He said, "Now, don't you never touch that n'more." And they never did come back with it. Cured'em. One operation cured'em. I never knowed it t'fail on one in my life.

Now this gal down here can cure thrash but I don't guess she knows it. I never have told her. I'm goin' t'tell her some a'these days. First time I think of it and I'm where she's at.

Let's see if I can remember any others. Law, it's been several years since. . . . Yeah, flour. Now that's good for a sore. Stops th'itchin'. And th'ol'-fashion' itch. You ever hear a'that? It's tormentin'. Lord, how tormentin' it is. When we'd get that, Mommy'd make us strip off plumb naked in th'kitchen and grease us teetotally plumb over. Th'way she made that itch grease, best I remember, was one large spoonful a'sulfur, one large spoonful a'homemade lard, a little mutton taller, a pinch a'salt, and th'gunpowder out a'one shell cartridge. Then she'd boil all that t'gether and put it in some kind a'container till we needed it. And it'd last right on. Might last for ten years. But, Lord, it'd stink. When we'd put that on, we'd stink like carrion. Had t'leave that on for three days. Shew! But it worked.

And poultices—Mommy knew how t'make lotsa poultices. She'd make a mullein poultice t'put on your breast if it was sore from nursin' a baby. And horseradish poultice for th'headache. Get those horseradish leaves hot by th'fire and then roll'em between your hands t'get'em all juicy, then bind those in a cloth t'your forehead. Fifteen minutes and your headache's gone. I do that yet. Sometimes I bind one on behind my neck and one t'm'wrist, and that works, too.

Then she made hot ash poultices for your heart; and for vomitin', she ground up horseradish roots in a sausage grinder—'r beat'em up with a hammer —and made a poultice t'put on your stomach. She learnt me lots about th'doctorin' business.

Then t'stop bleedin' if you're cut, hold your hand over th'cut place and recite Ezekiel 16:6 one time and it'll stop. And puttin' pot hooks around your neck'll stop th'nosebleed. I know that works. Somethin' about that cold metal, I reckon. And punch a hole in a dime and put that round a baby's neck on a string and that'll help it cut its teeth. It chews on that, y'see?

And warts—I buy them. I betcha I've took hundreds of'em. They was a whole crowd come Sunday last t'have me take off warts. They come in and said, "We've got some warts we want you t'buy," and I give'em a coin 'r two—I give one a'them boys twelve cents for all he had—and I said, "Now you just keep this money a little while and they'll go off." If any a'you'uns has any warts, I can take'em off for y'.

They's lotsa things like that if I could just think of'em all.

But anyway, we did th'most a'th'doctorin' ourselves. When we absolutely had t'have a doctor, we could send word t'Doc Nevilles and he'd come. They wadn't no better doctor in th'world than Doc Nevilles was. And he loved t'come t'my house t'eat pickle' beans worse'n anything. He always made it convenient t'eat in my house, and he always got pickle' beans. Boys, he loved'em th'best a'anything in this world. If he ever come t'my house, I sure got him a good dinner. I reckon he loved my cookin'. And he always made it t'th'beans!

Now th'first time he come, it was th'year [1918] th'flu was s'bad. We all like t'died with it. Mommy *did.* She took th'flu on th'third day in March and it was June when she died. She wouldn't give up. I know two'r three more that died, too, but I can't think a'their names right now. Boys, that was hard times. Poppy didn't take it because he had it once before, but th'rest of us did. It like t'got all of us at th'same time. I had it bad, but still I had t'do ever' bit a'th'cookin' for two families. I was waitin' on two families with th'flu and never went t'bed. It's a thousand wonders it hadn't killed me. But I waited on our family, and th'family that lived about from here t'th'ridge down here. His wife took th'flu and she couldn't do nothin'.

So we sent for Doc Nevilles, and you'uns don't know about th'winters we use t'have. You couldn't get in and out t'save your life. Well, he come down on th'train. Th'train stopped at Otto at that time. So he come down on th'train and Mount—that's my baby brother—he met him down there with a horse and Doc Nevilles got on horseback t'come t'our house. I don't guess a doctor'd do that now.

He seen th'shape we was all in and he done what he could. He give me a handful a'medicine. I counted th'doses and they was thirty-two doses of it. I never will forget that as long as I live. But that kept us alive. It was a hard time, though. Our house was built separate—in two sections. It was built t'gether under one roof, but still y'had t'go out on th'porch in th'air t'go t'th'kitchen. But I done all th'cookin' for us and them, and Poppy carried their rations back'erds and forwards. That was about as far as from here t'that bridge down there at th'end a'this road. And their boy come and stayed with us, too. Doc Nevilles seen th'shape he was in, and he told Poppy t'take him out a'th'bed and wrap him up good in a blanket and carry him t'me and turn him loose in our good warm house. We had a good house. We sure did. Not like this house. And that's what he done. And that poor little ol' youngun. I can see him yet. Buddy, he was just tickled t'death t'get t'that house. He was just big enough t'be right cute. He sure was. Big enough for Poppy t'carry him t'my house.

But that flu was so contagious that if anyone else from out in th'community ever come t'see 'bout us, they'd come in th'yard but they never would come in th'house. They was scared of it. They'd come and look in th'winder and ask us what we wanted and go t'th'store and get it and set it on th'porch. That's th'way they waited on us.

Well, we ever' one got over it 'cept Mommy. If it hadn't a'been for Doc Nevilles doctorin' me, though, I'd a'not been here. And I believe that as much as I believe I'm a'livin'. He was a awful good doctor, and if he ever got mad 'ary time, I never knowed it. He never got mad—'cept one time. Leanner had th'pneumonia fever, and she *had* it, too. Oh-h-h, she like t'died in spite a'all of us—doctors and everbody else. Her and her husband was just newly married, and he didn't know what t'do. One-room house and a little ol' side shed was all they had. Set up on top a'that hill down there. It's tore down, now. It burnt up. And it was a a-a-w-ful bad day that day, and Doc Nevilles come ridin' up and he said somethin' t'me and it didn't strike me just right, and I said more back t'him than he did t'me. I didn't care nary a cent. I says, "I ain't gonna take things off a doctor! I'm half white and free born." And I didn't take a word of it. I couldn't help her bein' s'sick, and I couldn't help her bein' s'bad off. But I left my home and went down there and stayed day and night with'em. I guess she'd a'died if they hadn't a'been somebody t'stay and take care a'her. She just come within a peg a'goin'away from here. That's been thirty year ago. Last year my Irish taters didn't do too good, and her husband dug his and he asked me did I want some Irish taters. I said, "Yes, I want some Irish taters."

"Well," he said, "how much you want?"

I said, "Two bushel."

And when I went t'pay him, y'know what he said? He said, "You paid me for them over in th'holler that time."

But Doc Nevilles was a good ol' doc. He was as good t'us as he could be. Right down here, th'horse got scared and run off th'road and throwed me out a'th'wagon and broke my arm. Course we had t'send for th'doctor. Doc Nevilles come and fixed my arm. Poppy said he just thought he was th'roughest man with my arm he ever saw in his life. Said he looked for it t'break in two again. Nevilles didn't do it, though. He knew what he was a'doin'.

Boys, how I did hate it when he died. Daisy Cabe and one a'her younguns was up there when Doc Nevilles died. He was in th'doctorin' room in his house. This is what they said, now. I don't know if it's right 'r wrong. He'd went t'some state on a pleasure trip and come back and course went right back t'his practice, y'know. Course he was hungry when he got back, and his wife cooked some kind a'pie—seems t'me they said apple pie—that day for dinner. He eat too much of it and died before dark. Daisy was there, and she said she never felt so bad as she did when Doc Nevilles died awaitin' on'em.

As much sickness and everthing, it's been pretty happy from beginnin' t'end. Course now you can't be happy when people are sick, but now I've never had no long face round sickness cause that just will not do. Talk and laugh and laugh. Make'em think you're thinkin' somethin' else whether you are 'r not. And I never see'd many people in m'life but what I could out talk. Now you take a crazy person. I could out talk them and they never knowed no difference, and I never told no difference. Y'don't let people know what you're doin' and you can manage'em better. You understand me? Younguns, remember that. I hope t'God that you'll never have t'put up with crazy people, though. 'Bout th'worst thing that I done was takin' care of a crazy person. I oughtn't t'tell you'uns but I'll tell you so you'uns'll be expectin' it. I didn't have nobody t'tell *me.* When you're waitin' on a crazy person, now, you've got your heart full and your head full, too. And your hands full, too. Now I've tried that.

See, now Aunt Avie—that was Ulyss's stepmother—was crazy about eighteen months. She didn't know nothin'. She didn't know when t'quit eatin'

and I didn't know what t'do. She'd just eat till she'd hurt herself. So we had t'allowance her rations. Doc Nevilles said, "Just get you a tray and give her just what you want her t'have." That made her s'mad, oh-h-h-h, she'd just cuss me out, but I never let it cut no squares on my mind in no way, shape, fashion, 'r form. I done just what Doc Nevilles told me to.

And we had a hearth in there that had a big hole where th'rocks and th'floor met and she wore stockin's like I got. When we'd take her food she didn't want, she'd make out like she eat it, but she'd pull down her stockin' and put it down her stockin' leg and put it down that hole. That's th'way she done. Done that for months.

We had t'watch her. She took a shovelful a'fire one time and put it in a chair that I had a cushion in. It's a wonder we ain't been burnt up. You had t'watch her day and night. I'd take her medicine in there, in that other room in yonder where she stayed, and she wouldn't do nothin'. Crazy person just does what they want and sometimes part of it's meanness. I'd stand there till I'd nearly fall over dead, and keep starin' at her t'make her swallow her medicine, and just as soon as I'd turn my head, out behind th'bed that medicine goes! I stood there one night and I was tired t'death, and I kept starin' at her and she wanted me t'leave, and she didn't know how t'get it done so she'd make out like she was goin' t'hit me. "Now," I said, "you hit me and I'll slap th'fire out a'you." She said, "I didn't know I had any fire in me!" Ulyss's brother busted out t'laughin'. Just laughed. [Laughing.]

We had t'keep th'doors locked on th'outside a'her room. When she'd get up, she always kept up a racket. She'd cuss. Law, she'd cuss like a. . . . It'd just tickle you t'death t'hear her. Why I'd just sit and laugh at her. I oughta be ashamed a'myself. I do get awful, but I just simply amazed myself a'laughin' at crazy people. But I just couldn't help it. Always have done that.

But we had t'keep th'doors locked t'keep her from runnin' off. Why, she'd run off and she'd get out a'sight. She'd go day'r night. I've see'd her wade in snow that deep from here t'William Carpenter's. She wouldn't wear low-cut shoes. She'd put on her shoes and high tops, and she never did tie'em up, and she'd take this trail across this mountain here and go through th'woods t'William Carpenter's. He lived way on across this mountain.

Daisy and them come up here t'get me t'sew for her one day. She use t'live right down here on th'top a'th'hill 'tween here'n th'highway. I said: "Now I'll sew if you watch Aunt Avie and keep her from goin' off t'William's. She'll go 'r die." They'd watch her. Well, I missed Avie and I says, "Where's Aunt Avie?"

"Lord," said ———, she didn't know where she was at. We got out a'huntin' for her, and we finally found her down there at Charlie Bell's spring with a dipper under her arm a'goin' t'William Carpenter's. See, she slipped out at th'well and got her a drink and slipped out around th'house, and I was in here at work and didn't know it. "Now," I says, "that's th'last time I ever leave you'uns t'watch her." And I never left her n'more. No sir. They didn't like it, but I didn't care.

But that's th'way we done her. [Pause.] Ain't it funny how a crazy person does? They know what they're doin.' They do know and they're mean, boys, some of'em. My mother's brother had epileptic fits and he got t'where he was dangerous. They had t'send him t'th'asylum. Use t'have guns up over th'door, and when he'd go t'takin' one a'those fits, if you didn't grab him and hold him he'd get a gun. I don't know why he'd do that. He had that in his mind. Some of'em would take it out a'his hand. It's a wonder he hadn't knocked'em down with it. Uncle John Fulger was scared t'death of him. Now I never was a bit afraid a'him, though. Not a bit afraid a'him.

Another'n that takes epileptic fits is ———. You don't know her, do you? Well, she's crippled. She's worse crippled than I am. She goes up and down th'road a lot, swarpin' along. Poor ol' thing. I'm sorry for her. She's crazy. She takes some kinda fits 'r tremens 'r somethin' and, law, you'd think she was a'dyin'. She'll chaw her tongue off, nearly. Use to, when she'd go t'takin' those fits, Ulyss'd get up and leave this house. Oh, he wouldn't watch her. I didn't leave, though. I ain't afraid a'her. Actually, I ain't a bit afraid a'her in th'world when she takes them fits.

Y'have t'watch her, though. Last time she was here was Thursday evenin' before Christmas, I think it was. She come t'spend th'night. Well, I was a'settin' right here and she was over there. We was eatin' apples. I keep a knife here a'purpose so I can peel on apples. I believe it was this'n. See what a sharp point it's got? I don't know what she done it for, but you can't tell what crazy people does. Y'don't know if they do it a'purpose 'r if they do it by accident. Well, she got up over there, and I don't know how come her t'sling th'knife around, but she hit me right there with th'point a'th'knife and it hurt pretty bad. It like t'made me mad. Now I'll just tell th'truth, it come in a lash a'makin' me mad. Scared me, too. Lord, she just like t'took a fit. I never heared no one take on so in all my life. She hit me hard enough t'make th'blood go out. Just lacked a little bit hittin' me in th'eye. She'd a'hit my eye plumb out if she'd a'hit it.

Well, I just set here and studied about that, and studied about it, and she just kept on takin' on.

When it come time t'go t'bed, I got th'room in there straightened out. I always put her in that far room in yonder in that far bed and shut th'doors so when I go t'sleep, I'll know where she's at. Well, t'cap th'stack, that night she said, "I want t'sleep in Ulyss's bed."

I said, "Oh, Lord!" It was late then and pretty cold, just before Christmas, and I said, "Well, I'll go upstairs and get down some quilts. Ain't no quilts on that bed." I didn't have nary a blanket on it. I said, "You stand there at th'door at th'foot a'th'stairs and catch th'quilts." I can't walk up and down a'holdin' much, so I throwed'em down so I wouldn't fall down and get hurt. She catched one of'em, but th'rest of'em I just throwed down.

I can't hardly sleep a wink when she's here. I ain't afraid a'her if I see her, but then y'don't know what a crazy person'll do. I'm goin' t'say this, boys, the devil's in her; it's in her all th'time. Now that's awful t'say about your own folks, but it's there.

Now this poor ol' woman over here, I'm sorry for her. I can't get t'see her—can't hardly walk there and back. She lives a right smart piece. But she's blind and she's deaf and she don't know a thing in th'world. Not a single thing

Aunt Arie's remedies for curing stock:

When a horse gets colic, take a handful of homegrown tobacco, put it in a bucket, light th'tobacco and get it smouldering, and then shove th'horse's nose into th'bucket. Wrap a cloth around th'bucket rim and th'horse's nose so none of th'smoke escapes and th'horse is forced t'inhale it all. Keep th'nose covered until th'tobacco goes out and th'horse has breathed in all th'smoke. This cures th'colic.

When horses, cows, mules, or sheep get poisoned (sheep, for example, frequently get poisoned from eating rhododendron), take a lump of alum and beat it up fine. Do not mix it with water. Pull out th'animal's tongue and put one spoonful of th'powdered alum at th'back of its throat and hold its mouth shut.

After it has swallowed th'alum, turn loose and "Get out a' th'way when you turn'em loose, too, cause they'll throw up all over you."

in th'world. She's livin' with her son-in-law and she sees things. Sees grapes and apples and everthing down on th'porch. She'll tell'em t'get that, and course it ain't there, and then cause he can't get it and give it to her, he slaps her hand. "Boys," I said, "if that was *my* mother he'd not slap her hand." Boys, I wouldn't have slapped nobody's hand like that for nothin' I'd see'd. Course he's a good ol' boy and don't know no better, and she don't know no better than t'tell'em such stuff.

Waited on thirty-two sick people in my life, and dressed and laid out I don't know how many dead people. That's th'kind a'parties I had. Enjoyed th'last bit of it. Enjoyed th'last bit of it. I was a help t'somebody. I just enjoyed it. 'Druther go into sick rooms better'n anything that I ever done. Go and stay day and night and never eat a bite and just keep a'goin' on till I give plumb out. Then, course, I had t'quit, but I've had t'do it all my life. You do anything for forty, fifty years, you're liable t'want t'keep on just because it's t'help somebody.

If you'd see little ol' younguns suffer as bad as I have, you'd be like Doc Nevilles when he said, "I'm glad I could come." Now, when Annie Brown's baby died, they sent for him and he come and I was stayin' with Annie. Stayed there ten days. He got th'medicine ready t'give and said, "I'm so glad I come just t'help ease that youngun." That little bitty baby died in my arms. I knowed she was dyin'. I knowed she was dyin'. See'd too many of'em die. Annie didn't know it, but I did. Doc Nevilles looked at me and I knowed just as well what he meant when he looked at me, and I see'd he knowed hisself. Th'baby was done a'dyin' and I knowed it. But he looked at that little baby, give it some medicine, and he said, "I'm glad I come t'give it a little ease." Poor little thing. Now that was about th'hardest thing that's ever come my road in my life. A little newborn baby, just two weeks old. It was deformed. Boys, that poor little thing suffered —it was awful. It might near got th'best a'me. If I'd had a heart a'stone it wouldn't, but I haven't, and I'm glad of it.

Another hard one was ———'s mammy. They say they's never been a better woman in th'world than her mammy was. She took sick one day at dinner —that's been a long time ago—and she died before midnight. And this is what everbody thought, now—you can't hurt with your thoughts if y'don't think'em too loud—but everbody thought her daughter knocked her off.

Poppy was livin' here at that time and we was eatin' in th'kitchen. It was cold. I don't know where Ulyss' was at. And they come for me. Ever since I been in this family, when 'ary one got sick, they had t'run after me, *then* after th'doctor. So I went on down there quick as I could and left Poppy at th'table. Course Poppy knowed what t'do, and he went and took all th'things off th'table and fixed'em all so th'two cats wouldn't get on th'table, and I went on down there. I knowed she was a'dyin' when I went. Oh, I never felt s'bad in all my life. They didn't have a dime t'phone for th'doctor—didn't have a thing in th'world. Ulyss', he come on down there, and quick as he got there he turned round and went back t'th'house t'get a dime. On th'way, he just happened on Thomas and stopped him and got him t'go and call th'doctor, and Doc Nevilles come. Course she was done past knowin' anything in th'world when th'doctor come, and that was th'last a'that. Somebody dies unexpected that way, though, y'don't know but what they been killed. Y'can't help that suspicion.

Then I watched Aunt Mary Bates die out over there. That was Mommy's sister. It took her two days and nights t'die. Now that learnt me another lesson. Now Uncle Jim Bates, they thought th'world a'me, and they thought if I stayed there all th'time I could cure anybody. I don't know what makes'em do that. But they wouldn't let me leave there. I layed down on a little ol' lounge and Aunt Mary was sick in her head. Well, ever' time she moved in that bed, I knowed it. They said, "What made you do that?" I said, "Got her on my mind." Well, when death took her, Uncle Jim, he tried t'do this and tried t'do that. I was a'gettin' just as bad as they was. And she revived enough till when th'hawks got after th'chickens on th'outside, she heard it and said, "Th'hawks are after th'chickens!" And her a'dyin'! She stayed there two days and nights and struggled. Ever' once in a while she'd come to. I said, "That was my first time ever t'do anybody that way, t'keep revivin'em when their time has come, and it's my last. When death first strikes anybody it'll stay there, and revivin'em over and over don't help, I don't care what y'do. You might revive'em and keep'em with you enough till . . . you understand what I mean. Now I said, "That was my first'n t'ever do that to and that was my last'n." I said, "That's my last one."

It's mighty hard, knowin' you're standin' there a'watchin'em die. That place right along there. [Indicates jugular vein with a tapping motion approximating a heartbeat, and pauses, greatly affected.] You can tell when anybody's a'dyin'. If you've watched as many of'em die as I have, you'll know just exactly when they're dyin'.

Well, life's uncertain, death's sure.

But now I know God will reward me for all I've done. God always takes care a'his own, don't He? I believe that as much as I believe I'm a'livin'. You try and stay eighty year out here and see if you don't believe it. Yes sir. You just look at th'people that come here now and help me out bringin' me somethin' t'eat ever'day. Like that Floridy woman lives right across th'hill. She come in here a while back and stayed a half day with me. Here she come bringin' me a pack a'tater chips, knowin' that I love'em as good as anything in th'world. I said, "That's th'way they do me." And Eliot come yesterday and brought me a pack a'sliced-up meat. It was that big. Whew! Law, how good it was. I eat three pieces of it for breakfast. I sure did. And he brought some oranges. I said, "Well, I needed that." I've got plenty t'eat a'what I *have* got, but then somethin' extra's a heap better.

6.

"Some a' these days I'll be where I won't have t'walk in th'mud"

I've been goin' t'church all my life. Born and raised over there on Hickory Knoll and we walked t'church. And I mean I went all th'time. I didn't go one Sunday and miss a month 'r two. I went *ever'* Sunday. Enjoyed it. Law, how I did enjoy goin' t'church. And I miss it just as bad now as I enjoyed a'goin' then. But I haven't been there lately. See, when I was eighty-five year old, I still walked th'two miles t'th'Coweeta Church ever' Sunday. Ever' once in a while somebody would happen t'come along after I got t'th'main road and pick me up and take me th'rest a'th'way. And when I got there, they wouldn't let me walk back. I'd beg'em t'let me walk back but they wouldn't do it.

Then I took th'pneumonia fever th'thirtieth day a'December and I never walked and went t'church nary'nother time. Th'preacher'd come after me after I got well and take me in a car over there. Ever' Sunday mornin' I'd get up and run around here and get things cleaned up so that when th'preacher come after me, I'd be ready. Got ready one mornin' and put on m'coat and set here till eleven, and he didn't come, so I said th'next time I got ready t'go t'church, I wouldn't put on m'coat! And he'd took pneumonia fever and was in th'hospital in Sylva. Course I didn't know it, and he didn't know it. He was good t'me, though. How good he was. Poor ol' feller's got past doin' anything now. So have I—about it.

Now I set here ever' Sunday and listen t'church on th'radio. I don't cry. I don't cry cause I can't go t'church. Ain't no use. But it's not cause I don't feel like it. Set here by myself. But I'm doin' th'best I can. If you're doin' th'best you know how, that's all that's required of you. If I do th'best I know how, that's all God requires me t'do. And I'm expectin' not too many days from now, I'll be rewarded. Yes sir. I enjoy it. Enjoyed ever' bit of it. Many a time I set down and get t'studyin' about that. I can just see me a'comin' and goin' t'church just as plain as my hand.

Now, I'm a Baptist. I belong t'th'Missionary Baptist Church. I was baptized over across this mountain in th'creek. That's about th'best thing I ever see'd anybody do, is be baptized. And I'll stay Baptist till I die. I just don't agree with th'other denominations. Like th'Holiness. Some a'them does that snake handlin'. Baptists don't believe in that. I never see'd it, but I wouldn't look at it if they was t'come right out there and do it. What I don't believe in, I don't practice. And them Holiness try t'heal by layin' on hands. One time they come in and got a poor ol' lady whose leg was broke t'walk on it, and it broke again. She died. That turned me against all of'em. They oughta had sense enough t'know they couldn't cure that, but they's some people wouldn't have no sense if they met it in th'road.

I don't agree with them Jehovah's Witnesses, neither. They use t'come up here lots. Course I was glad t'see'em come. I enjoyed th'company, and I love t'talk about th'Bible with anybody. I do. I just enjoy that as good as anything. And then they always brought plenty a'literature and left it here. That helped cause that always left me lotsa papers t'start my fires in th'wood cookstove. I wouldn't a'made it sometimes without them papers! [Laughing.]

Old Coweeta Church

My daddy's folks was all Methodist. Mommy's folks was all Baptist. After they was married for a long time, Poppy joined th'Baptists and was baptized. T'get baptized y'have t'take a different set a'clothes with you, y'know, so you can change after y'get wet. Everbody walks down beside th'creek, and you wade down in th'creek and let th'preacher baptize you. He says th'ceremony hisself. Some a'th'people comes out a'th'creek shoutin', and you'd be as happy as anything in this world t'see'em. You love t'see people shout? I do. It's th'joy a'my life, yes sir.

Then we had at least three singin's a week here. Yes sir, we sure did. Y'know, I miss that till today. I just love t'sing. I use t'go t'ever' singin' that they was in Macon County. I use t'be a pretty good singer, I reckon. I went t'ever' Association Singin' Convention, too. They had three days and nights of it, and we all went. My brothers, all of'em sang, and we all went. I always went t'ever' one of'em. Sung at many a singin' convention, they called'em. I ain't been t'nary'n lately, though.

I was th'secretary a'th'church for years and secretary for th'Sunday Schools for years and a Sunday School teacher for sixty years. Teach your own Sunday School class for sixty-odd years and you learn t'love little ol' younguns. I don't care if y'ain't got none a'your own, you learn their way, learn their little bright eyes. Why, I can see them little bright eyes lookin' up at me till today. Smart as crickets, ever' one of'em, and just as spry as a basket a'chips. Expectin' t'meet some of'em some a'these days. I know some of'em's done gone on already, praise th'Lord, I know that.

And I never believed in *makin'* younguns go t'Sunday School. I just tell you, I don't like that. I want t'persuade younguns and tell'em what's right and teach'em t'go t'church without *makin'*em. I'm bad t'persuade younguns, and I never let a youngun get away from me in my life. I taught that Sunday School class for sixty-odd years and I never let one outdo me. I'd just out talk'em. Just commence t'sayin', "How do you like this, and how do you like that?" And always give th'little ol' younguns something t'do, and nine times out a'ten they'll be good. I tried that. I know.

At one point, Aunt Arie hadn't been to church in months, simply because no one had come to take her, and she was unable to walk there. A group of students remedied that, and surrounded her in the Coweeta Baptist Church she and Ulysses helped to build.

I've had some little mean boys in my Sunday School class. Even got out their knives in th'Sunday class one day, and I didn't know if they might take a knife t'me. I didn't know. You take a boy that's mean enough and if you was t'say anything they didn't like, they might cut y'. Well, I didn't know hardly what t'do. I just kept a'talkin' to'em. They was settin' on th'bench with their knives out. No tellin' what I said. I don't remember now. But next thing y'know, they was puttin' their knives up and never said another word.

I'd be teachin' Sunday School t'this day if I was able. I finally got t'where I couldn't hear good, though, and so I quit. Afraid one a'them younguns'd ask me 'bout somethin' and I'd not hear'em just right and tell'em th'wrong thing.

I wouldn't do that for nothin'—tell a little youngun wrong. Or not hear th'question atall and not answer it and make'em think I was ignorin'em. I just wouldn't do it. So I quit.

I hated it, though. I loved them little ol' younguns t'death. They'd be all round my knees, and they'd come alive just in a minute. I'll meet'em some a'these days.

And they's not a thing in this world in my life that I'm ashamed t'meet nobody with. You all remember that, children. That's th'first advice I would always say t'them younguns'd be, "Always do th'right thing." And one thing t'do for sure is never t'do nothin' they don't want their mother t'know. Now that's about th'best advice you can give a child—I mean, little children—is t'*never* do *nothin'* they *don't* want their *mother* t'*know.* For nine times out a'ten—ninety-nine out'a a hundred—if y'do anything wrong when you're young and that way, your mother will find it out. Yeah-h. [Laughing.]

And always be certain you're right before y'go ahead and do anything. Remember that as you go out on th'journey a'life, and you'll never have no trouble.

Always try t'be kind t'people, and I don't care at th'goodness y'do, you'll always get repaid double for it—fourfold. You children all remember that. Th'more y'do for people th'more they do for you. You cast your bread upon th'water and pretty soon it'll come back t'you. Now I've tried that. I have. I've tried that over and over—bein' good t'people. After while, I don't care if they appreciated it 'r not at that minute, it comes back. God does that. Yes sir. He'll see that you're took care of. I know that's true. I've watched it. And experience is th'school we'll all remember. God always does all things well. If y'live in a hell on earth before y'die, God will give you peace. Now you can believe that 'r not. I do. I believe that just as much as I believe I'm livin'. And always tell th'truth. People twist a lie t'suit theirselves, but y'can't twist th'truth. It'll be there today, tomorrow, and forever.

Obey your parents and your days shall be prolonged. That's th'only one a'th'commandments that's got a promise with it. Obey your parents!

At a dinner on the grounds during an all-day sing at the Coweeta Baptist Church to which Eliot Wigginton had brought her, Aunt Arie was surrounded by friends she hadn't seen in months.

And always remember: t'have a friend, be a friend. I've learned that by experience, too.

And then when th'last roll is called, you'll be ready t'meet and go where you're goin' t'spend eternity. I want you all t'remember that. I'd be glad t'meet ever' one a'you some a'these days, cause that's where I'm a'headin' for. Some a'these days I'll be where I won't have t'walk in th'mud. Sure will. I'll have a road t'walk on besides walkin' in th'mud.

You'uns know how we got our church? Way back yonder, Uncle Billy Carpenter—he was Ulyss's uncle—helped commence buildin' th'Coweeta Church. He got Uncle Jim Bates that lived right across th'hill here t'build a ol' log cabin church. Th'church didn't have th'money t'pay Uncle Jim Bates, so Grandpa Henson, Mommy's daddy, sold th'last milk cow he had and paid on that church. They used that church up till they commenced buildin' this new church that's there now. The termites got in th'floor a'th'log church and eat th'floor up. When you'd walk on it you'd sink down, so it got t'where we had t'have a new church. Me and Ulyss' talked it over and talked it over. Course, we both made a little money. I've worked hard t'make a little money all my life. Once in a while I'd get a little money with one thing and another. Use t'have a lotta chickens and eggs t'sell. Picked beans all over Macon County and got paid for that. Picked beans we growed and sold'em. And another thing, all our lives we always had one'r two good calves t'sell, and that helps some. Yes sir, it sure does. And I use t'sew lots. Sold a many a dollar's worth a'stuff. I'd sit up and card and spin up till two'r three o'clock in th'mornin'. Never paid it a bit' a'tention in th'world. Not a bit. Enjoyed it. They made me go upstairs t'spin so they could sleep!

So we made a little money, and we decided t'put a thousand dollars apiece on th'new church. We put th'money in th'post office. Y'know, you use t'didn't have much of a bank. Wadn't nothin' to it. So if you put money in

"This world's a wonderful place t'live in if you want it t'be."

Aunt Arie and Ulysses kept a careful penciled record of every donation—no matter how small—they received toward the construction of the new church. At her request, we totaled the amount donated at the top of each page, and then figured the grand total.

After we figured the grand total, Aunt Arie studied it in amazement.

th'post office you could get a little interest on it. Well, we started savin' some a'what we earned, me'n Ulyss' t'gether, and puttin' it in th'post office.

Ulyss' got his thousand dollars paid before he died. We had th'two thousand dollars paid, all but a hundred and sixty-five dollars. Well, he got down and couldn't do nothin' for so long, and he just decided we wouldn't pay that last hundred and sixty-five dollars. I said: "Yes sir! If I live I'll pay that." And I have. I got th'last dollar of it paid. Took th'last of it up there last year. Boys, they was tickled! Oh-h-h, you'uns never heared such slappin' a'th'hands in your life as when I told'em t'come and help me count it up.

[*Editor's note:* Aside from the two thousand dollars Ulysses and Arie donated to the new church building, they also collected donations, ranging in size from a dime to several dollars, from people throughout Macon County, and turned that money over to the church, too. Aunt Arie told us: "When people couldn't pay money, we took eggs 'r produce and sold that. Several times I've got a twenty-five-pound flour sack full a'eggs and carried'em into Otto and got th'money out of'em and give it t'th'church." Ulysses kept a careful record of all the donations in a small notebook, but before he died he had never totaled up what they amounted to. After we had known Aunt Arie for some time, she got out that worn notebook and asked us to add up the amount for her. The record went on for pages, so we got a calculator and figured it all up. To the amazement of all of us, the total came to $1,536.00. Aunt Arie was delighted.]

Ulyss' walked all over Macon County, almost, t'get that money; and I wouldn't a'believed it if nobody hadn't told me that he collected over a thousand dollars, but you counted it up! No sir, he wouldn't a'believed it either! And he died and didn't even know it. How I do hate that. I hate that so bad.

22 23 24 25 26 27 28

7.

"It's been a long time, ain't it?"

Several years after we had begun to visit Aunt Arie with some regularity, the students mentioned Will Seagle, a man they had met in a different interview situation. Aunt Arie reacted immediately, saying that she had known Will all her life but hadn't seen him for years. Both of them had reached an age that prevented their getting out and visiting. So Laurie Brunson and Mary Thomas and several others decided to drive Will up to Arie's house for a reunion. Several weeks later they did so, and they tape recorded the conversation. Both Arie and Will knew, of course, that the tape recorder was there, and the students were there also, so the situation was not a normal one by any means; but the resulting transcription was an interesting and rather moving piece of material, and we felt it should be included.

WILL: How long's it been, do you recollect, Arie, since I've see'd you?

ARIE: Law, I don't know, Will. It's been a long time, ain't it?

W: Yes, it has. It's been several years since I've been here.

A: Yes, it has.

W: It sure has, Arie. I've been tryin' t'get somebody t'bring me and they say: "No, I ain't got time. I ain't got time. Got t'go somewhere."

A: All that keeps me from goin' up there, Will, is I can't walk. Course I'm paralyzed on this side. [Indicates lump on her chest.] That's where I got hurt. It's growin'. I started in and up th'steps with a load a'wood t'go in th'fireplace and it was snow on th'ground, and I knowed better'n that, Will.

W: Yeah, y'ought to.

A: I knowed better'n that. I knowed t'lay that wood on th'porch and then come in and pick it up, but I didn't do it. Just too late. Well, I fell and that big long stick that I walk with—th'lower end hit on a rock and th'end hit me there. It's been done four year, and it's got t'growin'. Ruth wanted me t'go and have a operation. I said, "No sir, I'm not a'gonna have no operation."

And now I can't walk away from here. I tried it one day and got down t'th'road. I can walk without that stick, but I can catch with th' stick if I go t'fall and it helps me a'walkin', so I take it with me. So I started t'th'graveyard that day and I took a hoe t'clean off Ulyss' and Poppy and Mommy's graves, and I got right down below J.B.'s house and a sharp pain hit me right there in m'side and knocked me t'th'ground. I didn't know what t'do. I can't get up when I fall. I just can't hardly get up t'save my life. I'd throwed m'stick out a'th'way t'keep from fallin' on it, and I got hold a'th'stick and held to it till I got up, but when I got up, I couldn't stand up. I got about as far as from here t'th'bureau and down I went. I couldn't get up t'save my life.

W: Well, I'll be.

A: And I was right in th'route where th'cars go by. I said, "A car'll come along directly and kill me." I finally got out a'th'route, and here come one a'flyin'. I said, "That thing'll run over me!"

When it got by me I see'd who it was and I hollered. It was Alec, and he backed down there. Said, "What in th'world's th'matter with you?"

"Now," I said, "Alec, I don't know what's th'matter with me. I know I can't get up," I said. "I've done tried to."

Said, "We'll get you up." And he got me in and brought me home, and I ain't been out ever since.

W: Well, I can't, either. I'm in th'same shape you're in. I can't go without somebody takes me.

A: I miss goin' t'church, now, th'worst thing of anything that's come my road.

W: I don't guess they's a day passes without I don't think about how I stopped ever' Sunday and eat dinner with you'uns.

A: 'Bout near it. Ever' Sunday. You know I still miss that.

W: We went t'church t'gether.

A: Yes, we'd go that mornin' t'Coweeta Church and come t'my house and eat dinner and go t'th'schoolhouse that evenin' t'Sunday School.

W: Sure.

A: Done that for years. Law, time passes, don't it?

W: It passes. It runs on.

A: Yeah, we use t'be t'gether so-o-o-o much.

W: We went t'school t'gether and played t'gether when we was small. Is there just a year's difference between me and you? You're a year older, ain't you?

A: Yeah, I'll be eighty-eight year old m'next birthday.

W: I'll be eighty-eight September sixteenth. I was born in eighteen and eighty-six.

A: And mine's th'twenty-ninth a'December. I'd forgot when your birthday was.

W: Yeah. I never did pay no 'tention. I'd rather not have no birthday! [Laughs.]

A: I've give s'many birthday dinners here, Will. I think a'ever'one ever' time they

come round. Ulyss' and Uncle Bud and Aunt Avie and Poppy. They's been more birthday dinners right here in this holler than in any other place in Macon County. You can bet on that.

You remember th'weddin' dinner I helped t'cook for you?

W: Yeah, I recollect it.

A: I do, too. Never will forget that.

W: No, you won't.

A: No sir. All them good sweet tater custards.

W: Yeah-h-h.

A: I never will forget that while *I* live. Went one day before th'weddin' and cooked nearly all day there.

W: You cooked all day. [Laughs.]

A: Yes sir. That's th'way we use t'do. And I'll never forget what a day th'next day was. Rain! Law, it just poured.

W: Yeah, it just poured th'rain.

A: Is that ol' house tore down, Will, where you was married at? Is it tore down?

W: Yeah. It's tore down.

A: I wish I could have see'd it one more time before it'd been tore down. Somebody told me th'Vance house was tore down, too.

W: Yeah. It's tore down, too.

A: Y'know, I wish I could go back up in there.

W: I wish you could, too.

A: I wish I had th'strength. If I had th'strength in m'legs. . . .

W: Is Mount still alive?

A: Yeah. He's been sick all winter.

W: He has!

A: He's been bad off. I want t'go down there t'Toccoie so bad I don't know what t'do. They's no use t'cry about it.

W: I'm goin' t'see him if I can get somebody t'take me.

A: Boys, I wish you would. They'd be tickled t'death.

W: It would just tickle them *to* death.

A: Yeah. I sure do miss Maude goin' up and down th'road.

W: I miss her, too. I miss th'poor ol' thing. I hate th'way they took her and carried her s'far away.

A: Well, it's their business. Ain't none a'my business. But I never would want t'take Maudie away off down there and bury her down there. I'd a'buried her where her folks were if it'd a'been me.

W: I would, too.

A: Is Henry got pretty good health now, Will?

W: No, he ain't no good hardly atall. He's in pretty bad shape, Henry is.

A: And is Ider still livin'?

W: No, she's dead.

A: Is she?

W: Yeah. And y'know Rose—that's th'youngest—she died in Washington. They brought her back here t'bury her. And Minnie, she died at Canton. She's buried up there with Riva.

A: Well, is all th'girls dead but Laura?

W: All but Laura. Laura's th'only sister I've got a'livin'!

A: Well, is Henry still gettin' along all right?

W: Yeah. He's gettin' along all right.

A: Law, it's been a long time since I've see'd him. Got out their pictures and looked at'em th'other day. Henry and you. Got'em out and looked at'em th'other day.

W: Ah, yeah.

A: Van died out, didn't she?

W: Yeah, yeah. Died out.

A: I miss her. Lo-o-o-rd. When I got sick, she always come.

W: I miss her, too. Back before she died I got one a'them diggers they call'em, and I planted her garden for her.

A: Y'know who I miss th'worst? Floyd. After he went off down t'Atlanta—I don't know which one I miss th'worst.

W: Well, if I could get somebody t'bring me when you're makin' your garden, I'd come. I'd sure come t'fix it for y'.

A: Well, my garden. I ain't worked nary a minute in th'garden this year, Will.

W: You ain't?

A: No. Y'know who works my garden? Eliot Wigginton.

W: Well, my doctor says, "If y'want t'die, just get out and go on in your garden." I work yet anyway. She said if I got too hot I'd take a stroke.

A: I ain't been in th'garden today. A man and a woman come here th'other day and th'man charged me not t'go into that garden. Tickled me. I don't know who—he was a Floridy man. If you look you'll see plenty a'weeds in there, but I just couldn't hoe it. Will, y'can't hoe with one hand.

And th'weeds is this high out between here and th'toilet. I got off t'diggin' out th'weeds and I got wet and never finished. I give this little ol' boy four dollars t'come and mow out there and he never done a thing to it. I don't know what makes'em do me that way.

W: I don't either. I wish I lived close to you.

A: Yeah.

W: I've got a lawn mower.

A: Eliot hoped [helped] me this year—Eliot and his younguns—his kids, he calls'em. They come and hoed it out a time 'r two, but it's rained so much.

W: Rain lets th'weeds grow fast, Arie.

A: Yeah, they sure do. And they never got t'come back yet and it's just growed up. But I've got plenty a'canned stuff yet. Ulyss' and me'd go ahead and can way more'n we ever needed, and I do that yet. Have it t'throw away.

W: Yeah, I'd eat it, Arie, and not let it waste.

A: Well, I try to, but Lord, Will, I eat such a little. I don't eat over two meals a day.

W: Just two?

A: Uh huh.

W: Well.

A: I always go in there close t'one 'r two o'clock and eat me somethin'; and then I build me a fire in th'stove about five o'clock of a evenin' and get me a bite a'hot supper t'eat and go t'bed.

FOXFIRE: Is there anything you need? Flour or anything?

A: You'll have t'wait till I get m'check cashed.

FOXFIRE: That'll be all right. We'll bring you some and give it to you. You can have it.

A: Well, that's just th'way they do me. [Laughs.]

W: Well, ain't that good, Arie? [Laughs.]

Do you sleep good of a night?

A: Well, some nights I do, Will, and some nights I don't.

W: Just like I am. Sometimes I sleep good as I can and then again I don't sleep atall.

A: I'm th'same way. Sometimes two o'clock in th'mornin' I'm still not goin' t'sleep. I don't know what does that.

W: I don't either.

A: Gettin' unnerved some way'r'nother. I don't know what. Sometimes—you don't know how that hurts there. [Indicates lump in her chest.] When I go t'bed, if I lay down on that, in just a few minutes, oh mercy, it wakes me up. If I lay five minutes on it, I won't sleep. It hurts me and I wake up.

W: Yeah.

A: It's a wonder I ain't got scared here a lot by myself, but I ain't. But I have been lonesome many a time.

I miss Eliot. I know he works hard. He can't come ever' time I want him to, but I love t'see him. He's good t'me and I just miss him.

And I cried when that little ol' boy left me [a boy who was visiting Eliot and stayed with Aunt Arie for a week while Eliot was out of town]. I cried like a whipped child. I just cried and cried. Like t'never got over him. I was s'lonesome I thought I'd die. He helped me t'do everthing—washed th'dishes three times a day. I always got him a big dinner. I didn't make him do without. I miss him s'bad.

——— come here not long ago and him and his wife was gonna move a trailer in right over here and take care a'me. Next thing I know they've gone over yonder t'live. Went off and never said turkey. Ain't been back t'say nothin' 'bout it since. Well, they didn't come and I said, "Well, I didn't beg'em to." Ain't gonna beg nobody t'come in and be dissatisfied. I'd rather be alone by myself as t'be with somebody that's dissatisfied.

W: Oh sure.

A: Oh Lord. I never have been dissatisfied in my life and hope never t'be.

W: Well, do y'have much company, Arie?

A: Ever' day.

W: Ever' day? Well, that's good. I'm glad.

A: Ain't been a day missed here. . . .

W: . . . But somebody's here?

A: Yeah. Somebody about ever' day. If nobody else doesn't come, Marie does. She brings m'mail.

W: Good. I'm proud t'hear that.

A: She works all th'time. She's cannin' beans today. She was here a while ago just before you all come. Irene had her girls here yesterday, and when they started home they got on a snake right out there at th'end a'th' porch.

W: Well.

A: And one of'em come runnin' back and I said, "What's th'matter?" Said, "They got on a snake." And th'little girl, she wouldn't pass that snake. You couldn't a'hired her t'pass it. Tickled me! I said, "I'li get DDT." Y'know, snakes can't stand DDT. You sprinkle it round where they are and they'll not come back over n'more.

But I couldn't find any DDT, so I took hot water and kerosene oil and poured it out round there, and when I get some DDT I'll spray a little. But I ain't done it. I don't remember you and me ever gettin' on a snake, but me and you and th'boys went possum huntin' some.

I believe we did, didn't we, Will?

W: I know we did.

A: Did I ever tell you about th'time I shot that possum out for Ulyss'?

W: No, I don't believe you did.

A: Well, I don't know whether you'll believe this 'r not, but if y'do, all right, and if y'don't, all right. It's impossible t'believe it, 'bout near it. Now that's th'truth. Charlie Bell use t'live in that big ol' house, and he had a dog that talked. Rambler was his name, and he'd say "Rambler" as good as I could. If you give him a piece a'bread he would say it. If you didn't give him no bread he wouldn't do it. Well, me and Ulyss' both petted that dog t'death. One night along about two o'clock, Rambler treed somethin' right over there on th'hill. He got Ulyss' awake and got me awake and wouldn't let us go back t'sleep. He just kept a'barkin'. And I waited for Ulyss' t'say "Let's go." I was afraid t'say it—'fraid he wouldn't go. Finally, at last he said, "Let's go and kill that—whatever it is." I said, "Let's go. I'll go with you."

We got up and put on our clothes and got th'lantern and went over there and they was a big ol' sourwood tree, kinda blowed over way out across there. Well, Ulyss' was totally blind in one eye and just about blind in th'other'n. That's th'reason I always followed him ever' step he made all over this mountain. Well, we went over there with that lantern and they was a big possum had clumb up that sourwood tree. I said, "Ulyss', d'you see that possum?"

No-o-o, he didn't see it. I knowed he couldn't. I showed him where it was at and he still couldn't see it, so I said, "Let me have th'gun," and I said, "I'll hold th'gun, but I'm lettin' you shoot it." Ulyss' said, "All right." He give me th'gun and I helt it. I took a sight on that possum and I helt that gun right on th'possum and Ulyss' pulled th'trigger. Well, sir, when he shot th'gun out, it killed that possum and down it come! [Laughing.]

I said, "I couldn't do that again t'save my life." [Both laugh.] It was just a accident.

W: And you killed it?

A: Killed it, yes sir. We killed that possum. And ol' Rambler?

W: Yeah?

A: Well, he run off with th'possum. He wouldn't leave it for us. No sir. He just got that possum and he went t'Charley Bell's with it!

W: Yeah?

A: Went home with it! [Laughs, then pauses.] Many a hard trip you took up and down that mountain.

W: I sure have, Arie.

A: Picked blackberries and everthing else. It's a wonder that you're livin' now.

"Rags is honorable if your youth was kept well."

W: It's a wonder, Arie, that I'm alive. I don't see how I am. Lord's been awful good t'me.

A: Yes sir, Will. Lord's been good t'me. Course I tried my best t'be good. Seems like He's been better t'me than I have t'Him, though.

W: Well, that's me, too, Arie, but I'm a'tryin' my best. . . .

A: I live right.

W: And I pray ever' day.

A: Yeah.

W: I don't miss a day nor night.

A: I know it. Oh, we've had some good singin's t'gether, ain't we, Will?

W: Oh great goodness! I reckon we have. Lord, I use t'like t'sing. And I can yet! [Laughs.] I can sing th'ol' songs. I can't sing none a'them new ones, but I can sing bass on th'ol' ones as good as I ever did.

A: After I took th'pneumonia fever, it kinda took my voice away from me some way'r'nother. I don't know what it done.

W: You recollect—I'll never forget it—you recollect when I took th'pneumonia fever a'standin' down there in th'garden, and your poor old daddy said, "They's somethin' th'matter with Will." I had t'sit on th'creek bank. He said, "He's not workin' fast enough. They's somethin' th'matter with Will."

A: I know it.

W: That's what he said.

A: I remember things like that just as well as if they was just yesterday, Will.

W: Y'recollect all about it. Somebody come along with a wagon and took me t'th'house, and that night I didn't know a thing!

A: Yeah. I remember.

W: They took me in th'house and that night at midnight, I didn't know a thing.

A: Yes, I remember that. Me and Ulyss' and Poppy got up there and stayed with you of a night.

W: Sure.

A: Yes. We stayed with you right overnight. When I left th'house, Poppy went with me. I wouldn't go by myself. We always went after supper and went back before breakfast.

W: Sure.

A: Yes sir. That's what we done. Th'doctor said you'd die that night.

W: But I never. He give me up. He told'em I wouldn't live. He come and he told'em, "He won't live no longer'n midnight. But," he said, "if he *is* alive in th'mornin', let me know." And sure 'nough, I was alive th'next mornin'.

A: Doctors don't know everthing nohow. But sometimes we need'em.

W: I know some that's just after th'nickel as fast as they can be. I want t'ask y'one thing. What're they gonna do with it? They gonna take it with'em? And I know some of'em that's just as close with a nickel—why, they's no use in that.

A: Not a bit in th'world.

W: I believe in bein' savin', but I don't believe in bein' s'tight that y'can't spend a nickel.

A: Well, I've got enough put in th'bank t'bury me.

W: I have, too.

A: Yes I have, Will. I said I didn't want t'be buried on th'credit.

W: I've got seventeen hundred put away t'bury me, and it'll be right there when I die. And that'll put me away any time.

A: Yes sir. But t'put it another way, Will, there's no tellin' how long you'll have t'lay sick.

W: No.

A: Might take lotsa money still before y'die.

W: That's right.

A: Yes sir. That's th'reason I don't want t'spend what I've got. And I live off Ulyss's Social Security check. When he died, he was gettin' seventeen dollars and a half a month. Then after he died they took his and put it on mine and now I get forty-four dollars a month. I make it on that.

W: Well, I'm s'proud, Arie, I got t'see you.

"Well, we did a lot together.
And not for one day now and then.
It was for years."

A: Yes, I'm s'glad t'see you, Will.

W: I'm s'proud I got t'see you I don't know what t'do.

A: I'm s'proud t'see you, Will. I sure am.

W: I sure am.

A: And you needn't think I don't think about you ever' day. I just wonder how you are. I wonder *where* you are.

W: [Laughs.] You weren't expectin' me but knew me quick as I come in that door.

A: Never expected you t'be here t'see me n'more.

W: Yes sir. I'll never get over it now, I'm s'proud. I said, "I'm a'goin'," and these folks—boy, they good t'me—they said, "We'll take y'." They told me they'd be over here t'take me at one o'clock, and here they come! I was s'proud t'see'em comin' I didn't know what t'do.

A: Well, we did a lot t'gether. And not for one day now and then. It was for years.

W: No. It wadn't for one day now and then. It was for all th'time.

A: Boys, you get t'studyin' about all we've done that we can remember. It's wonderful, ain't it?

W: It sure is, Arie. It sure is.

A: If you'uns needed anything, we'd help you'uns. And if we needed anything, you'uns helped us.

W: Sure. Sure we did.

A: Yes sir.

W: We helped one another.

A: Had a pretty tough time. But still, I've enjoyed it.

W: I have, too. I've enjoyed it.

A: Laughed all m'life. I've laughed more'n ary two people could count.

W: I guess so.

A: Yes, I have. I've always done that.

W: I believe that.

A: I was just born that way.

8.

"Livin' by yourself ain't all roses— and it ain't all thorns"

The nineteenth day a'November, I'll be here seven years by myself. When Ulyss' died, they didn't want me t'come here and live by myself. I don't know at th'people that wants me t'leave here. They don't want me t'stay here atall, but I never have been afraid a'*nothin'* s'bad that it would make me move away from here. They said, "You never have been afraid?" I said, "No!" They thought since people has got so mean, somebody might come and scare me, but it's just as peaceful here as it can be. A night 'r two ago, I thought I heared somethin'. I'm as easy waked as a cat. I never have got bad scared, though. Not since I been here.

Besides, I've got enough of a temper t'take care a'number one. I don't let nobody run over me. Th'Bible tells you if anyone slaps you on th'one cheek t'turn th'other cheek. I don't do that. I don't. I don't want nobody slappin' *me* about! I told Ulyss' once, "You go t'strike me a lick, you make *sure* and make it count cause you'll never strike me another!" I'm half white and free born and I never have took a lick off a'nobody, and I ain't a'gonna commence takin' nothin' off a'nobody now! If y'let people commence runnin' over you, they'll tramp you under their feet. I don't do it. I'll say somethin' back. I'll say it even if I have t'say somethin' and run! [Laughing.]

And I've got a good number twelve shotgun in there if I need it. I've shot it many a time. I use t'shoot with th'boys, and I was pretty good with a gun. Use t'be. I ain't shot none in a long time. Last gun I shot I killed that possum I told you'uns about. That's th'only thing I ever shot at t'kill it. But I know how t'use it. I was raised with boys, and I mean I was *raised* with'em, and I done just what they done. Yes sir. They was always lotsa boys at our house that come there t'be with my brothers, and I've shot with'em lots just t'be out in a gang a'boys shootin' at spots.

Some of'em wants t'buy that gun I've got, and they're not gonna get it. I've got it hid. I hope t'God I never have t'use it, but I might sometime. I don't know. Y'don't know what you'll do. Some people make you do things you won't do.

I know one woman who got her a pistol. I'm scared t'death of a pistol. That's th'truth. I never shot a pistol in my life. She said I oughta have a pistol up here t'protect myself. I said, "Lord, I ain't gonna have no pistol." I might get shot with it. I might.

But she got her one because they was some mean boys down where she lived that done her wrong. She had a grapevine right below th'house and them mean boys'd slip under her grapevine and steal her grapes till they'd hear her open th'door. Then they'd run down th'hill and they'd laugh like they'd die. Didn't care for her feelin's a bit more'n a big groundhog up there on th'mountain. She got tired of it and got her a pistol. They calmed out and she never did have t'shoot none. I said I wouldn't a'cared much if she *had* shot *at*'em. I don't mean *shoot*'em, but shoot *at*'em and just scare th'hell out of'em. That was meanness. They never did do me that way. I wouldn't'a shot'em, but th'first time they'd done me devilment they'd a'got run off, day'r night either one.

"It's a long lane that never has no turns."

And I'm not a'gonna be like Grandma Henson. She was afraid a'anything. Th'mules got loose one day and come towards th'house, and she seen'em a'comin' and she run up on top a'th'springhouse! Yes sir, she sure did. That's just how afraid she was a'anything. I'll not be like that.

Livin' by yourself ain't all roses—and it ain't all thorns. On real dark lonesome nights when a thunder comes, 'r lightnin' comes right down there, and I'm settin' here and it comes all around me, and it seems like it comes right down on th'house, I get in th'bed pretty soon! I do. I ain't afraid of it. I just ain't what you'd call *afraid* of it. But it uneasies me. Now I don't know whether you'uns will agree with me 'r not. If you don't, you don't, and if you do, you do. It's all right. You ever heared tell that if it comes a storm t'lay down on a feather bed and you never would get struck? That's what I do. I got a feather bed. [Laughter.] You don't know how little you feel layin' there by yourself, though.

But I ain't like ol' Maggie down here. Now with all due respect t'her and all th'women in th'world—I don't mean t'make fiddle and fun a'nobody—and if she's afraid of a storm, she's afraid of a storm. She can't help it. Well, when a storm comes she just cries her eyes out, nearly. She cries like a whipped child. She just can't stand it. Now I don't cry and I don't get scared, but you feel bad. You set down here by yourself and know y'can't make nobody hear—I couldn't holler and make nobody hear—well, y'don't feel good. Then's when y'know God is takin' care a'you. You feel it. You understand it. Yes sir.

Still, it gets a little bit lonesome—'specially if y'get t'hurtin' right bad. When there's nobody here but me, and I feel bad, I lay down pretty soon. Now my heart took a bad spell a'hurtin' th'other night—aw-w-w-ful. I don't know what done it. I went on t'bed. I lay there and tumbled and tumbled and tumbled and I couldn't go t'sleep and I got up 'bout two o'clock and took another aspirin tablet and finally went t'sleep. Sometimes this hand hurts and keeps me awake. It took a spell th'other day and it like t'drawed me t'death. I put alcohol on it t'keep it from drawin', and if I go t'bed and take a bad case a'th' "slick foot," I call it, and can't go t'sleep, I get up and take me a aspirin tablet and sometimes I get t'sleep. I have m'bottle filled at th'drugstore. I get Ruth t'take it and have it filled for me. I don't do without it. If I do without, I can tell it just in a few minutes. I *want* t'do without it, though. It costs like everthing. Just a little ol' thing like that cost three dollars. One time I said I'd just do without it. Ruth, she begged me not t'do it. I said, "Next time I get out a'that little ol' medicine,

I'm gonna do without it awhile." Shew, I done without for two'r three days and my hand commenced t'drawin'. That's what it commenced t'doin'. I just can't do without it. If I have t'sell this place t'buy my medicine, I guess I'll just do that. I'm just gonna live so long, anyhow.

That and high blood medicine is th'only kind a'medicine I use. Dr. Kahn makes me take that ever'day a'my life. He's a good doctor. He's been here t'see me two'r three times. I got s'tickled at him. He come one time and I was layin' on th'lounge, and he hadn't been here before. He come in through th'kitchen door and set down there and wanted t'take m'blood pressure. I had on m'dress, and he got out his knife and I wished you'd see'd that man rip my dress sleeve. He never cut no hole in it. Just cut along th'seam. Just as particular with it as he could be. And I set there—laid there, I couldn't set up—laid there and laughed at him. He was particular with it as he could be. Way on after that I went t'his office. I asked him if he remembered rippin' m'dress. He said, "Yes, I do." I said, "You was so particular; you that afraid you'd cut m'dress? What made you so afraid?" He said, "I was afraid you'd cuss me out." [Laughter.] That's all he said. That just tickled me t'death.

Dr. Kahn's a good doctor. He's good t'me. And I've got good neighbors. They's hardly a day passes here without somebody comes t'see about me. When nobody comes is when I get worried. Then's when I wonder if I'm doin' th'right thing, stayin' here. It's not all sunshine, I can tell you, stayin' by yourself. I hope you'uns'll never have t'do it. I do. I hope you'uns never have t'do it. But if y'do, and if y'live t'be as old as I am, you remember what I tell you'uns. [Slowly and deliberately.]: You *learn* t'make yourself do lots a'things that you *never* did think you *could* do. I have t'*learn* t'make myself not be lonesome. I have t'do that a lot here lately since Ulyss' is gone and nobody here but me, cause if y'give out a'heart, ever'thing goes t'th'bad right *now.*

I nearly go into fits when I have t'set here all day when it's rainin'. I just get s'lonesome I just can't hardly live. It's them days when I think bedtime'll never come. Y'listen t'th'radio, but y'listen to it, and you can't say nary a word *to* it. When y'listen t'*somebody,* they can answer you back 'r you can answer them back. But y'learn t'pay no 'tention t'things like that. I do. I turn off that radio sometimes. I get s'aggravated with it I don't know what t'do. [Makes a blah-blah-blah sound.] Half th'time I don't know what it says! Course I love a good program on th'radio. I do. I couldn't do without my radio. But still, it's not like havin' somebody here.

Somebody asked me th'other day didn't I want a telephone. I don't believe I could hear good enough t'answer it. I don't believe I could. And I don't want no television. Ain't got a bit a'use for television in th'world. Th'way it flitters it hurts m'eyes. You look at that wiggly thing too much and it'll ruin your eyes, and m'eyes are th'best thing I've got. That eye specialist I went to examined m'eyes and he said he couldn't find a thing wrong with'em and me as old as I am. Yes sir. If God was t'take my vision away from me, what would I do? Course I don't see as good as I *did* any more. You'uns get my age and I guess you'uns'll not see good neither. [Laughs.] I *hope* y'do. Hope you can see as good as *I* do.

Yes sir. That goes with th'Cabe generation. My grandma Cabe, now she died and didn't have t'use specks. I don't have t'use specks now. But they's some a'that little tiny print on th'medicine bottles that I can't read. Another thing I can't do is run a reference in th'*Bible.* That's somethin' I hate s'bad that I don't know what t'do. I still read th'*Bible.* It's a good pastime t'me. I've read it plumb through more'n once. You teach Sunday School class sixty-odd year and see if you don't, too. Commence from one side and go right out th'other. Not all at one time, but you know what I mean. And I still read in it, but now them little bitty letters when they run a reference—I've got so I can't see that good, and that worries me.

Readin's good, though. I read more, I guess, than I ought to. They bring me th'Asheville *Citizen* and th'Franklin *Press* and all kinds a'papers up here and let me read'em. I'm awful t'read. I'm a paper bug. I sure am. But it's not like havin' somebody here, either. I'll tell y', there are some times you get pretty lonely. Sometimes you get mighty blue. Sometimes you feel like gettin' up and goin' *somewheres*—no tellin' where. Th' "allovers," I call it. And if it wadn't for walkin' and s'many snakes crawlin' round here, I'd go many a night down here

As Aunt Arie's eyesight failed, it became harder and harder for her to read the references in her Bible.

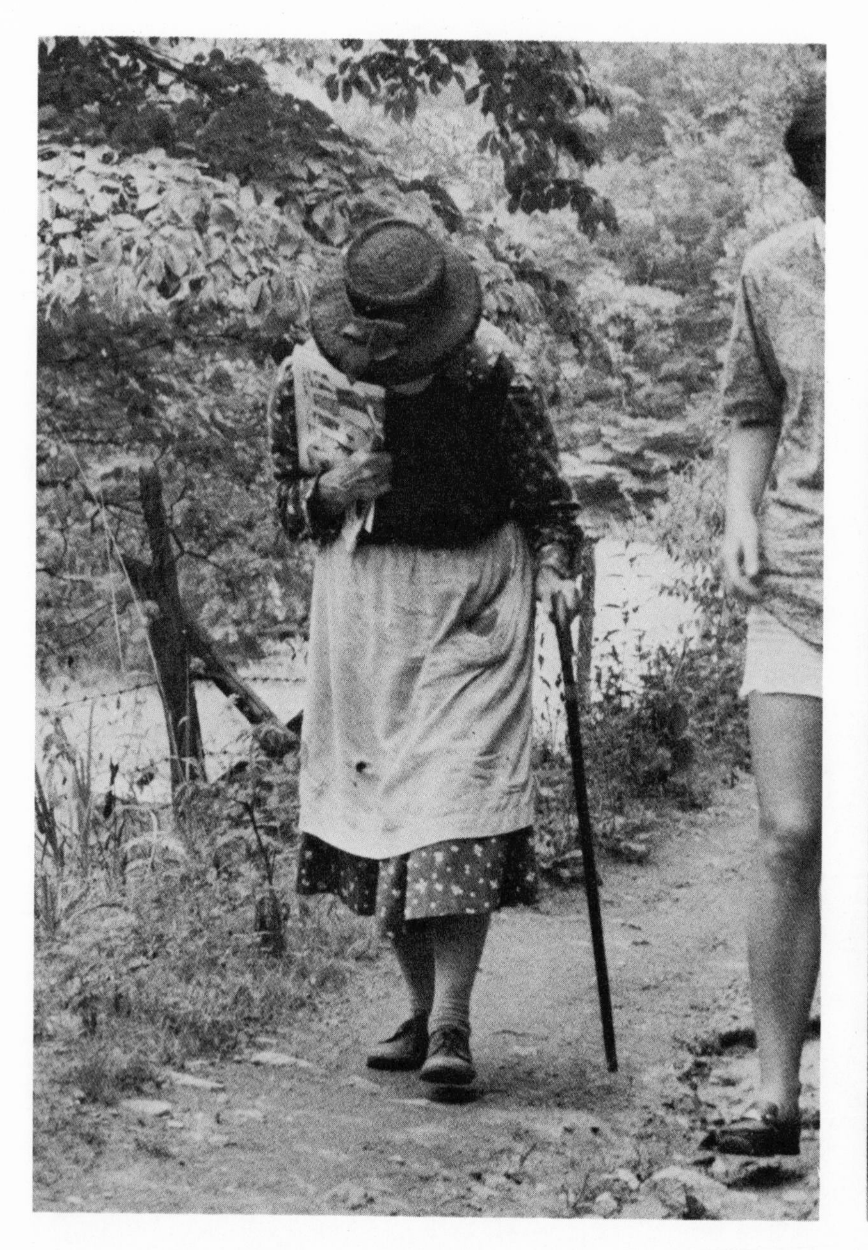

A walk down the gravel driveway to the mailbox often led to the discovery of a bundle of fan letters from strangers, some of which, to Aunt Arie's unending mystification, contained money "just to help out."

t'supper and come back. I can't hardly do that now, though, and that's hard when you've always been use t'goin' on where y'please and comin' back when y'get ready. Th'worst time is winter when they's snow on th'ground. Now when it's warm weather, in th'daytime, if nobody comes t'visit, I can walk t'th'mailbox and see somebody. I can even do that in th'rain. But when it snows I just about have t'stay in day and night. I just about freeze myself t'death and can't walk in it. I just can't walk in th'snow. I said this winter, when I had such a hard time a'freezin' t'death and couldn't get nothin' done much, that I didn't believe I'd try t'stay here by myself nary'nother winter. I keep a good fire in th'livin' room here, but I just have t'stay and I never get out th'door. I use a chamber [pot], y'know, cause I can't walk in th'snow t'save my life. I just squenge. It squenges me all over. I've learned when it snows t'stay at home. Yes sir.

Winters are th'hardest time. One winter not too long ago, that food cellar door out by th'well got froze shut and I like to a'starved t'death. I got sorta uneasy then. Now that's th'truth! [Laughter.] When they fixed my cellar that fell, they left a seam right in front a'th'cellar door, and when it come that hard freeze, it froze that seam till it pushed up and locked my cellar door. I couldn't open it and I didn't have a bite of a thing in th'world in th'house, only bread t'cook. Not a thing. I had a-l-l my taters and everthing in th'cellar. I couldn't get it open. I got me a rock and beat on it and beat on it and beat on it t'see if I could rock off th'hinges. Boys, I sorta got scared. Y'can't get your hand on nary thing t'eat, cook. . . . I can cook but couldn't get m'hands on it *to* cook. So I said, "Well, I reckon th'next thing best t'do is t'boil a big kettle a'water. . . ."

First thing I done when I went in th'kitchen th'next mornin' was t'go see if my door'd open so I'd have somethin' t'cook for dinner, and it opened just as pretty as it could be. Lord, I rejoiced! I did. I rejoiced and run in there and got me a can a'beans and put on t'cook. You set down t'nothin' t'eat but only bread, and y'can't hardly eat that by itself. No sir. [Laughter.] Y'*could* eat enough t'keep from gettin' hungry, though. I'd betcha that. [Laughter.] Yes sir, y'sure could.

I wadn't as bad off just by myself, though, as I would be if somebody

Winter snows trapped Aunt Arie helplessly indoors. They were beautiful in one sense—lovely, stark, and pure—but they imprisoned her as surely as bars or chains, and she huddled in front of her fireplace. If the supply of firewood on her front porch ran out, and no one came to help, she retreated to her bed and burrowed under layers of quilts.

was t'come in and I was thinkin' I oughta give'em maybe a little somethin' t'eat. "A little nothin'," I call that! A little nothin' t'eat! [Laughing.]

But I'm makin' it all right. Stayin' right here. I don't know what I'll have t'do before I die. May have t'lay out in th'rain somewhere. I hope I don't. I think God will take care a'me. And they's lotsa pleasure in bein' alone. They's nobody t'quarrel at y'. And when I need'em, I've got awful good neighbors, I'll tell you. Y'know how t'live and make neighbors? Be a neighbor. Be a neighbor and you'll have neighbors. I've tried that. Now I've tried that by experience. I do try t'be good t'everbody, and there's one thing I'll never do is insult anybody in my house. Mommy taught me that when I was young.

I try t'treat everbody just as I'd have them treat me. Do unto others as you'd have them do unto you and you'll have a good time. Well, anyhow, that's what I do. And look what I've got in return. There's Marie. She helps me do anything and everthing. Comes nearly ever' day. I can't do without her hardly, and that's th'truth. And Ruth comes up all th'time. I don't never have t'tell her t'come and bring m'rations. She brings m'coffee and medicine and sees about me. I just can't eat without coffee, I don't reckon! I'll tell you what I use t'do, now. I use t'drink nine cups a'coffee a day. You'll think that's awful, and I do, too. Three for breakfast, three for dinner, and three for supper. I quit th'coffee and never drunk a drop for three years. Now, like I did today, I pour me a little out in a saucer. I never do pour me out no coffee in a coffee cup. Hardly ever. Pour it out in a saucer and drink it while it's hot.

And then these neighbors that live up there in that trailer are as good t'me as they can be. They bring me stuff t'eat, already cooked, and ever' time I go up there they want me t'eat somethin'. Last time I was over there I said, "I'm gonna quit comin' up here. Ever' time I come you want me t'eat!" He said, "We don't care if y'eat everthing we got!" Tickled me, and I said, "Oh my, I can't do that." Th'other afternoon when she come up here, she brought a piece a'ham meat already cooked. It was ever' bit that big. I guess my hand wouldn't cover it. All I'd have t'do was warm that. I built up a fire. My hot plate's gone t'th'bad and I have t'build up a fire now. I just don't eat cold rations. I took me a knife and stripped that into three pieces and laid that in a fryin' pan and poured cornbread gravy on it. And it was *so* good.

Then I get lotsa visitors I don't know. Course I never see no strangers. They're all just as welcome as they can be. Four'r five boys come th'other night. I didn't know nary one of'em, not nary one of'em. As it happened I was eatin' when they come. Somebody come t'th'door and knocked, and course I hollered, "Come in!" Sometimes they'll come in and sometimes they won't. Now you'd come in if you was t'come here cause you're use t'me. But a lot a'people ain't use t'me and they won't come in. I got up and went and started t'th'door, and they all come on in, and of course they all told who they was. I'll never remember even one name. Use to I never forgot nothin', but m'mind ain't as long now as it use t'be! It just can't be. It's been wore out too much!

Then there was a man and a woman come here a'Sunday. Said they had drove four hundred miles a'purpose t'see me. They stayed here and took pictures all out there and developed'em while they was out there. I wanted one of'em s'bad I didn't know what t'do, but I never said a word. They didn't give me one and I didn't tell'em to. I just hated to. She said she'd a'brought me somethin' if she'd knowed for certain she'd a'got t'see me, and when she got ready t'start she give me fifty dollars in money. Said she had read all about me in th'*Foxfire.* I said, "Yes, who ain't?" [Laughter.] Poor Eliot done me a good favor.

Use to I didn't know what t'do when people give me money like that. First time it happened this man was here, and when he left, he left a letter in th'mailbox. I opened th'mailbox and there was this letter about so high stickin' up in th'back, and there was a twenty-dollar bill in there. He never said what t'do with it. Never said what t'do with it. Y'know what I done with that? I kept it two year before I ever spent it. I put it on this road. I finally said, "Put that on th'road." Spent four hundred and forty dollars and so much on that road. That's how much they charged me, gettin' that road fixed. That took all I had and more, too. But that twenty dollars helped out, and I never asked for that.

You don't know how bad I hate t'ask people t'do things. Like that clock there on th'fireboard. Now I can't wind that clock t'save my life. I just can't.

"You all remember that if you ever have th'chance,
come anytime and stay just as long as y'please.
Now, while I think about it, I hope ever' one of you

The Puerto Rican students, with Laurie Brunson, visited Aunt Arie several times during their stay in

a safe journey through life. And if y'ever have th'opportunity t'come back in here, remember the door's open; come pull th'latch string anytime you'uns wants to."

Rabun County. Before they returned to New York, they presented her with an Easter basket.

Well, just as quick as anybody comes, I ask'em t'wind m'clock for me. I hate t'do that. Use to I wouldn't do it. But when it comes t'*have* to, children, you don't mind it a bit in th'world. You just go ahead, and I don't believe anybody in this world cares a bit t'help me do things like that, and I appreciate it from th'bottom a'my heart. I can't express th'appreciation that I have for what people does for me. I just can't do it.

They come in here and help me do anything and everthing in this world: plow, fix th'garden, fix th'bean patch. Th'poor ol' feller that plowed my bean patch last time done it all wrong and it had t'be done over. I'll say it this way, with all due respect t'him and everbody else—I was tickled t'death, honest I

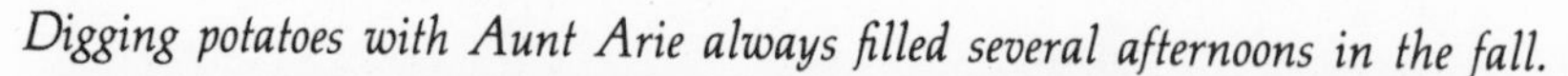

Digging potatoes with Aunt Arie always filled several afternoons in the fall.

was—but I was s'sorry for him I didn't know what t'do. He laid them bean rows off straight as a gun barrel. He sure did. That was all t'do over. But he's a big help t'me. They all are. Th'other day he said he was goin' t'bring his son and his son's wife and children if I didn't think they'd run me crazy. I said: "You think I'd run crazy? Ever' youngun on th'hill comes up here, and I'm not run crazy!" No sir. I'm use t'younguns. Love'em t'death. I'd rather see younguns come as t'eat sugar. Course I enjoy when *anybody* comes t'see me. And I'm just tickled t'death whenever anybody comes t'*stay* a few minutes. I'll tell y'what I don't like. I don't like it when anybody comes in this door and goes out that door and never sets down t'stay there a single minute.

I always have time—*take* time—t'set down and talk a few minutes. Mr. Stiles come yesterday evenin' and I was in th'garden. I went on in th'house, and he come in and he said, "Can't stay but a few minutes." I said, "You can stay a *few* minutes!" And he did; he stayed a few minutes. And these boys come this mornin', while I was fixin' pickle' beans, and they helped me. They helped me fix ever' one of'em. I was tickled t'death with it.

So God does all things well. Just look how he's blessed us. Boys, you need t'never fear t'trust th'Lord. Cause I don't care what you do, if you do it in th'right way and in th'right spirit and do it for th'glory a'God, He'll return you fullfold. He'll sure do that. Now I've tried that. Me and Ulyss' both tried that. Yes sir.

And I've had lotsa happiness in my life. I guess th'happiest was when they was all here—Poppy and Uncle Bud and Aunt Avie and Berthie and Ulyss' —and all havin' a good time t'gether just like we are today. All happy as we can be, I call it. That's th'happiest time in your life. Lord, I tell you time passes by, don't it? Now I never quit talkin'. Ulyss' said I could out talk a flyin' jenny! Oh goodness alive! [Laughing.] When I had that stroke a'paralysis, y'know it got half of me. Yes, it got half of me. Even half a'my nose. But I said I was s'glad it didn't stop my tongue I didn't know what t'do! If I'd get t'where I couldn't talk, I don't know what I'd do. [Laughing.]

Yeah, I talk a lot. Wouldn't be a woman if she didn't talk. That's th'reason they out talk s'many men! Oh Lord have mercy! [Laughter.] I just keep clatterin' away. That's all they is to it. I know I've talked more'n Ulyss' has in his life. He was a pretty good talker, but he wadn't like me. No sir. Y'have t'get up before daylight t'beat me!

And I'll tell you another thing that was th'happiest time in my life was when we use t'have a revival meetin' in Coweeta and everbody in th'church would get t'shoutin'. That's th'happiest time I ever see'd in my life. Everbody was as happy as they could be. You don't see many a'them days now, though. Scare a body t'death if they's t'see anybody shout nowadays, wouldn't it? [Laughter.] Sure'nough, I ain't seen nobody shout lately. That was th'happiest time in my life, when I got back t'that church. Now that's th'truth. Words can't ever express th'feelin' you had. No sir. I was just th'happiest that I could be.

Course there were th'sad times, too—seein' your mother and father go out and knowin' they'd never be able t'speak t'you again. Knowin' that's forever. I don't believe anyone in this world can express that feelin'. I can't. Words don't come t'express it.

Ah, you get t'studyin' back over where you've been and what you've done, I get amazed t'death. I certainly do. I don't see how I ever done it. Eighty-eight year t'tag up and down this road is a long time.

I use t'be awful stout. Worked pretty hard. I enjoyed it, though. I'd rather work as t'play. Heap rather work as t'play. Still that way. I'll tell you th'hardest work I do nearly is drawin' that water out a'th'well t'wash with. That bucket's heavy. Yes sir. Sometimes I can't hardly make it go. Busted one bucket all t'pieces. Let it go and down it went. And there was two'r three days there when I done without fresh water. Just couldn't draw it, so I drunk ol' warm water. Now they come and wanted me t'put a pump in th'well and I coulda, but Ulyss' didn't want me to. You may think just whatever you please, but I hate t'go ahead and do things that Ulyss' didn't want me t'do. Now that's th'truth. Ever' time I go t'do somethin' he didn't like, I remember that. If he was here now, I don't guess he'd care a thing, but still it's there. Yes sir. It's right there.

Then th'other day, I tried t'do a little bit in th'garden and found out I couldn't do that. Come in here and set down and rested a little while. Then went t'th'mailbox, come back, and went in th'garden again. I thought I *could* do *somethin'.* So I took that chair out there and set it in between th'rows and set down in it and got t'pullin' weeds out a'th'peppers. I love t'work, but now I'm as slow as cream a'risin'.

Th'saddest thing that's come my road, though, is not bein' able t'do near what I use to. I can't get about and get stuff t'give people like I use to. I use t'have a lot a'stuff t'give t'people, but I just can't do it now. Can't give away quilts now like I use to cause I can't quilt. Can't cook'em somethin' good t'eat and give'em a good drink a'water like I use to cause I can't hardly cook.

And there's s'many things I'd love t'be able t'show you younguns how t'do, but I can't now. Can't crochet any more. Can't card and spin any more. Can't make willer baskets and bottom chairs any more. Can't do hardly anything I use t'do.

But I can still love.

Tributes:

"No One Could Out-Give Aunt Arie"

FORMER FOXFIRE STUDENTS

This book would hardly be complete if it did not include some comments from those who knew Aunt Arie, telling what that experience was like. Linda Garland Page, a former *Foxfire* student herself who preceded by one year our involvement with Aunt Arie, interviewed several neighbors (Tom Shope, and Marie Dills and her mother), and contacted as many former students as she could locate who had met Aunt Arie while they were working with *Foxfire* as high school students. A dozen responded with written recollections. Staff members Mike Cook (also a former student—and one of the first to visit her) and Margie Bennett also contributed written pieces.

When I look at the pieces written by former students—young adults who knew Aunt Arie when they were barely teenagers—I am struck by two things. One is the fact—and a fact of life in many rural counties like ours—that of that group, only one, Mike Cook, still lives in Rabun County. We've lost the rest, but they've carried Aunt Arie's energy out from Houston to Tampa.

The other thing that strikes me is the startling clarity with which they remember and prize the experiences they had with her. It is that fact that leads me to continue to affirm the worth of making this kind of thing happen at high schools across the country—for *every* community, no matter how small, has its own Aunt Arie Carpenters, sitting alone, largely unrecognized, waiting for company.

With an independent spirit and a zest for living, Aunt Arie had much to give to those of us who shared time with her. Her knowledge of practical living often seemed boundless. Her philosophy was unique.

Her greatest lesson to me, however, was her unashamed love of home. As a teenager it was sometimes difficult for me to acknowledge that I was born and raised in a small country town, naïve and unaccustomed to big-city ways.

Aunt Arie taught me that that didn't matter. After the summer I spent interviewing and visiting her, I returned to college with a new attitude about my heritage.

I had learned through her reminiscences, her struggles, and her camaraderie with the land just how important family, roots, and tradition are. They are lessons I'll never ever forget.

JAN BROWN BONNER,
librarian in
Easley, South Carolina

What I remember most about Aunt Arie is something very rare: She was keenly aware of those around her, always patient and understanding, listening and

Jan Brown and Aunt Arie braiding a corn shuck foot-mat.

David Young watching Aunt Arie stringing leather breeches.

helping (*if* she saw or felt the need to help was there—she never interfered when she wasn't needed). She possessed all the traits found in someone who sincerely cares about others.

JOHN DAVID YOUNG,
attending architecture school at the University of Florida, Gainesville

Aunt Arie was one of my favorite people, as I'm sure she was to so many others. She was very special to me because the first interview I had for *Foxfire* was with her. She made a city kid like me realize that people need to care about other people, not just themselves. Friends are so important, and kindness can go a long way. I could listen to her for hours. She had so many stories to tell, and there was never enough time. There will never be anyone else like Aunt Arie because of her warmth and strong will. You don't see people like that any more because everyone is moving too fast to stop and realize who they are, what they have, and what we all had.

ANNETTE SUTHERLAND DICKERSON
housewife and mother,
Atlanta

The entire *Foxfire* experience changed my outlook on life and Aunt Arie definitely was an influential part of that experience.

She was the most beautiful older person I've ever met—inside and out. When I think of her I always see her outside her house greeting us with a big smile and sparkling blue eyes. She was always so excited to see us. And then she'd buzz around the kitchen cooking and talking and laughing, but always saying something meaningful that you'd never forget.

What impressed me the most was how she always showed *by her actions* what was most important in life—love and sharing with others. She was never prejudiced and always accepted everyone. She was a very open-minded person.

She made me appreciate the small things in life—the moments of sharing and spending time together. And that's something that no one can ever take away. She always made the past part of the present—something to be proud of and to learn from. She was a dynamic person, "one in a million," someone you'd never forget.

KAREN COX TAYLOR,
runs a seven-acre nursery
with her husband,
near Tampa, Florida

I am sure she knew she fed me, shared her life experiences with me, and once gave me a place to sleep in a bed that was stacked one foot high with quilts. But

I doubt that she knew that she renewed my faith in mankind and taught me what unselfish generosity was. No one could out-give Aunt Arie. I never left her place without something . . . a full stomach, vegetables from her garden, a strangely good feeling.

Aunt Arie also taught me that things like honesty, caring, loving, selflessness, trust, and faith in God were legitimate, honorable virtues—virtues that you didn't have to be ashamed of possessing. In fact, Aunt Arie proved to me that "good guys" don't always finish last.

Aunt Arie knew right from wrong like night from day. She didn't beat around the bush, pull punches, or straddle any fences. She told it like it was and meant every word she said. She had a great sense of self-worth and inner peace. She didn't care what others thought of her. She knew that she was a fine person and had lived a good life.

Aunt Arie also reinforced the fact that we need to take the good with the bad and meet difficulties head on. She impressed me with her ability not to

Gary Warfield helping Aunt Arie read fan mail.

Don MacNeil enduring a visit from the neighbors' dog, Charlie, while stringing leather breeches.

gripe or complain and not to wallow in self-pity. Aunt Arie took pride in everything she did. Even though she drew her water from a well, cooked with wood, and lived in a house that only slowed the wind, Aunt Arie was optimistic, happy, and "up" on life. She always had a kind word to say and a positive outlook. I rarely saw her angry; when she was, it was when she would relate some injustice or inherently wrong circumstance.

Aunt Arie also impressed my hard head with the fact that I wasn't the brightest, wisest soul in the world. I learned shortly after our first visit that the longer one lived, the more one learned. It was evident that Aunt Arie knew more about life and people than most individuals ever will. And what is amazing is the fact that she probably never traveled more than fifty miles from where she was born and wasn't well-read or college-educated.

I hope that in the twilight of my life I will have Aunt Arie's vitality, enthusiasm, dignity, and inner peace. I hope that, like her, I can "set my feet under the table" with friends and dine on the cornbread, leather breeches, and lye hominy of my time.

GARY WARFIELD
is a veterinarian
near Watkinsville, Georgia

My first interview for *Foxfire* was with Aunt Arie Carpenter. I carried a camera and I'm sure there were tape recorders, but I don't remember being very concerned about either.

I thought I knew all about Aunt Arie from working my first month at school in the *Foxfire* office. Her pictures hung like icons among the photographs of old folks, who seemed like celebrities to a young *Foxfire* trainee. Aunt Arie's picture was clipped from *Smithsonian* and tacked to the wall by the time of my first visit to her house. I was nervous about meeting this woman who seemed such a part of *Foxfire,* and I wondered what I could ask that hadn't been asked by the jeeploads of kids that had lurched up the same road I was now climbing. I saw the mist rising in patches on the mountainside, then the smoke coming from her chimney, then the house and out-buildings, and, finally, Aunt Arie on her porch waving. She was just a sweet little mountain lady, not a star—a lot like my own grandmother. She had probably been on that porch since breakfast waiting for us to arrive. I was no longer afraid of her.

Wig introduced all of us who hadn't met Aunt Arie only after she gave him a big hug as he climbed up on her porch. She called me Randy Barnes and never did get my name right. We sat by her fire and talked. I snapped pictures and she would laugh and wink at me and continue talking, mostly to Wig. I remember thinking how cold it must be in the winter to leave this fire where, even huddled right in front, you could feel cold air on your back while your face got red-hot. I didn't want to think about running through the snow to the privy. I was raised in Atlanta with central everything, and I'm not sure if up till that time I was aware of any other way of living. Once again I thought of my grandmother and her family. That day we had a meal of vegetables, chicken, and bread that I helped bake.

The next time I went to her house we worked around her house while talking, *always* talking and singing, and after that I went to her house with a crew filming her for a special *Foxfire* film. In the spring of that year we worked all day in her garden, chopping at the rocky soil. While we were eating supper with Aunt Arie I told her I was going home at the end of school and how much I would miss her. She said "Give my love to your people in Atlanta, Randy Barnes." That was the last time I saw Aunt Arie. Now I see her in every older person I take the time to get to know.

RANDY STARNES,
with Channel 36
in Atlanta

Aunt Arie was one of the most insightful persons I have ever known. Soon after I met her, I felt that this was a person I could confide in and seek guidance from. Her days were filled with more hardship than I suffer in a year. She drew water from a well, used an outhouse, heated her house and cooked with fire, and never seemed to mind or notice that her life was extremely difficult. The example she set for people was astounding, and you never heard a complaint from her.

Aunt Arie combined all that is good in people with a rugged independence that will serve as an example to me and everyone who ever met her.

DON MACNEIL,
a stockbroker in Houston

Aunt Arie was living proof of the fact that persons in direct control of their own destinies are the most energetic, the most vibrant human beings. Today, with technology easing the responsibilities of mankind, people increasingly complain of being robbed of their individuality, their humanness. In such circumstances, we should turn to the examples who have passed before us, but not with a nostalgic attitude, for this brings a sense of loss and hopelessness when we must finally acknowledge that a mode of life has all but vanished in technology's wake. If we value the world's Aunt Aries only in this respect, then we miss the point. Aunt Arie lived in difficult physical surroundings, much more so than any most of us can imagine.

Aunt Arie was energetic; she was a positive, untiring, unselfish force for good throughout her long life. This is the important challenge she left to all who knew her.

CARLTON YOUNG,
just returned from Denmark
to his home in
Highlands, North Carolina

My father was in the monument business, or, as you may prefer to say, he sold and set tombstones. That's how we came to find Aunt Arie. Daddy set her and Ulyss's stone. Daddy said she was Patsy Cabe Kelly's great-aunt. Patsy just

Andrea Burrell with Aunt Arie in the garden.

happened to be a good friend of mine. So one day Patsy went with us to meet Aunt Arie.

It's been eleven or twelve years since that teenage girl traveled up a dirt road to Aunt Arie's. Most of that girl is gone, but the memories of that little woman, as strong and loving as the mountains we live in, will always be with me.

I like to think that some of that strength rubbed off on me, but that's not true. Her strength came from enduring hardships I'll never face—hardships she would never want me to face. Not that she talked of hardships; it was just something you could see.

She kept us smiling. She was such a warm and happy person. Even now when I think of her I smile—so, Aunt Arie, I'm still smiling with you.

ANDREA BURRELL POTTS,
runs a crafts shop
in Macon County,
North Carolina

When I first met Aunt Arie I was a twelve-year-old city boy who thought it would be great if the whole world looked like Atlanta, Georgia. Boy, did I have a lot to learn, and Aunt Arie was a tremendous influence. Imagine shucking popcorn (I didn't even know it grew on an ear like regular corn), splitting wood, digging potatoes, and drawing water from the well. I was doing something for someone else for a change instead of thinking only of myself. We went to help her because she needed help, but we never left without a meal prepared on her wood stove and a refreshed outlook on life.

I am not sure if she ever remembered my name, but she left an impression on me that I will carry all my life. She was genuine. She worked hard, she loved with all her heart, and she never passed judgment on the countless people who came to visit her. All were welcome. What more is there to living? I do not remember many of the specific things she said, but I remember feeling at home a long way away from my family. I treasure half a dozen photographs of her that I keep in a worn manila envelope. I often show them to friends of mine who never met her, even though the photos cannot fully express the unique beauty behind her smile.

RAY MCBRIDE,
restores historic homes
in Savannah, Georgia

FOXFIRE STAFF

Aunt Arie had no children of her own but enveloped each of us with a love that kept bringing us back to her house.

It was easy to plan a Christmas gathering for her, because no matter what we did, she'd be delighted. Just before Christmas vacation we'd load up gifts for her—all the goodies and decorations and *Foxfire* kids we could find—form a caravan of pick-up truck, van, and jeep, and head for her house as soon after school as possible. We'd decorate a tree from her woods with strings of cranberries and freshly popped popcorn, a string of very conventional Christmas-tree lights, chains of little colored construction-paper rings, and silver-foil icicles. We'd warm the typical Christmas foods we'd brought—ham, sweet-potato casserole, green beans, and more—and she always baked loaves of her biscuit bread in the oven of her wood stove.

We'd stay till seven or eight o'clock, when it'd be pitch black in the mountain cove where she lived. Naturally no one ever thought of bringing a flashlight into the house when we arrived, so a few brave souls would pick their way out to the vehicles and turn on the headlights to guide the others. We always took a long time with our "Good night" and "Have a Merry Christmas!" but I don't think any one of us ever stopped to think that one year there would no longer be old-time Christmas parties at Aunt Arie's with the *Foxfire* students.

MARGIE BENNETT,
Foxfire Advisor

A visit to Aunt Arie's was smiles and tears, the smell of wood smoke, flowers, a garden, the well, a small gray cat rubbing around your legs, the look and feel of weathered wood in the sun, old-fashioned dresses, wood stoves and homemade bread and stringbeans . . . a thousand stories and thoughts . . . the warmth and caring and genuineness of the little half-crippled woman who wouldn't give up and who really loved us all.

MIKE COOK,
Foxfire teacher

FRIENDS AND NEIGHBORS

"As far back as I can remember, I've known Aunt Arie. Seems like wherever her and her family was, there was always people. When she was young, first growed up, why, I've heared Will Seagle tell about how a whole bunch a'young people would go t'church on Sunday. Everbody walked, y'know, and they lived off up that creek, and everbody that went with'em t'church would come back t'her daddy's and eat dinner with'em. They'd have t'set extra places—have two'r three tablesful t'feed ever' Sunday. Aunt Arie and Will, they was about th'same age. She lived up on th'mountain, but he lived *way* up on th'mountain, Seagle did.

"I remember th'first time I ever see'd Arie and Ulyss' together. We was chestnut huntin'. These mountains use t'be full a'chestnuts. I don't guess you remember nothin' about'em, but they use t'be lots a'chestnuts, and a whole bunch a'us would go back up on th'head a'th'creek chestnut huntin'. Well, Ulyss' and Arie was up there and they'd just started goin' t'gether then. I always remember what my mother said that night. She said, "Looks like that's a'goin' t'be a weddin' someday!" I didn't remember th'weddin', but I remember right quick after we see'd'em chestnut huntin', hearin' that they'd been married.

"As long as I knew her, she was always doin' somethin' for the Coweeta Church. On th'thirtieth of May, people use t'go t'th'graveyards and take flowers and clean up th'graves and put flowers on'em, and they called it "Decoration Day." They call it "Memorial Day" now. She raised a whole lot a'flowers—roses and dahlias—and she'd always be there, and she'd take a bunch a'flowers, and Ulyss'd be there and he'd help clean off th'graves. He'd get'em all cleaned off and she'd put flowers on'em and then she'd stay around and see if there was goin' t'be flowers put on all th'graves. If there was some she thought they wasn't goin' t'be no flowers put on, why, she'd go back home and get another load. She'd always see that they was flowers put on ever' grave in th'Coweeta graveyard ever' Decoration Day.

"Well, I remember one time me and my mother was there, and Arie had all th'flowers that she had put down, and she said she was goin' t'stay around t'see if they was some on all of'em. Said she had plenty and there was goin' t'be some on ever' grave there before th'day was over. And there was a man that had had his arm took off and they had buried his arm. Folks use t'think that if y'had a limb took off and didn't bury it and bury it *right,* it would always hurt you. Like I've heared this old man tell about Doctor Lyle, a old doctor in Franklin, takin' off this boy's leg. They didn't want it burnt like they do nowadays t'get rid of'em. They wanted it took t'th'graveyard and buried. Well, they did, but th'boy just kept a'sufferin' of a night way after he had got well. His father went back t'th'doctor and told him: "You've buried that leg in a strain. Go and take that leg up and fix it straight and comfortable, and cover it up again." And he did, and th'boy quit cryin' with his leg then. [Laughter.] They's lotsa people who believes in that. Aunt Arie believed that. So she even put flowers where that man's arm was buried. They had took his arm and buried it in th'graveyard there, and she'd always put flowers over his arm. [Laughter.] She knew where it was buried, too.

"Th'worst thing I ever knowed a'people doin'em wrong was a man went there and wanted t'paint their house. He had a sprayin' outfit. They didn't want it done, but them high-powered salesmen, y'know, they kept on a'talkin' and said they'd spray it for four. Aunt Arie and Ulyss' thought four dollars, and when th'man got th'job done and they went t'pay him for it, they found out he meant four hundred dollars. I was over there just a few days after that and looked round at what he'd done. Four dollars would a'been *too* much cause he'd done her more damage than he done good! He went and sprayed and th'spray went through th'cracks in th'walls and went all over their clothes and beds and on their dishes in th'kitchen. It just messed up ever'thing in th'house! And it was a very sorry grade a'paint; it just wasn't worth nothing. I was glad that I didn't go about th'time he was chargin'em. [Laughter.] Yeah, they'd made a awful mess of it. They even got it on their clothes; I guess th'clothes Ulyss' wore t'church had paint on'em.

"And any time anybody was sick 'r had troubles a'any kind, she'd always go and visit'em. She was a wonderful ol' woman. Nobody ever said no harm against her. She was everbody's friend."

TOM SHOPE,
Aunt Arie's neighbor

MRS. DILLS: Well, I knew her for about forty years, and I lived—what y'might say—a door neighbor t'her for thirty years. I knew her long before we moved into this township. At Coweeta Church I'd see her, and it's been every bit of forty years since I first seen her. That was long before we moved in here from th'Franklin township.

MARIE DILLS: I always thought a lot a'Aunt Arie. She was a good person. Her and Mr. Carpenter both. And they was good neighbors. We lived nearby'em for just about thirty years, and they was good in sickness, and they was just good neighbors. That's all that I can say about'em. They didn't bother nobody whatsoever. I always thought a lot of'em. And they seemed real happy. I'd go up there on Sunday evenin' and they'd be sittin' by th'fire. She'd be poppin' popcorn for him if it was in the wintertime. She done a lot a'that.

MRS. DILLS: After Ulyss' died, she stayed a night or two away from home. She stayed over at my son's house a night or two, and then she stayed with Ruth some. Then she went back home. Said she'd just as well tough it out. That's where she said was home, and that was where she'd tough it out, and that's what she done. Long as she could go.

MARIE: Gosh, it seems like a hundred years t'me since she died. I saw her ever' day. In going t'get th'mail, she'd come down, y'know, and if she wasn't able t'go, why I'd walk down and get it and bring it up t'her. And you *sure* do miss her. It sure is lonesome. Oh gosh, I went up there one time when th'snow was above my boots and th'wind a'blowin'. I thought I never would make it up that road! I just had t'take it one little step at a time. I'd rest a while and here I'd go on. [Laughter.]

Another time I was walkin' her home, and I'm scared t'death a'those little tiny ants. We got up there near her house, and her foot log, y'know, it's just got them big ant mounds along there. Well, I'd just go a step or two, and she'd have t'rest. I couldn't hold her up good, y'know, but I'd stand and let her rest, and I just *knew* them ants was goin' t'cover me! I was a'shiverin'. [Laughter.] Oh, I'll never forget that! Oh goodness!

Well, it sure is lonesome without her, I'll tell you. Since she's been gone, I went up there twice, I reckon, and, oh-h-h, I could just see her—hear her comin' through th'house. I'd walk round her house there at the well and I'd just think, "Oh goodness, I miss her awful."

MRS. DILLS: We took Aunt Arie t'th'Macon County Fair one time. First time

On the spring following Aunt Arie's death, once benign flowering vines began to reclaim her home, tentatively covering the abandoned front porch.

I reckon she'd ever been. Oh, she enjoyed that! We enjoyed takin' her anywhere like that.

MARIE: Do you remember anything she liked most about th'fair, Mommy?

MRS. DILLS: Th'cattle. That seemed t'catch her eye. Went out t'where they had the cattle, y'know, that they was goin' t'sell in th'fair. And they had an old mammy sow with a bunch a'pigs, and that caught her eye more than anything that was there. Just small little fellers, and they was fat and pretty. She talked about that more than anything—that and th'pretty cattle they had there at th'fair.

But it wasn't much that she went with us. She'd go t'th'store once in a while with me at Franklin and sit and talk with folks till I'd get everything done and go back by and pick her up. Ever since she'd had that stroke, though, she always drug that foot. She just couldn't pick it up and walk normal, and so she always felt like she was hinderin' anybody if she made'em wait on her.

MARIE: Maybe that's why she enjoyed company s'much—because she couldn't get out. On Sunday, whenever they would be several come t'see her, why, she'd say, "What about anyone comin' t'see me and stayin' s'long?" She just enjoyed company. Oh, she enjoyed it. I don't think she ever met a stranger. Now, I don't. I honestly don't. It didn't differ night, day, 'r when—she'd go t'th'door. That's why I say I don't think she ever met a stranger. I'd tell her lotsa times that she shouldn't let just any and everybody in that she didn't know, but she would anyway. I don't see how she lived like she did without someone robbin' her. But she'd always be glad for company t'come. Especially you all from th'*Foxfire.* You was *real* good company for her. And she'd talk about Wig a'comin'. She couldn't think a'his name and she'd just say "Wig." And she'd come down, y'know, t'go t'th'mailbox, and she'd stop and say he was comin'. He'd tell her beforehand and she'd hurry home t'be there when he come. Then she'd tell me about how he'd bring in wood, y'know, for her fire; and especially, if he eat supper 'r dinner with her, about how she enjoyed th'company. She *really* enjoyed any one a'you all that come.

LINDA: What did she think about her pictures being in *Foxfire?*

MARIE: Oh, she enjoyed that! Yeah, she would let me look at her books.

MRS. DILLS: She seemed so pleased, y'know, that people would think of her and her "just an old woman," she'd say. [Laughter.]

MARIE: Yeah, and she'd say, "It doesn't look like young people like that would come see me and stay with me."

MRS. DILLS: And eat with her. That pleased her, y'know, when they'd come t'eat with her. She would say how strange it was that they would notice her, and think that much of her, and her an old woman.

Well, I can't get used t'her bein' gone. She was awful good t'have. Marie and I would go over t'th'barn and we'd always look over there toward her house t'see if we could see th'smoke from her fireplace when it was cold, and if we couldn't see no sign, one of us would go see about her. Seems like I look for that smoke yet.

MARIE DILLS and her mother,
both friends and neighbors
of Aunt Arie

"Can't do hardly anythin' I used t'do.
But I can still love."